ATTACK OF THE LOVESICK DRAGON

The spirit's voice broke off with a screech. A glowering rider mounted on a froth-flecked black steed bore down on them, glaring at them from dark eyes burning above a black face covering. He drew his saber, driving them towards the water. As Rupert stepped backwards, drenching himself to the knees, the sky suddenly darkened, the rider's horse shied, and the rider, not giving full attention to his mount, slipped sideways.

Grippeldice's front claws grazed the part in Carole's hair as the dragon overflew them and landed in front of them, flaming. The horse reared, screaming, and bolted, rider clinging desperately to its mane, streaming cloak trailing smoke and sparks as the terrified mount galloped heedlessly off down the trail.

The dragon beat her wings once and started to take off after it, but Rupert cried out and Carole, translating, stopped the dragon with a word:

"We *must* reach the desert before they discover we are coming. Otherwise, I fear we will never find Miragenia or the child again."

THE CHRISTENING QUEST

Elizabeth Ann Scarborough

BANTAM BOOKS
TORONTO · NEW YORK · LONDON · SYDNEY · AUCKLAND

THE CHRISTENING QUEST
A Bantam Book / August 1985

ISBN 0-553-25122-8

Published simultaneously in the United States and Canada

Bantam Books are published by Bantam Books, Inc. Its trade-
mark, consisting of the words "Bantam Books" and the por-
trayal of a rooster, is Registered in U.S. Patent and Trademark
Office and in other countries. Marca Registrada. Bantam
Books, Inc., 666 Fifth Avenue, New York, New York 10103.

PRINTED IN THE UNITED STATES OF AMERICA

O   0 9 8 7 6 5 4 3 2 1

For David Michael Ruthstrom, Minstrel Extraordinaire and Stalwart Questing Companion, with abiding affection.

Also for my parents, Don and Betty Scarborough, my brother, Monte Scarborough, and Greg Herriford, Jeannie Jett, and Charles and Karen Parr for their help and inspiration. Special thanks to Tania Opland for listening, and to Tim Henderson, songwriter and minstrel, for his special insight into gypsies.

I would also like to acknowledge Scottish songwriter & singer Archie Fisher whose song "Witch of the Westmereland" inspired the initial meeting between Rupert and Carole.

CHAPTER I

Banshee shrieks and shuddering moans pealed from the stone walls, bouncing from buttressed arch to arrow slot, lending the whole north wing all the peaceful charm of a dungeon. Rupert Rowan, prince and diplomatic trainee, winced and recrossed his long legs, sinking back into the velvet padded chair and trying to maintain his carefully cultivated serenity despite his sister's anguished wails from the other side of the iron-hinged door. He had wearied of pacing hours ago and now had settled down to present a good example to the occasional subject who passed by him in the corridor. Most of these subjects were women, and many of them pretended not to hear Bronwyn's caterwauling, which Rupert thought very decent of them. Bronwyn was supposed to be a warrior. Why did she have to choose a time when he was in earshot to give up stoicism?

A buxom wench with a pert face and a corona of golden braids smiled warmly at him, masking the expression he frequently saw in female faces with one of sympathy. "There now, Your Highness, don't worry. The hollering relieves the pains some, see? Every woman does it in labor. She won't even remember this when she holds the little one in her arms. You'll see."

He smiled at her, a bit pitifully, striving to present a visage that would inspire her to clasp it to her bosom. "You're very kind. Will it be much longer do you think?"

1

She smoothed the clean, white towels over her arm with one shapely hand. "Not much, I should think. Though the first always takes longer. Is it an Argonian custom to have a male relative in attendance, Your Highness? Forgive me, but we were curious, we girls, if you were here because Prince Jack couldn't be, being in Brazoria as I'm sure it's needful he be, though very hard on our young lady, your sister, it is. We think it ever so sweet that her brother should come be near her in her husband's stead. None of *his* folk offered, not even the women." She blushed a pretty pink and covered her pretty mouth with her fingertips. "No disrespect intended, milord."

"None taken, I'm sure. We all know what gypsies are like. As a matter of fact I—"

A particularly blood-curdling bellow emanated from the royal bedchamber. The girl started, gave him an apologetic smile and a half-curtsy, and scurried off, banging through the door hip and shoulder first.

He had been about to explain to her that the last thing he intended was to be at Bronwyn's bedside for her birthing. He had, in fact, only been stopping off on the way from his fostering in Wasimarkan, where he was learning diplomacy at the behest of his Royal Mother, Queen Amberwine. The Queen had rightly pointed out that with an elder sister as Princess Consort of Ablemarle (having lost the title of Crown Princess of Argonia when her brothers were born), elder twin brothers (one of whom, Raleigh, would be King, the other of whom, Roland, would be war leader), there was very little else for her fourth child to do that would be useful.

The Queen had declared with unusual forcefulness for a person of faery blood that she was not about to have a son of hers turn into a good-for-nothing knight errant bullying the populace and using his royal perogatives to rape and pillage. It had happened elsewhere, and Rupert was no less fond of the phenomena than his mother. He was a highly peaceable and loving sort by nature—so loving, in fact, that by the age of twenty, his frost giant ancestry caused him to be so unusually tall and well grown and his faery blood lent him such uncommon beauty and charm that he was a cause for alarm among the fathers and husbands in the Wasimarkanian Court. To the men he was called, behind his back (for it would never do to offend so powerful an ally as the Royal House of Argonia) Rowan the Rake. To the women, into whose eyes he gazed soulfully and whose hands he kissed tenderly, almost without regard for age, station, or pulchritude, he was Rowan the Romantic. He would miss those charitable and generous ladies, one and all, but his mentors, under pressure, had declared that with princesses of six major countries in a swoon for his attentions, he would need more advanced lessons in diplomacy than they had to offer. They referred him back to his own family for further instruction.

The stop in Ablemarle's capitol to visit Bronwyn had been an impulse. His ship was docking to take on cargo. He had not seen Bronwyn in several years, and she had always been his favorite in the family. She was as good a fighter if not a better one than Roland—at least on the practice field—and she had had marvelous adventures when she was still much younger than Rupert. When Rupert tired of hearing of those adventures, which he sometimes did since he always wanted to learn something new, Bronwyn was most adept at making up tales to amuse him.

He almost failed to recognize the wild-eyed creature who greeted him and clung to his hand, her face so pale that every freckle stood out like a pock, her wiry red hair loose and straggling in every direction, her belly great with child. The self-sufficient big sister of his youth all but pleaded with him to remain until her child was born, as it was to be any day, she begged him to stay since her husband, Prince Jack, could not. Rupert had failed to understand any more than the pretty lady in waiting why any masculine family member should be a comfort to Bronwyn in what was first and foremost and unarguably woman's work, but he could not deny her. He had stayed.

A long, gasping cry ended in an ear-splitting scream, was followed closely with another cry, this time unmistakably the squall of an infant. Rupert jumped to his feet and strode to the door, leaving his rowan shield leaning against the door. All the Rowan offspring usually carried the shields made by their father as birthing gifts on their persons, for the rowan wood was proof against magic. But he was in his sister's hall and far more excited than he had thought he would be at the advent of this new relative, and three strides was hardly an incautious distance.

The door flung back against him and the girl with whom he had been speaking bustled out, brushing against him, a whimpering blanketed bundle cradled against her breast.

"Wait," he said quickly. "Can I see?"

She lifted the triangle of blanket just above the crook of her elbow and showed him a wrinkled, red little face which began to screw itself into another scream. "It's a girl," the maid informed him. "Isn't she adorable?"

"Quite," he said, trying to sound sincere. "I'll just go congratulate Bronwyn."

"Oh, not yet, milord," she said. "She's getting her bath and then she must rest a bit. I'll be bathing this child to be presented to her when she wakes."

"A bath?" he asked blankly. "Oh, of course, the baby would be needing a bath. Well, um, may I watch? I've never seen a new child bathed before."

"I don't see why not," the girl said with a saucy, calculating look from under her lashes, "But you Argonians certainly have strange ways, if you'll pardon my saying so, sir."

"I'd pardon you almost anything, my dear," he said politely, and opened the door to an adjoining chamber for her.

The baby's bath was interesting chiefly in that Rupert thought it very convenient to be able to bathe an entire human being in a wash basin that barely fit his two hands. Otherwise it was rather messy. The maid herself was far more intriguing, and he proceeded to get to know her better while his new niece slept in her cradle, carved in the shape of a swan and newly decked with pink ribbons by the lady whose ear he was nibbling.

The enormous draft that blasted open the double doors took both Rupert and his companion by surprise, as did the fact that neither of them were able to do so much as raise a finger to lift themselves from the tiled floor where they had been flung. Indeed, Rupert could not so much as twitch his knee from where it undoubtedly inconvenienced his paramour, lodged in her midsection. He watched helplessly as a rather large rug whisked in on the blast. Two gentlemen with blue robes and bandages tied round their heads with blue cords lifted the baby from her cradle and onto the rug and whisked back out again. They failed to blast the door shut behind them and Rupert could hear doors banging, presumably all the way down the corridors to the main entrance, as the rug flew through unhindered.

Sensation returned to him as the last distant door slammed back again, and he jumped up, still stunned. The whole incredible event had happened so fast he thought perhaps he had been napping in his new love's arms. But the cradle was empty and when he ran to the arrow slit in the corridor outside, he could make out the outline of a flat flying object with two figures on it. Behind him, the girl scrambled to her feet, clutching her bodice together, and scampered into his sister's chamber. Rupert sagged against the arrow slit for a moment and watched the rug disappear over the city, over the masts of the boats docked in the harbor, and far far out over the line of greenish-gray that marked the vastness of the Gulf of Gremlins.

When no outcry erupted from Bronwyn's chamber even after several moments, he cracked the door, expecting to see her in a swoon. Instead, she sat up in bed, her hair splashing like blood upon the pillow, her eyes staring straight ahead. The ladies around her started nervously, but she quieted them with one look and bade Rupert enter with another.

"Bronwyn, sister, I don't know what to say," he began. "I was helping your nurse with the baby's bath and we had only just put the dear little one to sleep and were chatting when—"

She took his hand in both of hers and pulled him down to sit beside her, then wrapped her arms around him. She sobbed wearily and almost noiselessly, her face against his chest, her tears soaking his fine embroidered tunic. His own tears wet her hair, and he held her and rocked her until she was so quiet he thought her sleeping. Then she disentangled herself and lay back against her pillows, her face full of grief and something else that he could have been imagining as a reflection of his own shame at having been caught dallying when those who depended on him were threatened. The look on her face undid him, so that his own tears flowed anew. Her eyes turned outward, toward him, again and she reached up to mop his tears with the edge of her sheet.

"By the Mother, Bronwyn, I am so sorry. I had no idea—"

"I know, Ru. I know. I had no right to involve you without telling you but I thought they wouldn't strike so soon, that they'd wait until she was a little older, until after her christening—though why I imagined Miragenians respecting anything but their wretched Profit—"

"You know who they were?" he asked, incredulous.

She nodded.

"You knew this would happen?"

Another nod. "I never told you the whole end of the affair with the magic pomegranate I won from the sunken castle in Frostingdung. I had promised it to the Miragenians, in exchange for their help for our father in the Great War. They fulfilled their end of the bargain so readily I knew that the pomegranate must be of great importance. I learned that it had the power to undo all magic and sow disenchantment and despair in its stead. I could not, simply could not, place such a hideous weapon in the hands of those who care only to reap more profit than their competitors. As I told you, I disposed of it, or rather, Jack did, flinging it into the deepest crevasse of the highest glacier he could find. But the Miragenians demanded, as honorable payment of my debt to them, possession of my first-born child. Jack bargained with them until they agreed to keep her for only fifteen years—"

"*Only* fifteen years? Great Mother in the Ground, Bronwyn, how could you live with such a bargain?"

She shrugged, a mere hopeless twist of her mouth and clenching of her shoulder. "One never knows what will happen. We thought perhaps we would not marry, Jack and I, as we had planned, but even if we had not loved each other for so long, the alliance was necessary for both Argonia and Ablemarle. Then we hoped I would be barren, and tried to see that it was so but—" She rolled her eyes and sniffed, disgusted with herself for her failure to keep from her husband.

"I understand," Rupert said quickly.

"That's why Jack's away now, I know it. He couldn't bear to be here when they took her. He's been strange ever since I told him I'd conceived. And in truth, I don't blame him. I wouldn't be here either if I could help it. But I can't even ride after them and offer myself as my own baby's nurse. For the honor of Argonia, the bargain must be respected, hard as it is, and I cannot hope to see my child again until she's almost a woman. But, oh, Rupert, I did think they'd let me see her christened first, protected by the gifts we could give her. There wouldn't be many, of course, considering the circumstances. We've both been in secret disgrace all these years among our families because of it. The gypsies, except for his father and grandfather, are scarcely speaking to Jack—"

At that a black-haired maid who had been scrubbing the floor beside the bed slapped down the wet cloth, wiped her hands on her skirts, and with a passionate and unreadable look from coal-dark eyes fled the room.

"Oh, dear. I forgot about her. Gypsies are so sensitive." She collapsed into the pillow for a moment, then suddenly sat straight up, swinging her legs over the side of the bed.

"What are you doing?" he asked, restraining her.

"I know. I'll disguise myself as a man and go after them. I don't know if I can find Miragenia again but I did it once. I'll take the christening gifts with me so that even if I'm discovered, my daughter will have her birthright. . . ."

Her skin was hot and her breath came raggedly as she spoke.

"Bronwyn, you can't. You're not ready to be out of childbed yet. You're ill. Besides, you told me they have magic in Miragenia. You have none. You've no chance against them."

"I'll find Carole, our cousin. She'll help. She's a witch and she has magic. Besides, she's a priestess now. She can christen my child for me there. Yes. That's what I'll do. . . . She broke free of Rupert's hands and stood for a moment before blood soaked the front of her gown, turning it from white to red as she stood seeking to keep her balance. Rupert caught her as her knees buckled and tucked her in again, while her maids clucked about her.

"Where are the christening gifts you have?" he asked her, smoothing her hair back and paying no heed to the maids tending to the lower half of her body.

"Here," she said, reaching under her pillow and extracting a pitifully small packet. "They're runed spells to be burned and mixed with the christening mud. There's nothing else except . . . Take her my rowan shield, Rupert. She'll need protection."

"Hush," he said. "So do you. She'll have my shield, and I'll make myself another. Only promise me not to rise from this bed until your midwife says it's safe. I will find this cousin of

ours and together we will do what may be done for your baby."
He brushed his lips against her hair and rushed away to hire
another ship.

Less than a month later Rupert had crossed not only the
Gulf of Gremlins but Argonia, and rode across the snow-palled
plains of Wormroost Valley. The shadows of the great glacial
peaks reached out for him, chilling him when his path led him
through them. Snow slowed his horse. It burdened the boughs
of the spruces so that they drooped like old women with full
aprons. The deciduous trees were reduced to bare bones. The
sky was muzzy gray and wonderfully eerie. Wild animals
scuttled across the snow in front of him and beside him. This
was the wildest country Rupert had ever encountered. He felt
certain it was every bit as dangerous as Miragenia and began to
enjoy the perilousness of his mission already. Court was all
very well, but a man liked action and adventure occasionally.

Now here he was, heading into this fearsome border
country, accompanied only by his horse, a hawk, and hound
borrowed from Roland's castle, where he had spent the night.
He was readying himself to face a witch. Admittedly, she was
supposed to be on his side, but nevertheless, she was a
perilously powerful person. He remembered Bronwyn's tale of
her quest very well, and, at the moment, the part where this
particular witch had tried to drown his sister figured promi-
nently in his recollections. Also on his mind were the opinions
of his Wasimarkanian friends. Wasimarkan had little magic and
less regard for it, and the attitudes of the people who had most
recently raised him influenced him sufficiently that he felt he
was being put on his mettle to deal with a witch.

For her part, the witch was dealing with a great many
other problems of a distressingly mundane nature, and would
have preferred, as she had explained to the village seamstress
only the day before, to be almost anywhere else dealing with
almost anything else. But she had her responsibilities. The
villagers were used to a magically clean manor and common

dining hall and plenty of food on the board, something Carole's mother, Maggie, with her hearth magic, had always been able to provide with what seemed to Carole unthinking efficiency. For Carole, whose own powers consisted of being able to whistle or hum objects, people, and animals into dance, maintaining the same standards as her mother took a great deal of thinking and considerably more work. She could not simply wish a thing clean, but had to whistle a broom into an appropriately useful motion, a dustcloth into yet another, and the dishcloth, ladles, spits, polishing rags, and so on, each into its own movement. Chopping knives were a nightmare, and mending had more than once produced some bizarre results when she neglected to stop the needle in time.

And unlike her mother, she could not simply expand existing supplies of food but had to locate new ones as provisions ran out. Maggie had left in such a hurry to travel to Great Aunt Sybil's bedside in the Northern Territories that she hadn't reckoned properly what would be needed for the duration of her visit, which moreover had turned into a more extended one than she had anticipated. Consequently grain, fruits, and preserved vegetables were getting low and the villagers were complaining mightily about the extra ration of fish in their diet, since Carole was totally unwilling to whistle anything less cold-eyed and more furry to its demise on a supper table. Her father, Colin Songsmith, the noted minstrel, had attended the first town council where the villagers had mentioned their dissatisfaction with the arrangements. Thereafter, he hastily recalled an important seminar at the Royal Minstrel's Academy, far to the south and safely away from the valley whose government he was supposed to administer.

Then, of course, there were her other duties, those she had taken on with her vows as priestess. There weren't too many weddings in Wormroost, for most of the inhabitants were the age of her parents or older, but many sickbeds and deathbeds to attend, and officiating at the holidays, which

Mother be praised were mostly past now with no more due until surely, *surely*, her own mother, Maggie, was safely back.

Sometimes Carole had a sneaking suspicion that Aunt Sybil, who saw into other people's lives even as they were happening, had gotten sick simply to make sure Carole had enough to do to take her mind off the treacherous defection of her erstwhile suitor, Sir Brendan, formerly a knight at Castle Rowan, a week's ride from Wormroost, presently residing with his new bride in Queenston. Not that anyone cared, the witch reminded herself, hoisting her dip net and throwing on her cloak. Queenston was an overrated bore, full of lovely, costly goods and impractical activities and people silly enough to spend too much money on them. She had tried it once, fostering there between her fifteenth and seventeenth years, and had found herself longing for the valley and the villagers, who were unpretentious, if demanding. And here her magic powers ran only a close second to her mother's hearth craft and her father's persuasive musicality, rather than being lost in the smoky explosion of the grandiose and exotic abilities abundant at court.

When her parents were home, there was naturally less call for whistling things about, but her priestess work was necessary. She had ample time to swim in the talkative Blabbermouth River, enchanted by a previous witch occupant of the valley for companionship. She also liked to visit Sebastian, the amiable white beast who guarded the glaciers on the far side of the valley. She had ofted explored the ruins of the ice castle, without disturbing the sleeping ice worm whose breath in winter covered the town in mist. And there had previously been occasions when she rode to Castle Rowan for a party or weekend outing with Roland and his wife, who were dull but at least close to her own age. She liked watching the unicorns when they came to bless the river with their horns, rendering it not only pure but capable of sensible conversation (otherwise it did nothing but gossip and utter trite drivel of a personal nature). She liked seeing Wulfric, the wolf who was formerly a were, lope across the valley as he sometimes did when the moon was full, pausing to howl in greeting from a safe and lonesome distance.

She could do with a bit of a howl herself, she thought, dismounting her black mare beside the loop of the Blabber-mouth furthest from the village. She set her net aside while she stripped off her cloak and brown gown to reveal her bathing costume. A blue velvet, decently opaque, long of sleeve, with a divided skirt. The mermaids she had met when she was a girl would laugh at it, but her mother would settle for no less decorous attire and the villagers too were easily shocked, and certainly would have been by the standard mer costume of flashing tail and lots of hair with everything else bared to the waves. Sometimes she wished she had stayed with the mermaids, as they had desired, but though the singing was nice, she simply couldn't manage to develop a taste for drowning sailors. Besides, had she done so she would have missed out on the rest of the quest which was, except for priestess training—and she supposed she had to count Sir Brendan—the last interesting thing that had happened to her.

The hole she had hacked in the ice with a hand-ax had grown ice whiskers around the edges, but she was still able to plunge in, net and all, through the narrow opening into the chattering black waters.

Rupert, riding through the worm's-breath mist to the mumbling river, knew at once he had found the witch he sought. Who else was likely to be rising dripping wet and calm as you please from a river frozen solid? Her jet mare paced near enough for her to catch the tail of the patient beast and haul herself, whistling, from the hole. She hadn't the humanity even to shiver. Holding his rowan shield firmly before him, he flipped his hawk from his other gauntlet to circle her head, while the hound barked and whined. That should stop her from extending a witchy forcible swimming invitation to him, should she be inclined to do so. He would have had no doubt about handling an ordinary woman, but a certain nervousness around witches was, he felt, entirely justifiable.

The witch clung to the horse's tail and watched the hawk for a moment before blasting three short notes that sent the bird fluttering back toward Rupert. Its far-seeing eyes were crossed with confusion.

"Excuse me," she said, waving with her free hand, "Yoo-hoo, you there on the horse. Keep that creature on a leash, will you? Or jesses, or whatever you call them. The village won't be at all happy if I let some strange bird fly off with their supper, even if it is only fish." And she flopped a net full of them up on the ice and finished climbing out after them.

Rupert quickly swung down from his horse and gave her his hand, which she accepted in lieu of the black mare's tail.

"You were fishing?" he asked. "In there?" He looked over her dripping shoulder into the steaming hole behind her.

"Yes," she said. "Ice fishing. I realize it looks a bit peculiar, but water doesn't bother me much, even very cold water. Mer blood on my father's side, you know. But if you'll excuse me now, once outside the water I freeze as quickly as anyone, and you're between me and my cloak."

The last was punctuated with the clicking of her teeth and he snatched the cloak from her saddle, wrapped it around her, and watched as she rubbed the hood briskly against her hair and the cloak over her shoulders and arms before mounting her horse.

"I've come on an urgent mission, lady," he said, mounting his own and wishing to establish his credentials at once.

"Undoubtedly, since this is hardly the season for tourists. But excuse me, it's also urgent that I get myself and these fish to the hall." And the horse trotted smartly away. He caught up with her well before they arrived at the hall and followed her inside. "Make yourself at home for a bit while I dry off, will

13

you?" she called back and disappeared through a side door to reappear with her brown hair sleeked back from her strong-featured and rather saturnine face. She was clad sedately in a brown tunic, skirt, and wrapped boots not half so becoming as the wet blue velvet.

"Do I have the pleasure of addressing the Honorable Lady Carole Songsmith-Brown?" he asked, knowing he did.

"I sincerely hope you'll find it pleasant," she replied. "But I suppose that depends on who you are and what it is you want."

"I was about to say that," Rupert replied, so taken aback by the witch's lack of civility as to forget his own training. "If you'd be kind enough to let me get to it."

"Sorry," she said, not sounding so.

He smiled down at her. She was probably still rattled at having such a very large stranger as he was accost her alone in the wilderness. Though he could certainly be forgiven for not noticing, since she seemed quite a lot calmer than he felt. "I am your cousin, Rupert Rowan, fourth child and third son of His Majesty and—er—also Duke of the Eastern Salt Marshes."

She blinked twice, staring, to his satisfaction, with her mouth open, and sat down, belatedly extending a hand to indicate that he do the same. "My," she said at last. "What a pleasant surprise. You're little Rupert, are you? Pardon me if I failed to recognize you. I think you were about four years old when last I saw you. You've grown."

He nodded.

"Didn't I hear that you were abroad somewhere?"

"I was. Wasimarkan. I've learned all they have to teach me now, however, and am, as I mentioned, on an urgent mission for my lady sister."

"Bronwyn? You've seen her? How is she?"

"Sick with grief," he said, and told her the story of the

14

kidnapping, adding a few sword thrusts on his part and deleting the role of the nurse.

"Didn't waste any time, did they?" she asked with a brooding look into her mug of herb tea. She had prepared both of them a mug while Rupert spoke.

"Not even long enough to have the child christened, which seems to be what distresses Bronwyn the most. She was ready to ride over here in her nightgown to ask you to help her see that the child has full protective rites."

"But you came instead?"

He nodded.

"Let me throw together some food and get my cloak," she said, rising.

"You don't understand. They're already in Miragenia by now. It will be a long and hazardous quest."

"Oh, but I do. I'm quite prepared now, unless you're weary from your journey and want to rest a night?" Carole tried to sound merely cooperative rather than eager, but inwardly she praised the Mother for delivering her from the tedium of the past few weeks. And though the witch was sorry, in a somewhat abstract way, for the trouble that had befallen Bronwyn's household, she was not surprised and was certainly not displeased at the excitement Bronwyn's misfortune promised to generate. Not that Carole was enjoying the trouble exactly, just the opportunity to help her cousin out of it, as she had previously done when Bronwyn's curse had been a royal pain in the neck for herself and everyone else.

What marvelous timing. Just when she was about to march the entire village into the river, which no doubt would have made everyone very cross with her, Bronwyn provided her with a perfectly lovely excuse to chuck it all and venture forth to aid a beleaguered baby. No, not an excuse. A sacred duty. A family trust. A dire, drastic emergency. Even if one were extremely reluctant, one would have had to respond, of course, both as priestess and family member. Anyone would understand that. On the other hand, no one, especially the Prince, was likely to take kindly Carole's unseemly delight at the prospect, so she controlled her face and modulated her voice a full three octaves below the tones of squeaky excitement she was apt to emit if she wasn't careful. "You did say it was urgent, didn't you?"

"Yes, I suppose I did. I just thought you'd need more persuading."

"Under the circumstances, I can hardly quibble. Just let me drop those fish off at a certain town councilman's cottage on the way and I'll delay you no longer."

As she was grabbing her cloak, however, the long narrow windows of the hall began rattling and the massive furniture quivered. Presently there came a great noise, a periodic booming, as of some huge drum, passing overhead and quitting just as it cleared the manor house. A horse screamed. Rupert was on his feet at once, his hand to his sword hilt. Carole touched his arm.

"It's nothing to worry about. Just one of the dragons. Since I managed to persuade the council not to butcher the cow I set aside for her, she won't trouble your horse. Not unless she's unusually hungry that is."

Unreassured, Rupert raced for the door and around the building. In the farmyard was indeed a dragon, daintily covering with a loop of her tail a charred carcass from which she was chewing a haunch. She looked up, and belched, and to Rupert's amazement, blushed. He could tell she was blushing for her color deepened so that the lightest shade of pink in her scales, which was as delicate as the inside of a seashell, turned the same deep rose as her darkest shading. Her eyes were as large as his shield and the color of lilacs. They blinked slowly and incredulously, watching him.

"Ah, Grippeldice," Carole said, a pace or so behind him. "Good to see you. Meet my cousin, the Prince."

The dragon's eyes grew, if possible, larger, and then the

delicately veined lids drooped shyly over them and didn't look back up again. Her head dipped toward her rosy wing. Rupert knew the look, though he had never seen it on a dragon before. He didn't pause to wonder how Carole communicated with the beast. She was a witch, after all. He assumed she used witchcraft. He bowed his most elegant and courtly bow and said, "I had no notion we bred dragons so fair in this land, cousin," and, in a quick whisper from the side of his mouth added, "You can tell her I said so. You did say it was a *lady* dragon, did you not?"

Carole nodded. "Grippeldice is on mountain patrol this month. We provide her with stock in payment for her services."

Grippeldice emitted a low, hoarse growl, producing a cloud of steam. Carole nodded, and turned back to Rupert with an expression of amusement and a slightly raised eyebrow. "She wants to know where you've been all her life."

"I've been—see here, I'll pay you if you'll give me that spell you're using to talk to her. I've never spoken to a dragon before."

"Sorry, but it's no spell. It's Pan-Elvin, a magical language that takes years to learn. It's all in the silent letters, you see. So when I use it, it sounds like Argonian to anyone else but the creature I'm addressing, who hears the magical silent letters in its own tongue. When the dragon replies, she uses the dragonese version."

Rupert, who hadn't quite caught all that, scratched his head and shook back the curl dangling so charmingly over his forehead. "I must get you to teach me this language then. I really have to learn to speak with dragons."

"We have unicorns hereabouts, too, but they're shy unless—I don't suppose you're . . . no, silly of me, never mind."

Rupert was about to protest that she must tell him what she meant by that, too, until it dawned on him that he knew with whom, according to legend, unicorns were most friendly. He grinned and winked at her. "No, I'm afraid I wouldn't qualify in that respect, though I'm sure I could convince a unicorn of the purity of my intentions if only you'd provide the introductions."

Grippeldice, piqued at being left out of the conversation, breathed a slightly sulfurous puff in their direction. Carole made a quick reply. The dragon batted her eyes at Rupert again twice before launching herself upward, cow and all, and disappearing into the glacial peaks.

"That fish will be nasty if we don't get it delivered soon," Carole said, cheerfully linking arms with him. "And it might be wise to leave before the dragon forgets her cow and decides to take you instead. They're rather impetuous creatures, dragons."

CHAPTER II

The town councilman was far less pleased than Carole with her present and the knowledge that Wormroost would just have to cope without its resident witch and spiritual adviser for the time being.

"But won't that be hard on them?" Rupert asked as they left, very quickly, while the front door of the councilman's cottage slammed behind them.

Carole grinned a grin worthy of the Wasimarkanian version of a witch. "On the contrary, I think it will be very good for them. No doubt the Mother planned it that way. Still, we need to be well away from here quickly. I'm sure the stableman will be glad of the loan of a hound and bird for company and old Bernard may even remember how to hunt with them."

"Do you have the power of flight to transport us?" Rupert asked suspiciously. He did not mind taking her along, but he didn't much care for the way she was already trying to manage things.

"No," she said, "But I do have an extra pair of skis—that is if you're interested in a shortcut?"

"Back to Queenston?"

"Through the mountain, as Bronwyn and I did when we were girls, and to the sea."

"What then? Will your skis carry us across the sea to Miragenia?"

"No, but I think the mermaids might. Or they might let us ride their sea serpent."

Rupert, who had never been on skis, through a mountain, seen mermaids, or ridden a sea serpent before, was more than eloquent at persuading the stableman that the horse, hound, and hawk he had borrowed from Roland would be a great benefit to the entire village and were deserving of his tenderest care.

The skis were too short for him and the laces had to be lengthened to fit his feet, but once mounted on the skis, he watched his cousin glide forward with a half-stepping, half-skating gait, and soldiered bravely after her. On the river, he gained confidence and skill enough to pass her, but she stopped him with a gesture, and without explanation continued at a faster pace until she came to what looked like the side of the mountain, at which point she squatted down over her skis and plunged into some dead vegetation.

In a short time her voice called to him. "Come ahead. It's safe."

He did, gliding forward, squatting about where he thought he had seen her squat, and wondering what all the fuss was about when the bottom dropped out of the river, his skis flew out from under him, and he thumped down hard on his tailbone to slide through the dead brush and down into icy darkness.

"I thought you said it was safe," he said when he had recovered his breath to find her standing above him, waiting beside the frozen waterfall down which he had just fallen. They were surrounded by cavern walls pierced with holes through which pale light glittered on a wide rink, a pool of ice.

"Don't worry," she said, "You'll get the hang of the steep places after a while. There aren't many like that one. What I meant was that the river is frozen down here, too. I wasn't sure it would be, though I suppose I could have asked it. If it hadn't been, I'd have needed you to pull me up again so we could try the other way, but I believe this is going to work."

Rupert finished checking and decided he was still in one piece. Carole produced a pocket torch from her bag of supplies and lit it just outside the tunnel on the opposite side of the pool.

The tunnel was long and dark, breaking off at times into channels. The first of these forks baffled Carole for a moment.

"But didn't you notice them before?" Rupert asked.

"The swan was pulling us in a boat. I suppose she just chose correctly. I haven't tried the passage since. Just a moment. I'll ask."

She knelt down and used the flame of the torch to melt a deep hole in the ice. A thin voice burbled up. "Which is the safest way to the sea for us, Blabbermouth?" she asked it.

"To the right," it said.

"Thank you," she replied.

"Don't mention it. It's lonely down here, this time of year."

The next time she asked, the river was less than polite, advising them to go, "down the center, stupid." Carole explained to Rupert that the river was changeable as it ran its course, a statement that was proved out as yet later, the voice, dulled to a sucking whisper, replied, "All ways are the same to me" and a lot more nonsense Rupert couldn't make out.

Carole knelt longer at that spot, her eyes flickering up at him in the torchlight like a wild beast who had paused to drink at the puddle in front of her. "The spell wears off here," she said. "The river doesn't talk at all on the other side of the mountain. But the right-hand passage appears widest, don't you think?"

He did and reasoned that if it was not, they could always retrace their tracks and find their way upstream again.

When at last the cave broadened onto a horizon, it was a

darkened one, with an undulating ribbon of green rippling along the edge between the star-filled sky and the broad expanse of snow that was the eastern Blabbermouth.

They leaned on their poles at the mouth of the tunnel, allowing their eyes to rest on the green aurora and the stars. Abruptly, they found themselves staring instead at something quite different: All light was blocked from above when a cart-sized head dipped down from the top of the cave's entrance and an upside-down muzzle emitted sulfurous gusts of welcome while great lamping eyes blinked at them.

Rupert laughed. "How very clever. She followed us."

Carole felt unaccountably annoyed at the interruption. She had been enjoying the shushed ski through the mountain and the moonlight, the prospect of adventure in the company of her handsome and amiable young cousin. Surely just because she chose to delegate her own temporary duties there was no cause for every other creature in the east of Argonia to do likewise? "Grippeldice, why aren't you patrolling? You know good and well it's only us down here rather than invading armies or bandits."

The dragon did an airborne backwards somersault and landed gracefully upon her claws and tail in the riverbed ahead of them. She belched sparks at them.

"What did she say?" Rupert asked, smiling a puzzled but winning smile in the dragon's direction.

"Nothing really. She's just curious. She's a youngster yet and doesn't take her responsibilities seriously." The last came out in a somewhat self-righteous tone, considering the speaker, Carole thought, chiding herself.

"But if she's on patrol, perhaps she did think we were invaders. I had no idea dragons were so intelligent."

The object of his admiration regarded him lovingly and chirruped.

"I don't think so, Grippeldice," Carole replied quickly. "It doesn't fit in with our plans. Why don't you fly away now and tend to business? Dragons do not woo princes customarily, you know. You're a separate species. It would never work out."

Grippeldice hung her head sulkily. Rupert gave Carole an indignant look. "She's only trying to be friendly. You needn't hurt her feelings. Please tell her that I think she's very beautiful and that were I a dragon, I'd be sure to be smitten. As it is I hope we shall be friends."

Carole complied reluctantly. Her cousin might be a prince but he knew very little about dragons. She did know that even though her mother and father had dealt with Grippeldice's parents on occasion, their dealings were cautious. Dragons might cooperate with people sometimes, but they weren't to the best of her knowledge to be trusted as friends. The sort of behavior Grippeldice was displaying was so uncharacteristic as to make anyone with more brains than vanity nervous. Why, Carole and the dragon had all but grown up together and Grippeldice had certainly never offered *her* a ride.

Grippeldice cooed. Rupert skied ahead of Carole and reached out to pat the dragon. The beast lowered her head and nudged invitingly at him.

"Why, I think she means for me to ride her, cousin," he said, bending down to unfasten his skis.

"Your Highness, I don't think that's wise. No one has ever ridden Grippeldice that I know of and the coast is not too far to ski. Besides, the mermaids are—"

Rupert was not to be thwarted. "Nonsense. No one has ridden her before because she has not wished them to. I'm sure that if I request it, she will carry you also. Don't be such a spoilsport. I'll need a translator. Tell her I said you must come, too, and we will only ride as far as the sea coast. I don't want to miss seeing mermaids."

The serious young man who had so movingly related to her the plight of his sister seemed now more interested in trying one new thrill after another, but that was fairly typical of the jaded sort of person one found at court, Carole thought, her good mood at winning free of the village fading into irritation.

She couldn't resist mumbling into Grippeldice's ear as she climbed aboard that she hoped the dragon would be content with transporting them to the coast and then resume her more serious duties.

"Bother my duties, dearie," Grippeldice said. "They include invaders and *he* is the only stranger in these parts. I see more in a single day's flight than you would see coming in a week. I can spare the time, and still leave your puny domain safe. Why are you so all-fired interested in my duties all of a sudden anyway, hot stuff? You never said much to me before except 'Your cow is over there, dragon.' Trying to get rid of me? Don't blame you. I didn't realize they made mortals like *him*!"

Carole shook her head and settled down between two spines in front of Rupert. "They don't, dragon. But he's part of my family and part of the royal family besides. I just wouldn't want you to get so carried away you . . . forget yourself and treat him like one of your cows."

The dragon snorted at that but didn't reply.

Rupert was agawk over the countryside between the tunnel and the sea, pointing out every starlit bend in the river with awe and wonder. Unfortunately, by the time Carole finished her exchange with the dragon, the beast's strong wings had already carried them to the coast. Carole dismounted and stood staring out to sea. When Rupert asked if she was calling the mermaids, she didn't answer. This caused Rupert to look all the more avidly out to sea himself, while Grippeldice flapped nervously nearby. The dragon cooed inquiringly. Rupert gave her a half-impatient, half-apologetic shrug and continued his vigil. Grippeldice sighed warmly and departed, sensing herself dismissed. Rupert glanced quickly at his cousin, wondering when and how she was going to produce the mermaids.

Having returned to the spot where she first met the mermaids for the purpose of calling them again, the witch hesitated, recalling the less pleasant aspects of that other meeting. Weighing in her mind the merwomen's kinship with herself against their fondness for drowning anyone without mer connections, her own power against theirs, her wish to help Rupert meet the obligation he had incurred to Bronwyn against the danger, ultimately she decided that they had come this far and it would be much further to return, and not nearly so interesting. "Perhaps it would be better if you keep out of sight until I have a chance to talk to them again," she told her cousin finally. "They have a rather unusual view of . . . life, you might say, and can be dangerous to men, particularly. I would feel much better if I were able to see if I can persuade them to guarantee our passage before they meet you."

"You wouldn't just send them away before I got to meet them, would you?" he asked.

But his question was carried to sea with the same cold wind that blew the first notes of her whistled calling to the mermaids. He watched her for a while, reasoning that he would hide when he saw something coming on the distant sea, and then he paced, shivering despite his furlined cloak and gloves. He wandered in small circles, drawing patterns in the snow with the toe of his boot and still his cousin whistled. The tune was eerie and pervasive, rising and falling on the wind, but catchy, and soon he found that he too was whistling.

She batted her hand sharply at him to stop and he shrugged. "I'm not magic. Surely they can't hear me. And if they can, perhaps it helps."

"Don't—" she began but was interrupted as something large and narrow slid toward them through the waves. In the dark waters directly in front of them, two wet heads popped to the surface. Rupert was too busy staring to remember to hide, even if he still could have done so.

"Ooh, sweeting, I *love* how you modified that song of

calling," said the head on the right in a sweet, piping voice. Her hair gleamed wet and faintly green around her.

"Lorelei! How good to see you again," Carole said.

"It's good to see you, too, you sly little eel, but whoever is that behind you?" she replied.

"I think Carole's going to be her same old selfish self," the other mermaid said in a low and sultry voice, thick as honey. Her hair shone lavender in the starlight, and she regarded Rupert critically. "How about it, minnow? Are you keeping him for yourself or is he a present?"

"Cordelia, you haven't changed at all, have you? This is Prince Rupert, our King and Queen's son," Carole replied calmly. "Perhaps you remember his sister, Princess Bronwyn, who was with me when we met before."

"I don't remember *her*," Lorelei gushed. "But I do remember that delicious king."

"Yesss," Cordelia hissed, flapping up for a better look and giving Rupert a good look himself at what provided mermaids with some of their frontal bouyancy and a great deal of their charm. "My, my, how much nicer the family resemblance looks on the boys." To Carole she said, "Well, are you going to tell us why you went to all the trouble to make an introduction, clamface, or are you just going to stand there on your tail and pop your eyes at us all night?"

"Cordelia, don't be such a shark. Poor Carole, do stop being so awfully dry and come out here where it's comfortable," Lorelei said. "I don't know how we're supposed to talk about anything with you towering over us like that."

"Do you mind?" Carole asked Rupert, as if excusing herself to go to the privy. "I do need to talk to them—"

"Er, no, of course not. Never mind me. I'll just stand here and bask in the charm of such lovely company." The last was almost sincere, despite the fact that he was freezing to death. The bows of both mermaids were now above water, no longer concealed by the wet and clinging hair, and the sirens smiled at him flirtatiously as he talked to little brown Carole.

While the witch was stripping to her bathing costume Lorelei winked at him. "Why don't you tell us yourself what brings you so far, sweeting?"

"Why, tales of the beauties who dwell in the sea. A sight so wondrous I had to behold it for myself, fair maiden," he replied with a wink of his own.

"Fair mai—oh, you!" Lorelei squealed, and splashed him playfully. "Wouldn't you like to come in and play, too? Isn't it awfully cold and dry out there?" Her shining eyes grew large and fascinating as the sea while her voice crooned melodiously in his ears.

"Lorelei," Carole said warningly, splashing feet first in beside her. "He is *not* for drowning. Come on. I'm counting on you to help me persuade Cordelia to take us to Frostingdung."

"Do *you* want to go to Frostingdung, sweeting?" Lorelei asked, still gazing up at him and rewetting her lips with the tip of her tongue.

"In your company? Any man would be a fool not to."

"And our company is the *only* reason?" Cordelia asked, the calculation in her voice coated with honey.

"Other than a small family errand that provides an excuse for the journey, yes, ma'am. A fellow can't refuse a service for his own sister, can he, especially when he's as great an admirer of womankind as I?" He leered a little to make the point, and even Cordelia fanned her tail coquettishly.

"Well, then," she said, "I do think we can help you. Ollie, accommodate the gentleman."

Carole, who had been vainly paddling around trying to catch someone's attention, watched with a rueful expression as a coil of the silver-spotted sea serpent previously lolling just beneath the surface slithered ashore. Rupert sat quickly and unceremoniously as the coil gathered him in its circumference. He straddled the slippery back, thrilling at the novelty of what he was about to do. Belatedly, he noticed Carole, still swimming, reach ashore to grab her clothing and supply pouch.

"Cousin, may I assist you?" he asked, leaning precariously toward her.

She handed up the parcel. "Thank you, no. I believe I'll swim for now." She sounded, and felt, a little helpless. She had been outmaneuvered by the mermaids and by her cousin himself at trying to obtain some guarantee of safety for him. But then, mermaids were far more experienced at luring men than she was at luring mermaids, so she supposed she would simply have to keep alert and hope for the best.

For a time it looked as if her worries were unfounded. Rupert artlessly engaged both sirens in conversation, questioning them about their domain and listening with flattering interest to their simpering replies. Before long his hair and clothing were glistening with ice formed by the freezing of droplets sprayed up on him by his excited hostesses. Most of their prey—guests—didn't care to engage them in conversation. It was fortunate for Rupert that he was inclined to do so, and restful for Carole, since talking kept the mermaids from trying out any of their siren songs on him.

Later, when they did so, they were merely showing off and he insisted on singing harmony in a competently melodious baritone.

"How nicely you sing, cousin," Carole said, when they had finished, chiming in before Cordelia and Lorelei could embark upon a more lethal tune. "One would think you of mer stock yourself."

He ducked his head, boyishly pleased at the compliment. "My christening gift from your father, Minstrel Colin. The gift of song."

Even the sea serpent responded to Rupert's own odd sort of spell. The monster turned its long flat head occasionally to gaze with a sort of bemused admiration at its passenger. This caused it to forget the rhythm of its humping glide through the water and at one point threatened to dump Rupert overboard, except that Carole was watching for just such an event and

28

spoke sharply. Ollie looked sheepish, for a sea serpent, when he wove his head back to set the proper course again.

Carole swam along to the left and a bit ahead of the mermaids, near Ollie's head. The cadence of her own stroking soothed her apprehensiveness somewhat, and the limitlessness of the sea pleased her in a way that made her wonder how she could have spent so long away from it. When she returned from the quest, perhaps she would build herself a retreat near the shore, and leave the village and her parents sometimes to go to it. Perhaps she would even live there, and people would have to come from afar to find her. If they would. She was not likely to be as sought-after as her gregarious cousin, holding court from Ollie's back. It seemed to her on one hand that everyone made a tremendous fuss over the silly young man, and she wondered why, briefly, as she looked into the sea. But when she glanced back up into the happy, enthusiastic countenance of the handsome prince, she decided that he wasn't all that silly, though the reaction of every living creature who encountered him appeared to be. She had heard of the glamor of the faeries before but this was the first time she had ever seen it in action. Her aunt, Queen Amberwine, was said to possess the quality in abundance, but was often ill or absent while Carole was at court so the witch personally had never observed her to any degree to form an opinion one way or the other. But Rupert, combining his father's imposing stature with the refinement of his mother's long and delicate bone structure, the King's bluff honesty with the Queen's charm, had some sort of magic that not even his rowan shield could subdue.

Whatever the source of his power over his fellow creatures, so far it was standing them in good stead, though in some circumstances it could forseeably be dangerous.

The mermaids' atoll was much as she remembered it, a bit higher in the water perhaps, with the fresh-water pool in the center a little deeper into the coral-rimmed circle. Carole sat on a water-smoothed ledge just above sea level hugging her knees as Rupert and Lorelei bandied further words. "Is that trove still down there?" she asked the mermaid suddenly. "The one with all the instruments you showed me when I was a girl? I'd like to dive down and see it again."

The mermaid started to nod and Rupert looked up, easily diverted from his flirtations. "A treasure trove?" he asked.

"You should see it, Your Highness," she began, but almost before the words were out of her mouth the mermaids were diving like ducks, fetching up one salt-soaked bauble after another for the prince's perusal.

He praised the gold-and-pearl harp, the ropes and garlands of gems from pirate chests, the emerald whistle, and the stringless tarnished silver lute, but it was a tiny, thin-spined comb made of a single opalescent fan-shaped shell that pleased him the most and he turned the thing, no larger than his own substantial thumbnail, over and over, stroking it. "What an exquisite piece. I can't help thinking, cousin, that if the poor child had had the usual, happy sort of birthing rites, this would have been the sort of thing she should be receiving—"

The mermaids immediately set up a sympathetic clamor, wanting to know which poor child had so aroused his interest. He told them of Bronwyn's baby, brushing a tear from the corner of his eye as he talked. Carole would have sworn, from her knowledge of the sirens, that had she pleaded for the baby on bended knee and wracked with sobs the mermaids would have responded with indifference. Rupert's account of the baby's plight instead seemed to touch their hearts, which previously had given evidence of pumping nothing but pure, cold, green seawater.

"If you think she would like the comb, you must take it to her, Prince," Cordelia said in an uncharacteristically impulsive gesture. "Let it be our birthing gift to the dear little minnow."

For once it was Lorelei who appeared mean. "*That*

comb?" she asked. "Oh, Cordelia, do you think, knowing what that comb does that a split-tailed child of no mer ancestry should—"

"And who would need it more?" Cordelia replied with kindness throbbing through her until it quivered her very tail. She turned her wide, gray stare back to Rupert, who perched on an outcropping above her, looking humble and grateful and awestricken at the marvelous gift. "My sister refers to the magic properties of the comb, Prince Rupert. And indeed, it *has* been a while since we gifted a mortal child with anything quite so fine, but any cousin of dear Carole's is a cousin of ours, in a way," and she batted her dripping lashes at him.

Carole looked into the heavens and tapped her toe, schooling herself with priestessly patience to refrain from mentioning that the mermaids had hardly behaved as generously to their "mutual" cousin, Bronwyn.

"Magic powers?" he asked, as if unable to believe his luck. "*Real* magic powers?"

"We'd hardly give you fake ones, now would we?" Cordelia said, the edge creeping back into her voice.

"Oh, pardon me if I sounded dull, my dear lovely lady. I am just so overwhelmed already at your generous gesture of giving that unfortunate little one such a beautiful object. And to think it also carries with it wondrous power!"

"Not all *that* wondrous," Cordelia said modestly. "It will only help her grow a tail as she should have had had she not been born into deprived circumstances, and to breathe properly. It's an old device, a recruiting tool used once when our numbers were small and our power great. Now, of course, we no longer actively recruit, since Lorelei and I admirably manage this section of the sea. But if the girl should care to be schooled, we would be happy to foster her. In fact, I believe there's another of these below, dear boy, if you should care to—"

Rupert held up the flat of his hand and said in a choked

31

voice, "Oh, no. No, gentle lady of the waves, you do me too much honor. This beautiful and powerful gift for my helpless niece I may accept for her sake, but already you have done so much, your hospitality, your transportation, your charming company, and all of the lessons you have taught me about your fabulous water world. I'm overwhelmed."

"Naturally," Cordelia said. "But that is no reason to dismiss our offer."

"I wasn't dismissing it. I simply—"

"You mortals are all alike. A person condescends to talk with you, gives you everything, and first thing you know, you're spurning the idea of even changing one little bitty thing to—"

"But wait!" Rupert cried. "I didn't."

"You didn't?" Lorelei asked. "You mean you will accept our offer and join us here in the sea? Oh, how wonderful! And don't worry about the child. Carole can easily take care of that, can't you, dear?"

"What I meant to say was that it was so kind of you to transport us and we're both awfully grateful and while I'd really like to come back and see you often, right now it *is* necessary that *both* my lady cousin and I find my niece and make sure she has the proper start in life."

"How well do you swim?" Cordelia asked, a definite nastiness polluting her nectared tones.

Rupert smiled innocently back at her. "Oh, I swim quite well, but not nearly so well as you or your serpent."

"Yes, Ollie is a remarkable creature. You can see why we wouldn't wish to risk him in monster-ridden waters such as those around Frostingdung. If you'll only stay a day or so more, we'll call you a ship. That would be much nicer for all of us than to risk getting eaten by monsters, wouldn't it?" Her smile left some doubt about who the monsters might be.

Carole thought that the conversation had gone quite far enough. She picked up Rupert's shield and handed it to him.

"Cordelia, Lorelei, you promised the Prince you'd help us," she reminded them reasonably.

"So we promised and so we did," Cordelia said. "We brought you here to where you'll meet the very first ship passing by. But surely *you* recall how it was with those horrors created when the split-tails in Frostingdung took out their war on the sea, emptying their vile magics into our waters. I thought you *liked* Ollie. Surely you wouldn't expect us to expose him to that? So, I think since we're all getting on so well you should just do as you did before and take a ship. Or, if you prefer, if you really think it's so safe, you could swim ahead, dear, and we would send the nice young man later."

Carole gave the last suggestion the attention it deserved and ignored it. "When did the last ship come by?" she asked.

"It can't have been more than two or three years after the one you took last time, can it, Cordelia?" Lorelei said with an optimistic and encouraging smile.

"Not a bit more. We'll keep you fed on delicious seafood salad, and, meanwhile, Prince Rupert can learn to use a comb. Oh, I think you'll be ever so dashing in a tail, sweeting."

"That's a fascinating idea, ma'am," he said, "But I am bound to fulfill this quest for now. What if I couldn't change back?"

"Just think! You'd be rid of your deformity forever," Lorelei replied.

Rupert looked a little frightened, Carole thought, which showed good sense on his part. He was in over his head in more ways than one. The time seemed ripe for a threat.

"Remember the dance I taught you two?" the witch asked the mermaids, as if reminiscing again. "Perhaps you'd like to perform it for Rupert—keep your shield up, cousin—and afterwards, we could discuss this again."

The mermaids hit the water with a drenching splash and swam as if their lives depended on it. Ollie trailed in their wake, ululating inquisitively.

Rupert turned a puzzled face to Carole. "What was that all about?"

"I danced them around on the coral till the scales fell off their tails the last time they wanted to harm friends of mine," she said with deep and malicious satisfaction of a sort most common to but by no means exclusive to witches.

"Do you think they would have harmed me?" he asked.

"I think they may still, unless we're vigilant."

"I don't feel very vigilant," he said honestly. "I feel tired." Little wonder in that, since dawn had already dawned and the sun was again high in the sky. "I don't think it's wise to sleep," Carole told him. "They'll try to sing you off the island."

"But surely you can do something about that? They're afraid of you. I have to thank you for intervening. I had no idea they'd take offense so easily. But sometimes people just want me to stay somewhere with them a longer time than I want to."

She smiled ruefully and patted his dangling foot. "You were born into the wrong side of the family. People are generally more than glad to get rid of Brown witches. Even town councilmen, however useful they might find us."

"Then they're foolish," he said warmly. "I think you are a magnificent person—riding dragons and sea monsters and commanding mermaids with no more than a song. I'm very glad Bronwyn suggested that you come along."

"That's good of you, but I'm afraid I'm all out of bright ideas now, if not tunes. I'm sleepy, too, and the sirens are canny enough to know that we will be. I could try to fetch help, but the nearest coastline is Frostingdung, and Cordelia may be right about the monsters there. I had supposed they might have died off by now, but apparently not. I don't suppose you would care to change your mind and accept the mermaids' offer? I could call Lorelei back?"

He winced.

She favored him with a considering look and sighed. "Sorry, but right now that seems the most practical thing.

34

Perhaps I could manage to hijack Ollie, though the others have a much closer connection with him than I do. Without diverting them somehow I don't see how I would cope. I can always swim back to Argonia but if you have no aspirations as a merman or a drowning victim . . ."

Her voice trailed off as Rupert's gaze lifted skyward. A bright spot like a pinkish falling star sped toward them, growing more distinct as its bulk blocked the sun.

"I must remember to write Sir Cyril about this," Rupert said with a certain misplaced pride. "I don't believe there have been any other instances of princes being rescued by dragons, do you?"

"Not princes, no," she agreed. Rescue by dragon had become, for her mother and father in their early years, practically a tradition. With Bronwyn and Jack on her own youthful quest, she had helped rescue both senior dragons and Grippeldice. She understandably resented the expression on the younger dragon's face when she landed. It could only be described as a dragonish smirk, as if Grippeldice knew all about mermaids and had known from the first that Carole's plan wouldn't work.

CHAPTER III

The most recognizable feature of the coastline of Suleskeria oddly enough was the sea monsters Carole had not expected to see. They wallowed brazenly offshore, in greater and more unhealthy abundance than ever, snarling, mewling, drooling, attacking each other, chewing, diving, lurking, and floating like dead things on the surface of the water. The mermaids, for once, had not been merely making excuses. Even a large beast such as Ollie would have little chance of reaching shore unscathed, and then only if sea serpents were not on the menu of any of the other monsters present.

Carole worried when she saw this that there would no longer be a village at which to rest, for the monsters had menaced the town with great ferocity even when their numbers were smaller. And indeed, there was no village. There was instead a mighty city, with six buildings over two stories tall, arched gates, and domed and spired houses with gardens and fountains. There was also a covered marketplace, and everywhere people bustled, dickered, hauled bundles, rode and led horses, donkeys, cattle, sheep, pigs. Nowhere could she see any of the iron-banded buildings that had been the trademark of the Suleskeria where she had landed previously. The river was filled with barges and small boats, and the fishing industry seemed to center there. No boats at all lined the seashore. The docks were empty, the nets that had once guarded the coast now dried beside the river. Everything looked cleaner and more organized, the folk dressed in graceful flowing robes and some sort of headgear, the streets clean, the vegetation restored.

The castle on the hill had undergone structural changes, too—two new wings adorned with domes and spires, arched entrances, the whole exterior accented with mosaic-tiled decoration.

Carole whistled with unmagical amazement. "Gilles and Rusty appear to be doing very well for themselves."

The men-at-arms of Castle Killgilles were understandably startled when a dragon circled their outer bailey. They couldn't seem to decide whether to send up a volley of arrows or stare with their mouths wide open. Rupert's diplomatic training was not wasted however. Waving in a broad, friendly manner and nudging Carole to do the same he bellowed, "Yo, the castle! Greetings, friends! How is the good—"

"Baron," Carole supplied.

"Baron?" Rupert finished.

The good Baron looked considerably better than he had nearly twenty years ago, as a matter of fact. His silver-gilt hair disguised any gray strands and the new lines of authority in his face became him. Notably missing was the haunted and wine-soaked demeanor that had characterized him in times past.

His wife, the former Mistress Ruby Rose Raspberry, known to her friends as Rusty, was adept at penetrating disguises, even those caused by time and experience; she recognized Carole at once.

"My dear, you're bearing up marvelously. And where *did* you get *that* stunning creature?"

"The dragon?" Carole asked.

"Don't be coy. That utterly charming young man, of course."

"Excuse me. This is His Royal Highness, Prince Rupert Rowan, my cousin. Your Highness, meet Baron Gilles Killgilles, governor of Outer Frostingdung and his wife, Baroness Ruby Rose. The Baroness is the daughter of Wizard Raspberry of Argonia. I'm sure Bronwyn will have mentioned them to you."

"Call me Rusty, please. Everyone does," the Baroness said, permitting her hand to be kissed. It was a rather grubby hand, covered with stains and the scars of burns from experimenting with her alchemist's oven. Rupert noted that her nails, though wearing their share of stains, came to wicked points.

Everybody agreed on how charmed they all were to meet everybody else.

"You're both looking extremely well," Carole said. "Life in Frostingdung must have improved somewhat."

"In a great many ways, it definitely has," the Baron agreed. "Most importantly, it has become so newfangled—as my father put it—that he got disgusted with the whole country, decided that it would never return to the way it was when he was lord, and gave up ghosting me to venture on to whatever one does next. He haunts and nags me no longer."

"That is my job these days. Mine and the Miragenian bill collectors," his wife said with a wry twist of her thin lips. Carole noted that Rusty still avoided smiling open-mouthed in a manner that would display her rather alarmingly pointed teeth, the legacy of her ogress-descended mother. Her foxy red hair was dressed to loop over her ears, concealing their pointed tips, inherited from her half-elvin father, though the sharpness of her chin and nose, the tilt of her green eyes, and the general impression she gave of being distantly related to a vixen was unmistakable.

"Between them they are more than making up for my dear departed Dad," the Baron said, passing a wrist over his eyes in mock weariness. "You must tell Carole and His Highness the amusing tale of how you nearly burned down the west wing trying to produce simulacrums of outrageous plants to feed the populace. The Miragenians charged us extra interest on the loan for the repairs and raised our insurance on the castle another forty chests of iron pieces."

"Only because they were not pleased when they learned my experiments do work with chickweed and in time will be successful in other areas," Rusty said proudly. Behind her hand she added to Carole, "They get cranky with anyone who makes any progress with magic not in their employ. I swear they run the country with a more tyrannical hand than Loefwin at his worst."

"Oh?" Carole asked. "I thought they were only going to provide temporary aid until your own magic could be restored."

"My wife exaggerates," the Baron said quickly. "They simply have given such fine aid and at such reasonable rates and credit terms that even when our own practitioners developed, we found they were far more limited in scope than we remembered and the Miragenians were able to offer better and more varied services. I don't know what we'd do without the technical advisors we have staying with us at Castle Killgilles. Emperor Loefwin just appointed a Grand Wazir from among the ones he has. The Company sent him a whole case of free samples of simulated dancing girls to acknowledge the honor. Didn't go over at all well with Empress Lily Pearl, as you may well imagine."

"The Company?" Carole asked.

"Well, certainly. We deal exclusively with Mukbar, Mashkent and Mirza since they have the contract here. They have advisors in all of the former kingdoms and have done wonders. Everything has changed completely—"

"I noticed that the sea monsters are still a problem."

"Well, yes, and that is unfortunate, but as the Company explained, Miragenia is desert-based and sea-going magic isn't really in their line of products. It keeps us a bit sealed off from the rest of the world, having the monsters out there, but we really do get on so well with the Company's help these days that one hardly notices."

Rupert fell in beside the Baron, asking questions about the castle and its architecture while Rusty said in another aside to Carole, "I swear Gilles is so peace-loving now that things have improved he fails to see the danger in anything. Sometimes I think his father stopped haunting him prematurely, but I can see why the old boy couldn't take it. It's 'the Company' this and 'the Company' that and them owning the gross national product and anything else we might manage to possess from now till the end of the world."

A thin ribbon of flame shot past Carole's ear and past Rupert's ahead of her. She turned to face a glowering dragon. "If you people are quite through with my fascinating companionship, I'll just cool my heels for a while in the river. I feel the need to freshen up in case the Prince—"

The guards, meanwhile, advanced with snarls and raised spears.

"Oh, dear," Carole said. "Tell them to stop. They'll hurt her."

The Baroness gave the required command but the men-at-arms looked none too happy about obeying. "I'm afraid it won't do to have a dragon here, Carole. Are dragons the usual form of transport in Argonia these days? Father hasn't mentioned it in any of his messages."

"No. Grippeldice developed a fancy for His Highness. She's actually been quite a lot of help, though I'd rather she'd leave the rest of our task to us and go back to guarding the border. I gather she's not exactly welcome. Perhaps you can convince her to go away. Your Pan-Elvin is better than mine."

Rusty walked back to Grippeldice and spoke to her quietly for several moments. After a time the dragon circled the castle yard, dipped her wings once in a poignant farewell salute, and sailed off. Rusty returned grinning a rather ghastly pointed-toothed grin.

"I gave her a speech about honoring one's king and country and she told me to mind my own business and not give her any warmed-over platitudes. I do believe she's going through some sort of dragon's adolescence. But she did mind when I pulled rank on her and reminded her that there'd be no cattle forthcoming here and that not only my guardsmen but my villagers are very nervous about large beasts and inclined to kill first and question afterwards."

"Wasn't that rather harsh?" Rupert asked, blunt in his dismay at losing his voluntary transportation and most ardent admirer.

Rusty looked up her long, pointed nose at him, "Your Highness, my dear young man, you're unacquainted with the history of this country, I can see. Had the beast remained here, we would have needed to stable her indoors, I'm afraid, for it is quite true that natives of this region fear anything less domestic than a horse or a cow. It is also true that regardless of the Company's admittedly excellent precautions, we still have creatures even larger and more dangerous than a dragon roaming the wilderness areas by night."

"Not hidebehinds anymore, however," Gilles said with a fond look at his wife. "Not around here. They disappeared forever, shortly after Rusty and I married. I do see why the royal family has associated itself with ogresses in the past. Pointed-toothed beauties have abilities not commonly credited to them by most men."

Rusty blushed. "Gilles, not here."

A gaggle of stylishly clad ladies appeared at the doorway, ostensibly at the Baroness's command. They covertly in some cases and not-so-covertly in others, watched Rupert with a certain hungry wistfulness.

"How perceptive of you, girls," Rusty said to them. "I was about to summon you to show our guests to their rooms."

"It was the dragon, mum," said the boldest one, with the squat build and wolverine-translated-into-human face, Frostingdung stock bred true and homely. Her eyes were bright and cunning, flickering from her mistress to Rupert, who acknowledged the attention with one of his more vacant smiles. "We thought it might harm you and—"

"The dragon was in more danger from us than the other way around, as I explained to her."

A slender young thing with fragile white-gold curls peeking out from a lot of pale blue wisps of veil favored Rupert with a seemingly shy glance made bold only by her kindhearted concern, which made her eyes larger and bluer than should have been humanly possible. "The poor thing. I just love animals. I would hate to see one mistreated. You must have been very worried about her."

"He'll survive, I'm sure," Rusty said with an amused twitch of one red eyebrow. Carole began to wonder if the dragon was the only one to be endangered by predatory Frostingdungians. Her doubts were confirmed when Rusty suggested the time had come for the guests to freshen for dinner. As one unit, the ladies closed in on Rupert. Carole was escorted to her chamber by the slowest of these, who spent the whole time asking impertinent personal questions about the Prince.

The feast was something of a surprise, too, like nothing Carole had previously experienced in Frostingdung, or in Queenston. The gown the impertinent maid brought her should have been a clue that there would be something unusual about the evening. It folded almost square, with the deep rectangular sleeves extending only slightly beyond the edges of the skirt. The material was blue-green silk so fine Carole's mind boggled to think how many threads must have gone into the warp to produce so sheer a fabric. The whole dress centered on the square-yoked neck, embroidered heavily with gold-and-silver metallic thread—as were hem, sleeves, and scattered clusters of birds and lily-like flowers. A hair veil accompanied it, in the same richly embroidered fabric, and Carole couldn't help hoping it would add some warmth. Though Frostingdung's climate was warmer than Argonia's, the drafty stone halls were still drafty stone halls, and chilly despite their cheerful tiled mosaic inlays. She slipped into the gown, shivering, and briefly considered wearing her customary woolen garb underneath, but her image in the looking glass warmed her considerably.

The banquet hall was not at all cold, lit with silver braziers and hundreds of wax candles, with fresh blossoms and trays heaped with various foods, nuts, fruits, vegetables, and a great many sorts of meat chopped into pieces and served on mounds of rice. The floors were piled with rugs and the ceiling and walls hung with silken hangings and more rugs. Shields and weapons anchored them at strategic points.

Rusty wore an olive-and-gold garment similar to her own, while Gilles sported sapphire trousers of a full cut, a handsome silver jacket that matched his hair, and a scarlet sash. Rupert was clad all in dark blue satin, with only a strip of white embroidery trimming his jacket. His modest apparel did not keep the eyes of the ladies from him. The guests were seated on cushions opposite their hosts, facing a long, low table on which the food had been arranged.

Rupert was seated on Carole's right, while on her left sat a swarthy man with black eyes and beard, wearing a robe and headwrap of emerald-and-white-striped wool. Apparently the inappropriately flimsy Miragenian dress was adopted only by the foreigners. The Miragenians still had sense enough to wear the winter versions of their own traditional garb. On Rupert's other side sat the blond beauty of the morning, who, as it turned out, was a fostering noblewoman from one of the further-flung Frostingdung affiliates. To the lady's disapointment, Rupert addressed most of his conversation to the Miragenian on Rusty's left. Pointing with his dagger to the crested shields decorating the hall, he asked, "I note that all seven Frostingdungian states are represented, but I'm not familiar with Miragenia's shield. Is it among them?"

The Miragenian shook his head and smiled a very white and toothy smile, reminding Carole of a gypsy conducting a horse trade. "No, Your Highness. We have no shield because we are an anarchy, you see, a collection of independent businessmen specializing in the magical, miraculous, and marvelous. We have no central government to boast a crest. Our own company naturally has a trademark, but this is more suitable for our products than for military paraphernalia."

Rupert nodded wisely. When the man's attention was diverted by the lady on his other side, the prince turned to Carole and asked. "Where *is* the place, anyway?"

"From what Bronwyn said, I got the distinct impression that it moves," she told him. "I don't suppose your new acquaintance would volunteer the information?"

For once Rupert's diplomatic training came to the fore, countering what she had come to think of as his characteristic naivete. "I don't suppose so," he agreed. "And I also don't suppose it would be a good idea to speak of our mission in front of them. What do you think?"

The Miragenian on her other side leaned forward to proffer a remark so she nodded and returned her attention to him.

"His Highness and Lady Carole have been expressing interest in the way your company's products have changed life here in Suleskeria, Samir," the Baron said to the man beside Carole.

"Truly? Perhaps you would be needing some of the same commodities in your country, Your Highness?" the merchant said.

"Perhaps. I was just wondering what . . . form your products take."

"Ah. Many forms. We specialize in spells and potions of all sorts, curses, charms, amulets, talismans, magical beasts, transport, and servants—though the latter items are, as you may guess, rare and costly, and available only to our wealthier clientele."

The prince gestured in a grand and worldly manner, and said, "Naturally. But could you give us an example say, of something in this room for which your . . . merchandise is responsible?"

"Why, the feast you see spread before you. Begging the charming Baroness's pardon, but no lady could prepare such a banquet on such short notice without our help." (Carole scoffed to herself. He had obviously never seen her hearth-witch mother in action.) "The fresh fruits and vegetables were procured by our excellent magical servants, who helped speed the preparation as well, using magic of time and distance available only to such entities as they are."

"How clever," Carole said. "Can we meet one of them?"

"Alas, no. They have all been returned to their containers to await further service and they are most retiring by nature. But there would be little to see in any event. They are not particularly intriguing visually. My deepest regrets that that which I control can be of no profit to you in that regard, dear lady."

"Sir Ahmed and Sir Samir have been doing the most wonderful rehabilitation work with the river monsters, Your Highness," the blond girl exclaimed in a blushing gush.

"Rehabilitation?" Carole said. "That should please your sister, Princess Daisy Esmeralda, Rusty."

When Rupert looked puzzled another lady leapt into the breach and elucidated. "The Baroness's elder sister, Empress Lily Pearl,. is married to our Emperor Loefwin, Your Highness. Her other sister, Princess Daisy Esmeralda, is married to our Prince Loefrig, the Emperor's younger brother. Princess Daisy Esmeralda loves animals—as I do myself, dear little things. Except monsters, of course."

The blond girl, not to be outdone, butted in, "She means

those these wonderful gentlemen haven't helped with their restructuring potion. They've made many of the nastiest monsters absolutely adorable."

"And very tasty," the animal-loving lady added with a smile that showed a pointedness of tooth more pronounced than Baroness's. The lady quickly hid her smile behind a lace handkerchief and batted her lashes over the edge.

"I seem to have heard that you are acquainted with our homeland, Lady Carole," Ahmed remarked.

"Now where would you have heard that, I wonder?" Carole said, deliberately fluttering, something she had learned to do watching the seamstress's sister, a former dairy maid who now fancied herself a milliner. "A relative of mine once visited your land. Perhaps that's what you heard. I understand that it was very . . . exotic."

"Ah, a relative value, dear lady," Ahmed replied. "But the exotic is highly esteemed by both Samir and myself as well. That is why we prefer field work as technical representatives to remaining in the Company headquarters."

Rupert proceeded to question them at length about their work, questions which they answered vaguely and with a hint of condescension.

After the feast, when the gentlemen retired to the library for port and pipes, and the ladies, at least Carole and the Baroness, retired to the newly restored alchemy laboratory to watch the retorts bubble with the results of the Baroness's latest experiment, Carole was able to tell her old friend the real reason for her visit.

"We dare stop only long enough to get a good night's sleep but I had hoped you might have some clear-cut notion of how we could locate Miragenia."

"I don't. But I would very much like to give you a present to take with you for the child. Bronwyn is absolutely correct in assuming her baby will need all the protection she can get. The Miragenians are interested in little but power and profit, from what I can see. Why they should want a child is beyond me, but I'm very glad it isn't *my* child."

Carole nodded gravely and waited.

"The only question now is what it shall be. What would be appropriate, I wonder? I've never been good at this sort of thing. What are you giving her?"

"I haven't decided, to tell you the truth. I thought of giving her that invisibility pill you once made out of hide-behinds when we tried to escape Loefwin's castle, but the child might swallow it accidentally before she had real need of it and on someone that small, who knows what the proper dosage would be? She might well be *lost* until she's fifteen or twenty years old."

"My dear, if you believe that, your experience of babies is even more limited than mine. They howl most alarmingly if their needs are not attended to. Whether she could be seen or not, if the child was deprived of food or a diaper change for any length of time, she'd make herself highly visible. If I were you, I'd save that capsule for myself. Miragenians are sneaky in the extreme. It won't hurt to have something on hand that can help you be sneakier. Which gives me an idea. Hand me that parchment over there, will you?"

She sat at a counter for a quarter of an hour, carefully lettering runes onto the parchment with special ink, tossing sand over it to dry it, though it still smeared somewhat, and rolling it up to present to Carole. "There now. That should stand her in good stead."

"What did you decide on?"

"A hunger for knowledge, a sharp eye for detail, and an avid taste for trouble. Not the usual precious baby gifts, I know, but they're traits sufficiently related to me that I can pass them on with my blessings. She should give the Miragenians a run for their money, growing up endowed with such a gift. I also added a rudimentary knowledge of Pan-Elvin. Coupled with the other, she should have several dialects mastered by the time she's six or seven. Children tend to be fond of animals; if the people are beastly to her, the company of real beasts may give her some comfort."

They departed the next morning amid general consternation and a few tears from an uncommonly drowsy-looking lot of lady's maids, who were not used to arising quite so early but who refused to miss the opportunity to catch Rupert's eye a final time during his leave-taking. The baronial carriage took the cousins as far as the river, where they boarded a sleek, private sailboat with magic wind, courtesy of the Miragenians.

"Damned decent of them," Rupert said. "I begin to admire these people, for all their haste in running off with the children of others. Baron Gilles told me some of the most amazing facts concerning their participation in the rebuilding of Frostingdungian magic."

"Their replacement of it with their own, from what Rusty told me," Carole replied. "I just hope there's not a time limit on this wind. The Emperor's castle is a good long way from here and I know of no place closer where we might rest for the night."

Carole found the riverbanks were more densely populated than they had been on her previous visit, and the boat traffic much heavier, but by mid-day their boat had passed beyond those powered by more prosaic means of propulsion and had likewise left behind all but the thinnest habitation.

Alone with none but his cousin to impress, Rupert was quiet and placid, staring contentedly at the shadows of the bare trees striping the sluggish gray-green river, watching the banks for animals, replying to Carole's occasional sally with a vague smile or a monosyllable. The magic wind ruffled his buttery curls and the sunlight glinted heroic bronze from his face and hands. Carole, to whom the sort of country through which they were passing was no novelty, felt restless, and inclined to be pettish that the youth so full of charming conversation for other females had little to offer her when they were alone. Perhaps his tongue was tired, as well it could be. From what Rusty reported, the Prince had continued to hold forth among the admiring throng long after she had retired.

The sun sank ahead of them, directly in their line of vision, bouncing blindingly off the river. Carole thought they must be approaching a town again, for she heard hoofbeats through the woods on the left bank and the rustle of someone or something plowing through foliage closer at hand. Rupert stared straight ahead, into the brilliant light, and seemed not to hear the noises. Though Carole twisted to try to see what was making them, her eyes were too full of spots from peering into the brightness to be able to clearly make anything out. She thought she saw a rapid movement and a wisp of green before Rupert gave a strangled cry and sat bolt upright.

The green wisp transformed itself just in front of the bow, outlining a cool, slender shape against the glare of the sun. The shape undulated seductively before him, beckoning him closer with a wink of a rounded green ray here, a come-hither twitch there, a blink of incandescence, and a wonderful rhythmic crackling of exuberant energy.

To Carole the light was different—green with black bars, the crackle menacing, surrounding her, imprisoning her, threatening her with an overwhelmingly searing jolt if she so much as leaned forward to touch Rupert.

Rupert could see nothing to one side or the other, but could only stare straight ahead at the ladies of light, who were cajoling and beckoning him, whispering promises of secret tales more intriguing than any he had ever heard, of perfections beyond what he had thought possible, of sensations of softness and comfort and ease not dared dreamed, of grace and voluptuous warmth coupled with wild excitement. He rose slowly, intently, to his feet and stepped forward.

Carole cried out as the boat dipped toward the bow and the sail slackened. No sooner did she cry than from somewhere beside her, another angrier cry broke through the crackling. The foliage rattled again, and the green lights flamed up with a whoosh and blurred off the way they had come, leaving only the dazzling sunlight.

Rupert half-fell back into the boat with the recoil from the release of the spell. The rowan shield he wore at his back clacked against the boat's hull. Simultaneously, in the brush along the river, another rustling of leaves was followed by hoofbeats and the patter of running feet. A tag-end of green curled and disappeared behind a tree root and Carole, watching intently, grabbed an oar and turned the boat, paddling for shore. The magic wind deserted the sails and they hung slack and unresisting as she altered the course. Rupert recovered rapidly, and helped her paddle. They put ashore near the tree where the last of the green vanished. Carole climbed out and scanned the area. The crystal bottle was shaded by the tree root, all but one edge, which glittered like a peridot in the sun's rapidly dying light.

A silver-inscribed stopper dangled from the bottle's neck by a silver chain. Carole stuck it rapidly into the mouth of the container. Something about the bottle felt unsavory, disquietingly sly and somehow unnatural, tricky.

Once the bottle was sealed she held it to the sun, trying to look through the green-tinted glass to see what swirled murkily within.

"What is it?" Rupert asked.

A pair of eyes opened abruptly inside the bottle, staring out accusingly at them. "Take out the stopper," a voice commanded silently.

"Oh, no, you don't, my dear," Carole said. "In you went and in you're going to stay."

"Who are you to keep me here? You aren't one of the masters." The voice was huffy.

"No, but neither am I someone you can order about," Carole said. "If you didn't wish to stay there, why did you return?"

"It's . . . my place, of course. The only place since . . . since I've been in service. But without the stopper, I am free. You are not a master. You can't keep me." The voice wavered from sounding as if there were a blank space in what it knew of itself to a belligerent determination to cover up that lack of knowledge.

Carole was not fooled. "No. But if you want out of there, you'll need to answer a question or two. You're one of the Miragenian servants I take it?"

"Fancy that! So much power over the helpless and clever, too! How did you figure that one out? Let me guess, the bottle—"

"The spell you cast on us, for starters," Carole said. "Who put you up to it?"

"What? That little love charm? Surely you're not miffed about that? Obviously some lady wanting to impress that large fellow looming over your shoulder."

"You nearly killed him."

"It's not my fault if he's clumsy enough to fall in. She just wanted him back. The masters hire us out for profit, you know. The results are not always guaranteeable. Don't hold me responsible. Let me go and I promise never to do it again. How's that?"

"I'll let you go when you tell us where Miragenia is and how we can get there."

The eyes closed and opened again. "Why?"

"Why what?"

"Why do you want to go there? Big contract for the masters, eh? More profit to their coffers?" The voice seethed with a stew of hostile emotions and the eyes all but burned a hole in the crystal bottle.

"Hardly," Carole answered. "And why is none of your business. Keep that attitude up and I can assure you you may stay stoppered in there for good. Frostingdung has quite enough monsters loose already."

The eyes blinked again, wetly this time, and were half-veiled, but the voice was stubborn. "Are you bringing them more business?"

"We can't say," Carole replied.

"Then I can't tell you," the voice said, choked to a near-whisper.

"No," Rupert said from behind her. "Not to do business. Not exactly."

"Ah!" the voice said, brightening. "Make trouble then?"

"I wouldn't say that," he said.

"What would you say?"

"We need to tend to something they have that belongs to us," he answered cagily.

"There's a smart lad. If they have something that belongs to you, you'll be lucky to see it again."

"Then you'll tell us?" Rupert asked, encouraged by the voice's obvious lack of good will toward Miragenia and Miragenians.

"I'm thinking about it."

"I have ways of making you talk," Carole warned. She would feel no sillier making a bottle dance than she did having an argument with one.

"You've bullied me into it," the voice said cheerfully. "I hope you feel better. Like heroes, eh? Pushing mists around. Don't think you're forcing me, either. Anything that will cause the masters trouble is fine with me. To get to Miragenia, you need only cross into the desert, and if they want to see you, they'll arrange to come to you."

"But they don't," Rupert said. "We already told you that."

"There are magic words, in that case, but you mustn't let it get out. I only know because you overhear a lot of things sitting in a shop window. To make them think they want to find you, you have only to keep repeating the motto of the profitable client—"

"Which is?"

53

"'I want to get rich quick—'" The voice broke off with a screech as a snakelike flash of black wrapped around it three times, missing Carole's fingers altogether and snatching it deftly from them. A glowering rider mounted on a froth-flecked black steed glared at them from dark eyes burning out above a black face covering. He drew his saber and bore down on them, driving them towards the water. Only the fact that his attention was divided while he stuffed the bottle into a bag slung across the horse's back saved them. For as Rupert stepped backwards, drenching himself to the knees in the river, the sky suddenly darkened, the rider's horse shied, and the rider, not giving full attention to his mount, slipped sideways and threatened to lose his seat.

Grippeldice's front claws grazed the part in Carole's hair as the dragon overflew the cousins and landed in front of them, flaming. The horse reared, screaming, and bolted, rider clinging desperately to its mane, streaming cloak trailing smoke and sparks as the terrified mount galloped heedlessly off down the trail.

Grippeldice beat her wings once and started to take off after the horse, but Rupert cried out. Carole stopped the dragon with a word.

"Tell her we need to find that desert as quickly as possible now," Rupert told Carole. "We have no way of knowing how long the Miragenian was listening, or when or if he will compel the bottle to tell him of our conversation. We must reach the desert and use the magic words before they discover we know them. Otherwise, I fear we will never find Miragenia or the child."

CHAPTER IV

Carole deeply regretted the haste, for she had looked forward to visiting the Imperial Palace again and seeing for herself the changes wrought by Miragenian decadence. She had also hoped to visit Princess Anastasia and her sisters in their castle in the Nonarable Lands. Both places might have yielded some very useful christening gift for the child. She and Rupert needed to find Miragenia and use the magic words before they were altered or in some other fashion the cursed place managed to elude them. They couldn't expect to find so many neglected bottles that they could afford to waste the information they had gleaned from the first.

They flew several hours before the desert appeared as a beige sea on the far side of low, rugged foothills. The heat reached out and grabbed for them even before they cleared the hills, and the dragon relaxed, flexing her wings more fully, luxuriating in the sensation.

"Let's see now," Carole said. "The magic words were what? 'Now to get rich quick . . . how to get rich quick' . . . ?"

"I want to get rich quick," Rupert said. "I want to get rich quick."

"I want to get rich quick," Carole chanted. "Fine. I don't see anything yet, do you?"

The desert was closer, but just as empty as before.

Rupert shook his head. "Neither do I. Perhaps we're not saying it correctly. Tell me, have you ever wanted to be rich?"

She glanced back at him, her hair whipping in front of her eyes, "Why?"

"Well, I just thought if we could really say the words with conviction we'd be more likely to succeed. So I wondered . . . I wondered if you ever wanted to be rich. I mean, I believe I should enjoy it."

"But you're a prince. You *are* rich."

"Not exactly. I can't just suit myself. I must dress just so for each occasion, my spending is controlled by the exchequer, I go where I am sent. I never go hungry, true, but my choices are dictated for me by whatever someone else thinks is the good of the realm. Actually, I'm finding this journey more interesting than anything I've done in recent years. But back to my original question, cousin. How about you? What would you do if you were rich? What would you buy? Dresses, jewels?"

She considered. "That would be very nice but I actually haven't anywhere to wear such things. I would like a house facing the sea for myself, perhaps, and a lot of conch shells to keep songs and stories in, like Sir Cyril Perchingbird has in the Archives at Queenston. I would like to be able to come and go as I wish, and perhaps to buy one of those carpets or flying horses the Miragenians have, since dragons don't ordinarily find me to their liking."

"How about a dowry?" he asked slyly. "You're not too old to think of marrying yet—"

"Bite your tongue," she said crisply and finally.

"Well, pardon me."

"It's under consideration. If I choose to marry it won't be to someone who wants my dowry. Or anything or anyone else but me. In fact, it would be very nice to get rich quick simply so I would be wealthy and powerful enough that no one, not even princes, would feel free to ask impudent questions. Yes, indeed, I can see that as a very valid reason. With that in mind, I can say decidedly that I want to get rich quick."

Rupert was wondering whether to respond with a tart rejoiner or freeze her with silence when the dragon abruptly began downflapping and the heat shimmering above the surface of the sand suddenly coalesced into walls, spires, and gates rising from them, a city with the same architectural accouterments within its walls as those so recently grafted on to Suleskeria. "It worked," Rupert said, gaping.

"Magic words generally do," she said with somewhat contemptuous smugness, still smarting from his unintentional probing of her old wound.

A cloud of dust billowed around the walls, dancing motes on the heat waves.

If the elusive illusory city had any intention of scurrying away into the concealment of heat and dust, Grippeldice quickly foiled it for she flew so swiftly over the wall that she stampeded a herd of flying horses grazing on several of the flat rooftops. She landed on the largest of these rooftops, one covering a building large enough to be the great hall of some palace. It turned out to be a warehouse. This they learned when, dismounting Grippeldice, they saw a train of mules back a wagon up to the front of the building. The mules strained their harnesses upwards, shaking their heads and stamping, their eyes rolling as they tried to see the dragon they smelled above them.

The warehouseman, arriving at the door to inspect the cargo carried by the mules, followed their gaze and saw the dragon, who could not restrain her curiosity and looked back down at the man. Carole groped in her medicine pouch. Her fingers closed on the hidebehind capsule. Knowing that she was probably sacrificing it prematurely, but unable to think of any other way to avoid drawing further attention to themselves, she popped the capsule far back into the dragon's gaping jaws. Grippeldice, startled, turned from the edge of the roof to see what had occasioned the small interruption in her surveillance of the warehouseman, then vanished. Rupert and Carole stepped quickly away toward the center of the roof.

"What did you do to me?" the dragon demanded, shooting a warning blast of fire over Carole's head.

Carole ducked behind Rupert, knowing the dragon would hesitate to harm him, and quickly whispered her reply. "I gave you a pill that will make you invisible for a while. You'll recover. But meanwhile, it would be very helpful to what we have to do here if you'd find something to occupy yourself elsewhere. Two people can disguise themselves sufficiently to infiltrate Miragenia long enough to locate and christen a child. Two people and dragon are a bit more conspicuous."

"That is true," Rupert whispered. "Say that I wish her to leave now as well, that we appreciate—"

"Yes, yes," the dragon grumbled. "I can see I'm not wanted. Nevertheless, dear Prince, just holler if you're in hot water again. I'll understand and come. The language of love speaks with equal warmth to all creatures." And with a rush of hot wind she was gone, once more stampeding a herd of horses flying overhead.

The warehouseman and his helpers unloaded the cargo and carted it inside the building, no doubt assuming the dragon was just another transitory spell conjured on the roof by some competitor, or perhaps an advertising gimmick. Before anyone could change his mind and investigate further, Rupert hopped nimbly to an adjoining rooftop and urged Carole to do the same, springing from one of the closely packed structures to another until they were a good distance away from where they first arrived.

They had flown all night and found the desert in late morning. Now the day grew so hot that Carole found it difficult to stand, much less jump. Below them, the streets were quiet. People napped or ate inside their houses or under the awnings where they did their business. She could hardly believe her own eyes when Rupert, spotting several robes spread drying on a rooftop, scooped up two and began to don the larger, handing her the smaller.

The idea of tormenting her overheated, sweating, heat-drenched body with another layer of clothing horrified her. Her expression must have showed it.

Rupert turned to her cheerily, tugging at the robe's sleeves, which refused to cover him below the middle of his forearm. He pulled the hood up over his golden hair and lowered his burnished lashes, letting his chin touch his chest. "If we wear these robes like this, you see," he said, his words getting somewhat lost in fabric and the dust skimming the heights on a simmering breeze, "no one will ever recognize us for anything other than Miragenians."

"As soon as we've captured him, I want him measured for a proper robe," the chairperson of the board of Mukbar, Mashkent, and Mirza proclaimed. "Such an ill-fitting costume makes a joke of our corporate dignity."

"On an Argonian, mademoiselle?" the old man, Mashkent, asked with a sly twinkle in his eye. "What possible difference could it make to our corporate dignity what an Argonian wears?"

The board members were seated on deep cushions surrounding a circular pool of visions, and had just been entertained by watching the dragon land and disappear and the Prince and his companion deck themselves ludicrously in borrowed robes.

Mlle. Mukbar, heiress to old Mukbar's controlling interest in the firm, head of the household composed of herself and nine younger sisters, lifted her raven tresses with a langorous arm. Her eyelids, heavy with their fringes of curling black lash, veiled her almond eyes and her full, carmined lips pouted at her old uncle. "Naturally we'll assume control of such an outstanding asset as His Highness. Or weren't you watching? He is a fine figure of a man, of wealth, power, position and family connection. Just the husband my sisters and I need. With his past training, he'll make an excellent sales representative, once he gets used to us."

"And how do you propose to make that happen?" Mirza, sharp-faced and nervous in middle-age, his black hair threaded with gray, challenged her. He had rather fancied himself as husband to the Mukbar heiresses. Keeping the wealth in the family was not a bad idea in Miragenia. "He has come for the brat, of that you may be sure, and will neither leave nor stay and certainly will not do your bidding willingly until he has done what he came for. And that, as you know, is not possible. Are you so desirous of him as to use spells on him, mademoiselle? That would be damaging to the dignity of the firm also, I would think."

She laughed an earthy laugh from deep in her memorable bosom. "Nonsense, my dear Mirza. It is standard operating procedure among women of choice to use all manner of spells to procure the proper mate. My scruples will give my dignity no trouble whatsoever. Besides, he will be safest there, among my sisters and myself. He must be kept from the child until her destiny has taken its course."

Mashkent, ancient now, his whiskers wispy, his eyes sparkling with a certain magically induced artifice from behind clouded lenses, shifted on his bony shanks and cleared his throat. "You're your father's daughter, Alireza, to speak so. What are we to tell the parents when they demand their child back when the fifteen years allotment has passed? Will you have your pet diplomat make them some pretty speech about how she chose to remain in our service, only without her body?"

A golden-skinned, round-faced man with a thatch of black hair and a smug expression tapped the edge of the pool in front of him. "You grow addled in your old age, Illustrious One. You do recall my prophecy, do you not, that that child will bring certain ruin of the balance of trade? She is a liability, which the dear lady has in her infinite cleverness managed to turn into an asset, even while ridding us of the danger."

"Had we waited until the mother had performed her sentimental rites over this babe, we would not have had to deal with this princeling at all. He increases our danger a hundredfold, he and the witch."

"It all depends on your point of view, Uncle," Alireza Mukbar said, stretching blissfully. "The man's presence here is to my mind an unexpected bonus. We have not only profited from the brat, but I, at least, intend to profit from him as well."

"Greater profit might be obtained from our creditors by allowing him to find the child," Mashkent pointed out slyly. "He would be of great interest to them, you may be sure."

Alireza scoffed. "He'd never make it. The valley's guardian would intercept and spoil him, as she does all good things, and we would have no profit from him at all. Besides, isn't there a prophecy about that somewhere, too, Ali?"

"Assuredly, First Sale of the New Day," he said, using one of the Miragenians' most flattering terms for a beautiful woman. "If this prince becomes the prey of the valley's guardian, the profit-and-loss ledger will look even worse, for the woman will gain undue influence. Much as I would hate for you and your charming sisters to be no longer available for wooing, lady, I agree that, other than having him eliminated or transformed into some innocuous beast, allowing the prince to fall into your loving arms would be the safest thing to do with him."

"And his companion?" Mashkent asked. "The witch?"

"Surely a profit may be made from her also," Mirza said.

"What magic does she possess?" Alireza asked.

"Nothing of great note: a minor variation on the siren song plus an occasional borrowed trick like the one she did with the dragon. Still, she may cause disruption of trade if not handled properly."

"Neutralize her ahead of time?" Mashkent asked, pulling his beard. "We can safely do nothing to quell her power without further study of it. We can arm the security forces with wards against her, however, and distract her so that her power is concentrated elsewhere when we apprehend her."

"The competition won't interfere?" Mirza asked sharply. "We can't risk allowing anyone else to become involved in this. If our Gorequartz creditors learn of the presence of this pair from anyone other than ourselves, we may have a great deal of difficulty. I still think perhaps the best thing would be to send the man as a gift, disguised, up the Cashflow, avoiding the guardian, and let the Gorequartz priests do with him as they will."

"You're too cautious," Alireza chimed in, undulating her slender fingers at him in breezy dismissal. "Giving away assets before learning their full advantage to us is not like you, Mirza. I fear your little brush with the Guardian when you tried to obtain some of that cheap love potion to win my sisters and me undid you. The Gorequartz priests already have what they desire and if they know nothing of this prince, they will not miss him. I, on the other hand most certainly will. Nor is the witch going to appeal to our competition. Especially not if we surround her with a pall of bewilderment and strangeness. She will appear unprofitable, and none will wish to deal with her. Now then, my dear fellow board members, if I have eased your trepidations sufficiently, I will excuse myself while you deal with the witch. I must make my own simple preparations for acquiring her companion."

CHAPTER V

The first order of business was to locate Mukbar, Mashkent, and Mirza. Since the firm was large and influential, the cousins had anticipated no difficulty in learning its whereabouts. But each person they approached together turned from them to another task or customer.

"This will take all day at this rate," Carole said, shifting miserably inside her overabundance of clothing.

Her awkward fumbling was accentuated by a woman bargaining at the stall ahead of them. The other woman's movements were like a dancer's, fluid and graceful, golden bracelets clinking on smooth rounded arms as she gestured, fingers flying like doves, enhancing every softly articulated word. Rupert sighed as her beautifully formed head turned ever so slightly, the waterfall of black waving hair shifting beneath a sheer emerald veil, hooded dark eyes taking him in, nostrils flaring beneath the coin-rimmed veil, sweet flicker of tongue darting out to dampen lips suddenly in need of softening. He held her gaze for no more than a moment before she swirled, a fragrant, heady cloud wafting from her veils. She beckoned with a slim finger, her eyes darting back for another tantalizing glance.

"What did you say?" Rupert asked Carole, keeping one eye on her and the other on the swaying veils sauntering just ahead on the dusty street. Carole repeated herself snappishly,

63

but he replied with a blitheness born of relief. "Why, certainly it will take all day. This town is little used to strangers, since so few can find it, and two of us together bewilder them. We'll alarm them less if we split up," he said. "I'll do this side of the street, you do the other." And so saying, he trotted briskly after the departing green-clad figure.

Carole watched him, and hoped that the woman was as friendly as she looked. Perhaps their hunt would be over as soon as he caught her. Just so he proceeded directly with business instead of dallying about while his suffering cousin baked in the street. She watched the preoccupied merchants and approached the first. Tension and dread knotted her stomach. She suddenly longed for her recalcitrant villagers at Wormroost, lazy and spoiled and expecting her to take care of them. At least there she had some worth. Here people dismissed her and went coldly about their business as if she had never made a purchase in her life and wasn't about to start with them. She felt tempted to give them all dancing lessons, but it sickened her to think she had to dance people around just to get a little decent human cooperation from them.

A large animal with a hump in its middle, ridiculously attired in tapestry, tassles, and bells, brushed against her, nearly stepping on her foot. It gave her a supercilious look, very much like the one she and Rupert had gotten from the last vendor. She started to laugh, thinking that if even the animals in this place were unfriendly, she was being a ninny to allow the attitude of the people to cow her. The beast continued to glower at her, worked its jaws, and spat. She side-stepped the gob just in time, and ducked straight into the path of an enormous lumbering mud-colored animal with wrinkled skin and a nose that resembled a front-end tail. The beast was heavily laden. It was ridden by a small nut-brown man who threatened Carole with a riding crop. She wasn't too concerned about the riding crop, but the animal had a pair of horns situated on either side of its prodigious nose, each of them larger than four unicorn horns put together. She ducked again, tripping over a little brown hairy beast standing on its hands and juggling balls, which it dropped when she tripped over it. It jumped to its feet chattering and grimacing at her furiously. When she tried to retrieve the balls, it threw them at her. She longed for the animals of her home, work-hungry beavers, opinionated moose, dim-brained bears, rare and magical unicorns and even love-sick dragons.

In front of Carole a woman squatted beside a pile of glittering objects: mirrors with mother-of-pearl frames. The sun flashed from their surfaces. The woman eyed Carole suspiciously over a length of black veil much mended with inept embroidery.

"Mirrors for sale," she said dully. "You want to buy one?"

"Well, no. That is, I don't think I need a mirror."

"You think wrong then, girlie. I never saw one who could use it more. Take a look."

She thrust the mirror into Carole's face and Carole thought at first that a mistake had been made. This was no mirror but a moving portrait of a face that was beautiful, fine of feature, with milky skin rather than her own sallow complexion. The mirrored face was crowned with lustrous black waves, not with strawlike hair slicked back into a single brown braid. The nose was straight and patrician, lacking the Brown hook.

"Your mirror's defective," she told the merchant, handing the object back to her. "That's not me."

"It's what you ought to be. What you should look like if you was to do your duty and beautify the streets instead of being just another dowdy body taking up air. If you buy this mirror, see, you'll have the model before you, so you'll know what to strive for. With the proper accompanying spells and potions and maybe a judicious application of virgin's blood now and then to keep you young, you may come close."

"Thank you, but I think I'll pass," Carole said. "I was just going to ask if you could direct me to the firm of Mukbar, Mashkent, and Mirza."

"I could, but may I run at a loss if I will. I have business to do. If you want information, I suggest you go to them as sell it and let a poor woman earn her living."

She got a similar reception from everyone else on the street, even at a place where she parted with two of her small store of coppers to purchase an inedible pastry. Everywhere she was regarded with distaste and indifference.

She stumbled along, suffering with the heat, while trying to avoid the animal dung thick and steaming in the streets, she bumped straight into another vendor, who held her at arm's length. He brushed her off, and with a crazed expression lurched into his sales pitch. "You look like a lady who's going places. With my wares, you can so do pleasantly, safely, quickly, expeditiously, and without the need for such a fierce frown."

"Stop," she said. "I don't want to hear another word unless you can tell me where I'll find the firm of Mukbar, Mashkent, and Mirza. No one else will tell me and I'm not about to waste my time listening to someone who's going to be insolent when he's done with his own business."

"Ah, I can do better than that!" he said. "Though I have only myself just arrived here today. How, you may ask, did I manage to arrive so opportunely for yourself, just at the time when you most need aid. Why, by means of my wondrous wares, I answer. With the help of this marvelous item you too can be on hand for significant occurences among those who need you—even two during the same day. *And* have all of your adventures narrated to you in thrilling detail at no extra charge—"

"*What* are you talking about?" Carole asked, fanning herself with her hand and trying to stay patient. Crazed this character might be, but he was the only one so far who had heard her request and retained his eagerness to speak to her.

"Why, thissss—" he said, gesturing to the side of the road where a hollow stump lay and inviting her to follow him. "My magical, mystical travel log. I would be only too happy to give you a free demonstration."

"Sitting down on the log will be plenty for now," she said wearily. Before he could say more, a little round woman turned from the cartload of scrolls she was unloading and rushed to Carole, putting a restraining hand on her arm.

"No, no, my dear. Pay no attention to this man. He is a charlatan. I've been watching him and he's sat here all day. You're the first customer he approached. He may be a slaver. A young lady like you should be more cautious."

The man backed hastily away as the little woman glared at him. Picking his log up under his arm, he made a swift departure down the street.

Carole stared after him, stricken. "It's very good of you to be concerned for me," she said, "But he promised to help me find the firm of Mukbar, Mashkent, and Mirza. No one else will. I can't afford to buy anything."

"That is very plain. I just didn't want you to come to any harm. You may not buy today and still be a good customer in the future. You have the look of one seeking employment to me. I'd offer you a job if I could, but my business is run on the good will of my customers and I'm afraid you would not engender good will, no offense. Still, if you promise to keep away from slavers, I'll tell you where you can find the competition, and perhaps they'll be able to hire you so that you can someday come and look at my wares with a more positive eye, poor girl."

Toward evening, following the woman's directions, Carole stood before a shop front remarkable only in that it boasted a permanent awning and a recess in the wall, unlike the barrows and tables and spread-cloths of the other vendors. In front of a collection of pots, an elderly man sat on one rug while weaving another.

Carole was about to speak to him when two men sneaked up behind her, grabbing her arms in tight grips. They panted through guilty grins at the old man. "Here she is, Illustrious Employer. The witch you sought."

"Indeed," the weaver grumbled. "Very brave of you, capturing her just as she was about to introduce herself." The rug upon which he was seated rose high with his indignation. It plopped abruptly to the ground as the weaver said, "Stand by, but unhand her."

He spun around as the guards obeyed, the rug turning with him, and regarded her through rheumy eyes alight with some uncanny glow that made her think he might have fireflies behind his milky-white lenses. He beckoned her to come closer, and shook the clawed end of his weaving comb under her nose. "So you came to find us, did you? I thought you might. But I'll tell you it will do you no good. A bargain is a bargain, and you were present when it was made, even if you were too young then to have better sense than to do commerce with that redhaired liar girl and the cheat of a gypsy boy. You heard the deal as it was signed and sealed, and we have taken delivery, to the Profit of the righteous. If those who welsh on deals are not happy, let them think again before depriving their buyers of prepurchased goods."

Carole sank to the ground, crossing her legs, and facing him tiredly. She watched his righteous wrath rise and fall with his breath and decided that behind his eyes the fireflies were laughing at her. His pretension to an ethical argument was a sham. He had merely assumed a bargaining position, in quite the same way as the seamstress did when a lady from Rowan Castle was negotiating the amount of embroidery embellishing a new gown. "I'm glad to hear that you don't deny taking the child," she replied at last. "And there's really no need to be unpleasant about all this. As you say, I was there. I'm not challenging your basic position, just your timing."

"I see." Mashkent slitted his eyes and folded his hands, regarding her impassively, waiting for her to say more.

"In your haste to collect your debt from Bronwyn, you

spirited the child away before she could be christened. I don't know how familiar you are with the ceremony, but it will add inestimably to her value to you."

"How good of you to be concerned for our investment," he said. "Perhaps you would care to enter my home in order to estimate for us somewhat closer the inestimable value of this ceremony of which you speak?"

"That would be very nice," she said demurely, thinking thirstily of long drinks of water. Also, now that she and Mashkent had found each other, there would be no further need for her cumbersome, suffocating disguise.

"No sooner said than done," Mashkent said, inclining his head and smiling a sweet old man's smile full of fatherly kindliness and consideration. He clapped his hands once, resoundingly.

Tendrils of varicolored smoke slithered forth from the shop, curling toward her. The tendrils were very like the ones she had seen enter the bottle on the river bank. She watched them so intently she missed the disappearance of the old man. The tendrils wrapped themselves around her arms and legs and bore her gently aloft, so that she rested as if on a down mattress, very comfortably on her lower side. Nevertheless she had to duck her head to avoid injury as her translucent guides transported her through the low doorway leading from the cluttered shop to the garden that was the heart of Mashkent's home.

At the heart of the garden was a magnificent pool, surrounded by many peripheral pools. The group was connected with a web of blue-green tiled gutters with what seemed to be overflow rippling between them. Mashkent sat near the largest pool. It contained no fewer than thirty-five fluting fountains, showering the pool on seven different levels. The whole thing was larger than the finest, biggest mill pond in the east of Argonia, the new one just constructed at Little Darlingham.

Carole's vaporous guides deposited her on a silken cushion, wisped away momentarily, and wisped back with silver trays full of cut up bits of fruit, nuts, smelly cheeses, dates, and a sweating silver goblet of a tart fruit drink that was more thirst quenching than the water she had hoped for. She ate and drank as daintily as possible. Her host did not join her, but studied her with every evidence of benign pleasure in her pleasure. He made occasional friendly remarks about the garden, the varieties of flowers growing therein, which bird was singing at any given moment—they were all larks or nightingales or doves or something melodious and romantic, it seemed.

When Carole was quite finished her host clapped again and the vapors deftly removed the trays. Swishing around Carole like the ghosts of silken cloths, they wiped her hands and mouth.

Belatedly, Carole thought of Rupert. "Perhaps, actually, I should wait until Prince Rupert finds us to discuss this matter. He was . . . detained."

"Ah. Was he? But surely you need not delay your mission. You are in accord on this matter, I take it?"

"Yes, but, well, I—"

"You are distressed on his account, no doubt fearing in your womanly fashion that he has no place to dine and rest as you do. That is commendable, but a misplaced concern, I assure you."

"Nevertheless—" she said, fluttering her hand in an imitation of the gesture she seen Miragenians use, the one that meant "I need not explain the rest to you."

The old man's smile tightened momentarily, his patience strained, then he clapped his hands again, saying to her, "I shall undertake to settle your mind in this matter." To a solid and refreshingly human-looking minion, a boy of about eight, he said, "Check the pool and report to me if Prince Rupert is safely settled for the rest of the day, if he is comfortable and in amiable company, and has dined."

The boy bowed low and scuttled to an adjoining pool, over which he leaned low.

Carole sat erect, straining to see beyond the child into the pool. She recalled Bronwyn saying something about these pools that acted as crystal balls. She supposed that was what this was all about. She caught vague billowings of curtain-like draperies, soft, dappling light, and a bare glimpse of a familiar tawny head, eyes closed, breath sifting through the hairs of his mustache.

Mashkent laid his hand on her arm, restraining her from rising to see more of the picture. "I consult the pool as a courtesy to a guest. If you wish to consult it yourself, there will be the standard fee, of course." He accepted the boy's report that the Prince looked very comfortable indeed. He settled back onto his own cushion, calling for a pipe attached by a long tube to an ornate bottle filled with colored water. "Now then, perhaps you had better tell me of this matter which weighs so heavily on your mind. Tell me of your part in this—and of what you intend to do. Thus I can better determine what terms we might negotiate between us."

Carole shifted, the backs of her legs and her sweat-soaked gown sticking to the silken cushion. Now what? It was all very well for Rupert to be peacefully napping, but he was the trained diplomat, not she. Setting terms and negotiating was supposed to be his bailiwick. "First," she said, "I would like to see the baby."

"No doubt," he replied. "But I am afraid that is quite out of the question."

"There was nothing in the agreement forbidding visiting rights," she pointed out, "and we have come a very long way."

"You should have made an appointment," he said, and she sensed beneath his firmness a certain squirming. "Many regrettable matters could have been avoided had you not failed to do so."

"The same could be said of your firm," she replied calmly. "The question of timing I referred to revolves around just such an omission of securing a convenient time for all concerned. My cousin says you took the baby without announcing your intention to do so. Whatever your opinion of Bronwyn, your methods strike me as a singularly callous way to treat a new mother and child. I would think that even your people share with us certain human feelings that would—"

"Even my people? You have an unfortunate way of expressing yourself. Naturally we have a high regard for human sentiments of all varieties—births, deaths, marriages, love affairs. All of these experiences not only affect us in the usual personal aspects of our lives but are also sacred to us for reasons far deeper than your own. All such happenings are highly profitable. People lose their senses under the influence of strong emotion. They throw caution to the wind. They would do anything to gain this or that. So yes, assuredly we share those human feelings of which you are so fond and revere them, but in the case of your cousin, a deal is, you understand, a deal." He shrugged. "Surely as a fellow vendor of magic, you can see that. Among my people, it is written, 'He who fails to collect a debt shall himself soon be a debtor.' It is one of the most fundamental laws of the Profit."

"I wouldn't know about that," Carole said. "I don't consider myself a vendor of magic at all. I use my magic to help others. They pay me only by providing me with things I haven't the time or skill to provide for myself."

"Even if you believe such drivel as you are telling me, it is fundamentally the same thing," he said.

"It is not. I'd never demand someone's baby, even on loan. But if I did I would certainly give them a chance to practice their own birthing rites on it first, so they'd be sure it was safe and protected from harm, and wouldn't worry themselves sick over it."

"I thought you said this rite would enhance the value of the child. Now you tell me its function is protective. And you have yet to mention what your role in the affair is."

"Very well," she said. "The rite would enhance the child's value by providing her with protective personal attributes, but it is difficult to explain to an outsider. I was depending on my cousin for that. He is representing the child's parents. I am a priestess of the Mother, authorized to perform the rite."

"Ah, a functionary of your faith, rather like our own accountants?"

"Rather like an . . . uh, well, I suppose you could put it that way." She didn't wish to demur on what would be a minor point to the old man and thereby break the fragile thread of understanding so perilously spun between them. "Truly, I think I've said enough that you can understand why Rupert should be fetched and we should be allowed to see the baby. Christening is very important for Argonian children."

"All Argonian children?"

"Yes, but particularly those of royal or magical lineage. It is the chief source of influence in early life, affecting personality, physical development, interests in matters both mundane and magical, skills, character, and the Mother only knows what else. If the child is properly christened, she will be much more valuable to you. From the family's standpoint, she will have the protection of the gifts presented to her by her kinsmen and their allies. There are so many forces automatically aligned against a child born to power, you see, that protection is a matter of primary importance."

"I find this difficult to comprehend. Can you give me examples of these valuable gifts? What were your own, for instance, and how do they affect you today? And which are you bringing for the child?"

The fireflies in Mashkent's eyes danced anxiously and Carole flinched from them.

"I'm afraid I can't, actually. I will not learn what the baby's gifts are until I perform the ceremony. As for my own gifts, why, that was very long ago. Perhaps by the time my cousin can be fetched I'll think of some to discuss with you. I can tell you, however, that the gifts are so important to our lives that if the child is not christened, you may find that inadvertently it will be you and your firm who violate the terms of the agreement. For without the protection of the gifts and the rite, the child may not survive her fifteen years with you to return to her parents."

If she had hoped this was a clinching argument, she was disappointed, for he waved the last statement away as if it nullified the parts to which he had been listening so avidly. "That would be sad for your cousin Bronwyn," he said. "She owes us fifteen years of the service of her child. If this one does not fulfill the requirement, we will be forced to collect her next one. Now then, I think it is time you retired to a place conducive to your meditations."

So saying, he clapped his hands and the two guards reappeared beside her. "Do not waste your breath on these employees of mine, my dear," Mashkent cautioned. "They have been given protection against your charms. We can arrange for them to place you in irons if you prove uncooperative, but that seems so inhospitable. I trust you'll find your quarters comfortable."

Alireza Mukbar's spells went for naught with Rupert, who had strapped his rowan shield around his chest to ward off any possible blows or spells from the hostile Miragenian populace. Instead, it was primarily prosaic if pleasant occurences that brought about his captivity.

He had followed Alireza's green hem through a rabbit warren of alleys until she passed through a gate. He thought it would not amaze her greatly that he followed. He was surprised, however, when a young girl locked the gate fast behind him and thrust the key deep into the bodice of her gown. Then she giggled. Her giggle was echoed by seven or eight others as a vast array of black-haired girls poured into the garden and arranged themselves around him, laughing and talking and—as they grew accustomed to him—touching.

When his green-gowned beauty reappeared with a goblet of wine for him and one for herself, and looked deeply into his eyes as they drank, he thought perhaps he had done something to transfer him prematurely into that happy land where the Mother sent all of her best children upon their demise. As the ladies pressed closer, touching, tittering, and gazing moonily up at him from big dewy eyes, he decided, on the basis of some of the touching, that he was far from deceased. Besides, he couldn't recall anything that might have put him in such a sadly permanent condition.

He accepted the wine. The women spoke to each other in a language different from that of the marketplace, one he found impossible to understand, although when his original prize addressed him, her purring voice was in a language he could follow, little more than a variation on Argonian, spoken with a slight accent, which he found utterly charming.

They settled him in a cool, breezy room, with a fountain singing in the middle and delicious things to eat and drink. Then they began haggling over him, sending daggered looks and shrill exclamations over his person, while pinching and patting him for emphasis. Even in his wine-soaked haze he began to grow alarmed. His green-gowned temptress returned just as he was about to rise to his noodle-like legs and bolt. She no longer wore a green gown or much of anything else except two long narrow handkerchiefs of sheer pink fabrics suspended from a golden belt, covering the center of her buttocks in the back and shifting alluringly from one thigh, to the other. A lacy vest of gold cloth might have been made for her when she was eight years old, now totally inadequate for its task, strained to cover her gleaming cleavage, which gleamed all the more fascinatingly when she clapped her hands, sending the other girls scurrying from the room. She lowered herself beside him.

"Do not think too harshly of my sisters," she said. "They are passionate and hungry for affection. They find you pleasing as I knew they would." Her silken fingers slid beneath the strap of the rowan shield planted awkwardly in the middle of his chest. She felt for the buckle, tickling, so that he involuntarily pulled her hand back.

"Very nice girls," he agreed. "As you say, affectionate. I'm glad they like me."

"I don't know why they were so greedy tonight. We will have to make out a schedule." She licked her lips appreciatively and ran her eyes from his own, down across his torso, lingeringly, to his toes and back up again. "I am sure there is enough of you to go around."

"Enough to . . . ?" His tongue was thick. Speech was made more difficult as she sought to impede his tongue with her own. She succeeded, for quite some time. "Enough to go around? I'm sorry. I don't quite understand. I believe we need to talk about this . . . ahhh, yes—well, then—perhaps not. . . ." and forgot to protest again for a dangerously long time. Nonetheless, he lacked neither honor nor will to such an extent that he failed to intervene when her nimble fingers, seeking to encounter something else altogether, closed on the mermaid's comb hanging inside his belt. He clasped her slender arm from wrist to elbow in his large hand and with the fingers of the other hand gently removed the comb from her grasp. "I'm sorry, but I'm afraid your family wouldn't like what might happen to you if you handle this comb. Perhaps we should talk, after all."

Her sweet musky perfume grew a tinge more heady, her skin under his hand a touch more velvety, and her voice purred more compellingly than ever, punctuated by moist flickers of her tongue tip against his earlobe. "You will be my family. My love. My husband. Our husband." Her fingers curled toward the comb again playfully. "Now. That's settled. Since it's all in the family, what is that? A gift for some other sweetheart? You'll find enough here to keep you busy, my darling. Give it to me instead and I promise you'll need none of the others to make you forget her."

He moaned.

"Don't you trust me to keep my promise?" she said, pouting.

"It's not . . . that," he said thickly, trying to unwind his tongue from the roof of his mouth where it seemed wont to curl from sheer ecstasy. He continued manfully. "It's just that the fact is, now that you mention promise, I have one to keep."

"Forget her," she breathed huskily into his ear.

"I can't."

"I will make you do so," she threatened, tickling the hairs beneath the rowan shield.

"You will not, for I can tell that you are a tender and loving lady. You would not wish me to forsake the poor little infant whose protector I am to, um, that is . . ." His tongue was cleaving to the roof of his mouth again and his diplomatic training was as if it had never been.

"For the sake of a dalliance? But a dalliance is hardly what we—I—have in mind. You are a splendid man, my love, a superb man, a man who, with a little work, will be worthy of me, of my dear little sisters. You must stay and be ours. . . ."

"Nothing would make me happier, I assure you," he said, his tongue coming unstuck the moment she reintroduced the subject of himself at the mercy of her voracious sisters—plus the little work and worthiness business. "But I must do so with a heart and mind free of distractions."

"Your heart and mind may do as they please," she said, laughing, gleaming again. "But the rest of you must remain here with us."

"Yes, but you don't understand. I must see to the safety of my infant niece, only child of my sister Bronwyn, to whom I have sworn a vow."

"Silly boy. You must not let your concern for some child prevent you from following your more adult inclinations. I happen to know that the child is quite safe and is being spoiled and pampered in accordance with her station."

"You know where she is? You can take me to her?"

"No, I cannot. She is no longer here and we emphatically desire that you be."

"Where is she? What has become of her?"

"Don't bellow so, darling, they'll think we're quarreling. Why, the little dear is being a first-born royal highness, as she was meant to be. Oh, my love, must we talk business?" She ruffled his hair and favored him with a petulant expression. "I know so many more interesting things to do."

He lay motionless, though it was a challenge worthy of a religious hero on the rack, and stared coldly at her until she continued. He decided that later perhaps he would discuss this incident with Sir Cyril Perchingbird and see if inaction under duress did not sometimes constitute sufficient merit to qualify one for a medal of some sort.

"But it's so dull, really. A barren queen wanted a baby and since the Company *had* a perfectly good new baby owed to them, with no one able to tell the difference if quick action were taken, it was a simple matter of transferring the child from the debtor to the client, who took it from there."

"But the child has a family. She was only to stay here fifteen years."

"The clients who asked us—I mean, the Company—to procure the child are renting her services. So you see, it's nothing for you to get tense about. It's not as if she's a slave or anything dismal like that which might have occurred if with my tender heart, I hadn't searched and searched to find just the right opening. I'm very good at my work. Gore . . . the country where the child now lives in splendor and luxury is a very affluent one, one of our chief exporters of magical goods, and the King and Queen will spoil the brat rotten." She flopped herself down, folding her arms under her breasts and pouting in earnest.

He turned and stroked her hair. "You have relieved my mind considerably," he told her, then added casually, "What was the name of this place again? It must be close by."

She was very good at her work; it took him a long time to learn the rest of what he wanted to know from her, and a great deal of effort, which was how he came to be sleeping so soundly when Mashkent's servant saw him in the pool of visions.

Carole found one commendable aspect of the Miragenian way of life: It apparently excluded the idea of dungeons. She was locked in a room that must have been no less luxurious than Mashkent's own quarters, and perhaps more so. Looking it over, she decided that it might be a showroom for the firm's products. This she deduced by the way the mattress floated in midair, lying upon a rug hovering above the multitude of jewel-bright carpets strewn one atop the other in colorful profusion on the patterned floor. A small cascade of colored water spilled down one wall. The soft light of the waxen tapers shining from various nooks and crannies in the carved recesses of the walls reflected from the satiny tumult quick glimpses of faces and figures, people, animals, and landscapes. The falls formed a pretty stream bisecting the room. The stream was bridged at intervals by steps or little arches with golden rails, in which the reflected candle flames danced with their own shadows. Huge windows in ornamental shapes faced the garden in which Carole had spoken to Mashkent, but the view could only be seen through a deeply carved lattice. In every row of lattices sat a row of colored bottles, each row a different hue, each bottle the prismlike crystal of the peridot-colored one from the river near outer Frostingdung.

A young woman, veiled and obsequious, bowed her way into the room just as Carole dropped onto one of the cushions.

"If madam does not wish to retire at once, perhaps I could explain a few of the distinctive features of this chamber," the young woman said, and, without waiting for an answer, continued in a persuasive voice undertoned with what seemed to be great excitement at the opportunity of sharing the information with Carole. Either she had not been informed that Carole was other than a rich customer or else she was so used to giving this particular pitch that she was unable to vary the routine to suit the circumstances.

"The bed will lull madam to sleep with a gentle rocking motion once madam has mounted it by means of uttering a simple command that will cause it to sweep you off your feet and onto your back as smoothly as the most adroit lover."

Oh. Marvelous. Just what she needed. An amorous inanimate object. Silently, Carole vowed to remain on the cushions for the brief time she intended to rest before deciding how best to find Rupert, grab the child (for if the Miragenians didn't care whether or not the baby survived her first fifteen years, it was quite out of the question to leave her with them), and go.

"In the window," the maid continued, "you will notice the display of finely-crafted Gorequartzian vessels. These vessels will explode into flames and poisonous gases the moment they are touched by unauthorized hands, instantly immolating the intruder in the most painful fashion."

Ah, so the maid did know Carole was a prisoner. And the bottles were there to detain her. Not the same as the ones in the river then?

"Lastly," the woman continued, "I am required to explain to you that the firm disclaims any responsibility for damage to yourself or your property if you fail to heed our warning and will also hold you responsible for any damages occurring to company holdings resulting from said failure. Peaceful sleep, madam." She finished, and bowed out.

Carole sat tapping her fingertips against her cheek for a time after the maid left. The bottles might or might not be dangerous. At the present time, she was inclined to think that they were. Otherwise, why leave a lot of valuable and potent magic lying around free for the taking? Not that under ordinary circumstances she was one to appropriate random bits of other people's magic, but if the bottles were like the one by the river, perhaps they were just what she needed to execute her task. On the other hand, they might be just what the Miragenians needed to execute her. If the bottles did contain entities such as the one she had previously encountered, they had no doubt been set to watch her, to prevent her escape, even if they wouldn't actually explode. The maid's warning was clearly aimed at making the firm's involuntary guest reluctant to experiment. Nor did Carole merely wish to escape. Not without Rupert and the child. She stared into the waterfall, considering.

As she stared, she noted that some of the faces floating past were familiar ones. Surely that was the woman in the marketplace appearing briefly in a widening of the water's spill over an ornamental stone, only to narrow back into nothingness as the strand of water containing her thinned and dropped into the stream. And there, on the other side, wasn't that Mashkent himself? And the woman with the mirrors? Yes, no mistaking that dull countenance so badly in need of help from its own merchandise. When Rupert's dreaming visage tumbled over the artfully carved rocks, she had all the confirmation she needed.

She whistled a long, low note and held it. Rupert hung there for a moment, suspended with his chin in the narrow part of the rivulet, his dozing eyes and peaceful brow with the yellow curls broadening out over the rock. As she lost the note he drained away.

Having spotted him once, she recognized glimpses of his face at other points in the waterfall and tried to whistle them to a stop. If she aimed badly, she stopped another face. That of the old merchant, she noticed during one such mishap, was still awake, and contained a thoughtful expression that made her wish she knew what was behind it. Trying to outguess strands of water was slippery going, and she found she had trouble puckering fast enough to stop the one she wanted, tending instead to be in the middle of inhaling just as Rupert slid down the wall.

How was she to slow down the images in the stream long enough to sort them out? Perhaps if she could think of a tune that would call to Rupert's image particularly. . . . Her magic supplied it from a snatch of a love song she had heard him sing for the entertainment of the ladies at Castle Killgilles. She hummed it slowly, like a dirge. The water backed up, as if dammed, flooding the tiled banks from where she sat back to the waterfall, water lapping the edges of the costly rugs before she could find what she sought in its depths. That wouldn't do. Water gushing out the door would attract the Miragenians' notice. She stopped humming and the water flowed back into its course.

Taking one of the candles in hand, she examined the pool at the foot of the waterfall. The sides of it were built up slightly so that one might sit beside it. If she didn't hum quite so slowly, perhaps they'd contain the initial flow of water long enough for her to locate what she needed. She hummed a bit of a lullabye at what she hoped was an appropriate speed. The waters slowed and an infant appeared: a child crowned with dark red ringlets outlined against water. A tall, glittering structure rose in the background like a huge pile of coins, mist encircling its base. The child was wrapped in the arms of a girl whose hair was straight and light brown. They seemed to be sitting in a boat of some sort, and the baby was bawling lustily. The scene flowed past. Carole allowed the water to resume its original level before she hummed the love song again.

Rupert's image dutifully slowed down to where she could observe it in all its slumbering glory. Why in the Mother's name was he sleeping his life away when for all he knew she was still alone in the Miragenian marketplace and the baby still remained missing?

Maybe the Miragenians with whom he was staying had looked into a similar pool to assure him that both cousin and baby were well. Maybe. But did they have such pools elsewhere? It occurred to her that perhaps the water with which she was presently dealing was the runoff of the pools in the courtyard, carrying the visions, which continued to flow even when they were no longer being examined. It made sense to her. Time and events flowed on no matter who was watching, so why not the images? Anyone lacking Carole's talent would have been unable to understand what the waterfall and stream contained, so it probably seemed to the Miragenians perfectly safe to have the water running free for anyone occupying the room to observe if only they could look quickly enough.

Old Mashkent flashed by again and Carole whistled him to a dribble with a song that resembled not so much a song as a chant of the back-and-forth bicker of the marketplace, the buy-and-sell, too-high-too-low cadence she had been hearing all afternoon, unaware until her magic plucked it from her memory. The old merchant climbed onto a hovering rug that rose above the shop to soar across the city. As soon as the image died she caught another, and kept track of the rooftops the rug passed, feeling sure that his trip was somehow connected with her own.

The rug approached a dome composed of stone carved so intricately it resembled heavily starched lace. At its base, the dome's skirt scalloped up in curving arcs above a garden. In this garden, the merchant was met by a lady swathed in a pink-and-gold gown like the one Carole had worn at Castle Killgilles. Though the gown was a different color, the luxuriant hair and the set of the head made Carole certain that this was the same woman Rupert had pursued from the marketplace.

The merchant asked a sharp question. The lady gave him a quick answer that failed to satisfy him. He scowled and asked another question. The lady shrugged, looking smug, and pillowed her cheek on her hands, eyes closed.

So. Now Carole knew where Rupert was. She had only to find the house with the carved dome. Simple enough, if she could first free herself from Mashkent's hospitality.

She eyed the bottle-decked lattices thoughtfully. If she could not touch the bottles, perhaps she could dance them from their niches. If she stood on the far side of the room while doing so and the bottles exploded, so much the better. They would open the windows for her. Otherwise, she would have to hope a piece of the lattice was loose enough that she could jiggle it out, making a space large enough for her to fit through. Fortunately, years of walking and swimming the Blabbermouth had kept her somewhat on the stringy side of the usual sturdy Brownwitch build.

She danced the first three rows of bottles out with the first bar of her song, but as she took a breath, she heard them clamoring. Even though her song was now directed at their counterparts remaining in the lattices, they continued to bounce about on the thick layers of carpet on which she had been careful to land them. The lot on the floor were colored violet, periwinkle, and fuschia, and from them arose a collective whimper when she whistled them to stop. As she returned her attention to the deep ruby row still lining the next row of lattices, one of the ruby bottles cried out. Carole cast a furtive glance at the door. She was trying to whistle loudly enough to move bottles from across the room but not so loudly as to disturb guards posted by her door.

"Shhh," she hissed at the ruby bottle. "Stop complaining. No one's hurting you." As the bottle danced down, it twisted. Within, she saw the glitter of accusing eyes.

"Not hurt us, indeed? What do you call keeping us locked up in here while you jounce us around as if you were trying to make butter if you don't call it being hurt?"

"Confined," Carole said reasonably, allowing the troublesome object to drop beside its fellows on the carpet.

"How would you like being confined then?" asked another protestor, this one from the jade row beneath the ruby one.

"I am, you know, and I don't care for it at all," she replied when that bottle, too, rolled onto the carpet.

"Is that why you're taking it out on us?" whined the ruby complainer on the floor.

"I'm doing nothing of the sort," Carole hissed back. "I'm just trying to . . . none of your business."

Finishing the jade row, she started the row of robin's-egg blue. "We could do business together," the first of these wheedled, winking at her. "You won't get through the window without my help, you know. I propose a fair deal. You get me out and I get you out."

"Don't listen to that one!" the ruby vessel cried. "If you free *me* I won't cheat you out of the other two miraculous wishes you're entitled to by terms of the oral contract."

Carole danced the last robin's-egg blue bottle down and frowned at the crystal-strewn carpet.

"Look who's calling who a cheat," the robin's-egg blue vessel scoffed. "Maybe it is three wishes, but I naturally assumed that this honest and warmhearted lady would not insist on more than a simple trade, since she shares our predicament. Of course, if she's going to be as greedy as our present masters, I suppose there's no—"

"Listen," Carole said, "I am absolutely not interested in your wishes right now. I have plenty of other trouble on my hands without the kind that would come from your magic. If the maid wasn't making the whole thing up about fiery explosions. Neither do I want to be accused of theft."

"Just what do you want?" the ruby bottle asked. "If you free us all, you're entitled to three wishes from each of us. I wouldn't dismiss it so lightly if I were you."

"I don't, but I certainly haven't the time to sit around thinking of wishes all night, nor do I have the pocket space to carry all of you or even one of you. If I open one, can't that one free the others?"

"If that is your wish."

"That's one of them. The others are to get me out of this room and to help me free Prince Rupert and the baby." So saying, she approached the bottles, took a deep breath, pulled the stopper on the ruby one and waited for it to explode.

"That was four wishes," the ruby one said. "I'll give you the first three."

The room exploded in a mass of popping stoppers and spraying colored mist, through which Carole hurtled, covering her head as she reached the window, only to find herself passing harmlessly through it as though it were no more than illusion. The world blurred around her, a spinning confusion of garden and crescent moon, stars, and spires, streets with closed stalls, and arched doorways, all stirred with ruby mist, until she sat down sharply in front of an elegant edifice topped with the intricately carved stone dome. In less than a heartbeat, a ruby dust devil swirled from above, bearing something large and solid, which thumped down beside her.

"I wish you had been a little more patient," Rupert complained, rubbing his backside. "I was going to come for you as soon as I had all the information."

Morning was breaking and Carole and Rupert fled Mlle. Mukbar's mansion for the cover of a ruined wall, behind which they hid, watching the marketplace come to life. In a very short time, the shops were besieged by blue-corded agents of

Mukbar, Mashkent, and Mirza. Rupert, watching through a peephole as the guards briskly searched the street, shook his head, smiling with a hint of pride. "Those Mukbar girls have taken quite a fancy to me," he said. When Carole looked puzzled, he gave her a carefully worded explanation of how he had fared since he left her.

His cousin took her turn at the peephole as he talked and now stepped aside, pointing, so that he could look.

"I wouldn't like to undermine your self-confidence, Your Highness," she said, "but I think those colored clouds might have more to do with the abundance of the Company's minions than does the devotion of your fiancees."

In the street, four guards were now running headlong through the piles of fruit being thrown at them as they were chased by streaks of violet, ruby, and jade. Evidently, the protection they had been given against magic was only proof against Carole's own or else had worn off after a short time and had not been renewed, because after a spirited melee in which the guards definitely came out the losers, the street in front of the ruined wall was clear of both guards and colored streaks. Angry fruit vendors cursed and gesticulated graphically to the departing disruption before stooping to retrieve their bruised goods.

"Were those bright streaks what I think they were?" Rupert asked Carole. She nodded.

He groaned. "How could you? I thought you were going to make things easier here. Instead, the moment I trust you by yourself while I attend to more urgent business, you run off with the private property of the very people with whom we need to negotiate, thereby managing with considerable imagination to violate the only sort of violatable law in this entire anarchy, making us fugitives, no doubt with a price on our heads."

"I didn't run off with anything," she said. "They ran off by themselves, and I can't say that I blame them. They're some sort of intelligent magical creatures with minds of their own. From what I can tell, no one has any business claiming them as property."

"That's your opinion and according to your customs, not theirs," Rupert said stubbornly.

"It is also my opinion that you've little room to criticize when you've done nothing more constructive than sleep through my efforts to help the child after you abandoned me to—"

"I wasn't abandoning you. I was researching." Witches! Pah! They were more trouble than their so-called powers were worth. His rear still smarted from his cousin's idea of rescuing him from a danger that was far preferable to the conditions he now endured. "It may interest you to know that the child is not here in Miragenia, but in a land called Gorequartz. Had you not put us in a position requiring us to hide ourselves, we would need only to stand out in the open long enough for the dragon to find us and we could have her take us there."

Carole was watching the peephole again and made a gratified sound. "There's the scrollseller again. Perhaps she can tell us how to get to this Gorequartz place."

She quickly rounded the edge of the ruined wall, Rupert right behind her.

"No," she said, fixing him with a stare that promised him a dancing lesson if he didn't cooperate. "You're too noticeable. She knows me. I'll be right back." With that, she darted out into the street. She crossed quickly, holding her borrowed veil close to her face as she dodged horses and dromedaries to reach the scrollseller. The woman spoke a few words with her, nodded to the northwest corner of the street, and shrugged.

A sudden flash, further down the street, caught Rupert's eye. A hag hunched over a pile of shining mirrors beckoned to a newly arrived blue-corded company agent. She pointed in Carole's direction. The agent tossed a coin in the air, where it caught the reflected glimmer of a mirror before landing in the woman's hand, from there going straight to her teeth. The mercenary turned backwards and called to someone behind him.

Rupert bounded around the wall and into the street, promptly tripping on an overturned barrow formerly containing melons. When he lifted his face from the street, three blue-corded guards swept past him to close on Carole. She trilled once, tentatively, and again, confidently. When he stood the mercenaries were reeling backwards, cursing their masters for the unprofitable planned obsolescence of their protective spells. Their curses were to no avail. They danced helplessly an arm's length or so away from Rupert, whirling slowly at times or kicking out with little hopping leaps, but basically doing a two-step that kept them well out of reach of his cousin, who was whistling for all she was worth. Rupert held his rowan shield before him as he walked around the dancers to Carole's side. He used his shield gallantly to protect both himself and the poor friendly merchant woman, who had been gracefully two-stepping all over her spilled scrolls.

The dance company grew larger as curious merchants from adjoining booths edged forward to see what was happening and were caught by Carole's whistle. The street resembled a somewhat sedate block party. Many of the merchants trampled their own wares or those of their immediate neighbors. No doubt the loss of the trampled goods would be another crime to be balanced against his and Carole's account, Rupert thought grimly. Nonetheless, the sight of the merrily dancing feet of the merchants topped by their fiercely scowling faces was so humorous he couldn't help grinning.

His grin died as a street musician arrived playing a set of pipes with a high skirling tone that totally drowned out Carole's song, setting everyone free. Rupert drew her back behind his shield as the crowd closed in on them. An almond flew through the air and struck him a blow on the left shoulder. It was followed immediately by a clay pot, smashing against his exposed elbow, causing the shield arm to drop numbly to his side. He collapsed against the wall.

Carole fell on top of him. The merchant woman behind them shrieked. Rupert hitched himself up, spilling his cousin into the crook of his knee as he used his right arm to support his lifeless left arm. No sooner had he raised the shield than a sword crashed down on it. The blade banged off the wood, rebounding to its owner, one of the blue-corded mercenaries, who jumped backwards to avoid its bite.

The shield would protect them as long as he had the strength to maneuver it, for it would repulse any magic and surely, in a magic-proud land such as Miragenia, most of the blades would have some little cheap enchantment on them.

Suddenly a violet haze shimmered above him, causing him momentarily to imagine he had been hit harder than he had first thought. Then the haze was joined by a ruby one and a jade, and the three colors gathered into a malignant rainbow, attacking the merchants with their own wares, the mercenaries with their own weapons.

The shield before them, Rupert and Carole ran down the street, dodging missiles, merchants, and mists. Rupert's long legs fairly flew over the pavement. Carole trailed him at an ever-increasing distance until he reached back with his large paw to catch her up and jerk her forward at arm's length. She was still a good five paces behind him. He dragged her around a corner and almost collided with a raggedy figure who suavely blocked their path.

"Good morning, gentlefolk. I see you are traveling, and traveling is what I am about. Ah, who's this? Why, if it isn't the young woman from yesterday! Having once availed yourself of the services of my splendid travel log, madam, wouldn't you like to try it again? Picture yourself and your companion journeying swiftly up the headwaters of the Cashflow River to the ancient scenic city of Gorequartz. See the sparkling rivers cut through the mysterious magical valley, feared by the most acquisitive of merchants. See the shining sacred temples of many-hued glasses. See the priests float in stately procession down flower-strewn canals in the glamorous barges of the rainbow god, following their quaint, centuries-old custom of parading through the city before presenting to the massive godhead guarding their harbor the human sacrifices that have made Gorequartz a byword to those trafficking in raw magical force and power."

Carole missed part of the speech, for her heart was still beating a hard tattoo in her ears, but she recognized the speaker. "Rupert, the woman in the marketplace said this man might be a slaver—"

"Nonsense, lady. I am a freeborn man, a traveler, and a slaver of no man as I am slave to none. Indeed, you should know as much and so should the woman of whom you speak, for you did no more than gaze at my travel log before it caused the women to provide you with that which I promised it would deliver: the best route, the most scenic and expeditious mode of travel to your destination. If you will but mount upon my travel log once more, this time while it lies atop other materials awaiting us in yonder river, you will once more experience the wonderful convenience and economy of my marvelous device."

Rupert looked down at Carole, dismayed. "Human sacrifice? But Alireza said it was such a *nice* place. . . ."

The travel log rolled back and forth in the bottom of a small boat. The boat also boasted a pair of sturdy oars to augment the log's magic, but despite Rupert's most powerful efforts, progress was slow. The boat kept drifting back toward the grated gate regulating river traffic in and out of the city.

"I thought the log was going to spirit us away," Carole complained, squirming.

"And so it shall," the merchant said, "just as soon as you start singing to the boat and dance it up river for us." And he lay back nonchalantly against the bow—or perhaps it was the stern. They both looked the same since the boat was sideways in the water.

Carole complied, but crossly. Her whistle was whistled out from the long night of herding watery images. Her lips still tingled from orchestrating the dance in the marketplace.

Rupert was no more pleased than she. "It was ill of you, sir, to offer desperate folk magical aid where you had none to give."

"Ah, but you're wrong. I had it, of course. I knew where the river was, which was more than you did, and between my log and this boat, I had all that we needed, save one missing ingredient. The power of my log attracted it—or her, as you see. The rest of what I promised, the so-charming detailing of the wonders of the journey, I shall be happy to personally, enchantingly provide."

"You've been this way before then?" Rupert asked.

"Would I offer you such expert guidance if I had not?" the man asked, sounding both wounded and distinctly evasive. By way of diversion, he launched into his narrative at once. "You have here, for instance, some very fine banks," he began expansively, throwing his arms out to embrace each side of the river.

"Let's forget the banks for a moment," Rupert interrupted. "Tell us more about this place we're heading, this Gorequartz, and why anyone would want to practice human sacrifice."

"As to the last question, my dear fellow, you seem to have me confused with a theologian. If you want me to give you proper guidance, you must let me do so in my own inimitable way, to describe for you each noteworthy landmark in its time, to give it full glory—"

Carole stopped, gasping, her cheeks aching with whistling, her lips buzzing from humming. "Who said we wanted such useless services? The boat would move upstream far more quickly if it had less to carry. It's in my mind that unless you prove very valuable very soon you would be of far more use to us dancing back to shore with your log in your pocket."

The man's eyes widened with terror, but not at her threat. Pointing behind her left shoulder, he gulped and asked, "How valuable would you consider it, madam, if I were to point out that at this very moment your lamentably neglected spell is singing us into the path of another very large craft?"

Carole followed the pointing finger of their self-proclaimed guide to see a huge, bulge-sided boat bearing down on them. "Oh, Mother," she groaned, but wasted no other useless words before breaking into a shrill if exhausted whistle at a fast clip. Her song was copied from that of wild running rapids, though she was fairly certain rapids never ran upstream.

No sooner had she begun to sing their craft away from the big boat than a squad of mercenaries burst through the town gate and onto the left bank of the river. They brandished spears, bows, and in some instances, lightning bolts, which they hurtled at the smaller boat. This seemingly uncalled-for belligerence did not please the occupants of the larger boat, which had so far failed to notice the true target of the aggression. Archers on the deck of the big craft fired back. Unfortunately for Carole, Rupert, and their guide, their own small boat was far more susceptible to the rain of arrows than were the attackers on the river bank.

Carole dipped and dodged, ducking arrows so vigorously that breathing was chancy and whistling nearly impossible. Meanwhile the bow of the greater vessel loomed ever nearer, while the smaller boat wallowed from side to side as its occupants sought to evade the variety of missiles hailing down upon them.

Rupert threw up his shield, but Carole could make no use of it while trying to sing her spell, however erratically. Just as she thought she could not tweet another note, the little boat shuttled like a water spider to the lee of the larger craft, which began crawling past, its bulk protecting the smaller vessel from the attackers landside. This left the mercenaries to concentrate their fire on their unintentional targets in the large boat while their original quarry crept upstream.

Carole heaved a deep sigh, rolling her eyes upward in time to see yet another feature of the Miragenian landscape so far unheralded by their guide. The underbellies, necks, pluming tails, and beating wings of a herd of flying horses swooped overhead. Every horse was mounted and every rider armed. These airborne assailants were not deceived by the cover of the larger boat and began chucking spears at the smaller boat with aim sufficiently accurate to pin Carole's skirt to the deck, through which the haft sank to half its length.

Another spear chunked past Carole's nose. As she lunged violently sideways, so did the boat, which flipped over. She splashed into the water and kicked free. The spear held the stout wool of her skirt and jerked her back. The last thing she saw before her head slammed against the side was Rupert and the merchant tumbling toward the bottom in a haystack of plunging spears and arrows.

CHAPTER VI

Rupert found that although his arms were very long, suddenly he hadn't enough of them. The shield broke his fall when he plummeted into the water, but the travel log seller had grabbed onto him while still clutching the allegedly magic log. Since the panic-stricken merchant held the log against his body with his arm instead of using it to help him float on the surface, the combined weight of water-logged log and water-logged merchant threatened to sink Rupert, merchant, log, and all.

Carole's skirts and hair canopied over them like a large jellyfish, the woman attached to them floating flacidly in their folds, alarmingly unlively. Rupert stopped his plummet with a hard kick toward the surface. He was very strong and it cost him little effort to move. To his surprise, he found holding his breath under water no strain at all. It felt almost natural.

He grabbed Carole's skirt, jerking. She bounced upward and he kicked after her, releasing the hold on her skirt to gain a hold on her waist while angling up between the shadows cast by the boats. The arrows still hissed into the water on all sides of him as he raised his face to breathe. Carole drifted listlessly, supported by one of Rupert's arms, but the log-laden merchant climbed Rupert's other arm, dragging Rupert lower and lower, while he tried with decreasing success to continue kicking to stay afloat. If only the merchant would unhand his arm, he could raise the shield and use it to buoy them up, but the merchant continued to claw at Rupert. Fingernails and log-bark bit through Rupert's tunic sleeve, pulling him off balance.

An arrow whizzed by Rupert's ear and the merchant howled into the same ear. In that instant, the iron grip on Rupert's arm loosened, replaced by a clawed hand groping for his eyes and nose. Rupert ducked backwards. The hand grasped his throat in a stranglehold.

His breath was knocked from him and he stared upward at the circling wings of the flying horses, the great vessel looming over him, the arrows plunging toward him. Rupert knotted his muscles, bracing them against each other to shrug off the merchant with a heave of his shoulders, but he waited, for he wanted to give the travel-logger as long as possible to come to his senses and allow Rupert to help him in a way that wouldn't get them both killed. Closing his eyes tightly, Rupert en-treated the Mother to take literally his prayer to deliver him from fools, and heaved. Whether it was the heaving or the praying that did it, at that moment the hand at his throat relaxed.

He opened his eyes, shut them, and reopened them, for a rosy glow pulsed toward him, thrumming in a familiar way, the glow dissipating as the thrumming grew louder.

The arrows turned magically aside as a strong wind chilled the Prince's wet hide to the bone. Against him the merchant shook convulsively.

Suddenly, the water exploded upward behind them as if something large had dropped into it. Rupert felt teeth graze the skin of his back and buttocks as warm breath and cold water touched his bare skin at once. He was hoisted by the seat of his pants into the air, through the arrows, through the horses, the merchant still clawing at one arm while Carole hung from the other. The leather belt with which he had closed his robe cut deep into his middle where the dragon's teeth pulled it tight, away from his back. He felt the material of his britches strain treacherously. It was sturdy cloth, but not that sturdy.

As if things weren't bad enough, Carole struggled to wakefulness just as the dragon lifted them up through the herd of hostile horsemen. His pants loosened another fraction as he adjusted his grip to hold onto Carole while she squirmed. He thought his arms would burst from their sockets, for he was already overburdened without her making matters worse.

Fortunately, she quieted quickly, most intelligently taking in the situation almost as soon as she woke. She moved not at all except to shake her head, spraying water, and twist it slightly as if to listen to something. She adjusted her grip so that she clung more securely but with less encumbrance, tight against Rupert's chest and shoulders.

The merchant fought Carole's hands and she batted at him, causing the wind to increase at Rupert's backside, the belt to tighten so that, breathless, the Prince issued a whuffing grunt.

"Be still, you cheesehead, and cooperate," Carole told the merchant. "If you keep causing my lord cousin to make such pitiful noises, the dragon will burn us both from the sky to save him further discomfort."

The wings beat her voice away from their hearing, but the merchant reared attentively and painfully against Rupert's arm. "Eh? Dragon?" he shouted into Rupert's ear.

The Prince groaned again and the muzzle pressed against his hindquarters trembled with a deep ominous rumble.

In his other ear, Carole shouted, "Grippeldice wants to know if you're safe and shall she set us down somewhere?"

Rupert nodded with a necessary economy of motion that nevertheless contained an abundance of passionate enthusiasm for the dragon's proposal.

The three of them dropped sickeningly as the dragon swooped low, skimming the water quickly. The line of scrubby greenery separating desert and river blurred past them. Ahead the desert floor dropped and rocky hills rose sharply from the flatlands, breaking into austere red-striped rock slabs, backed by higher slopes sparsely dotted with dark green, followed by wave upon wave of misted blue mountains with white ridges bleeding down into spiderleg veins.

Into this landscape Grippeldice carried her live cargo. For a time she still followed the river, which narrowed somewhat beyond the first few mountains where various streams fed into it. Past the second set of slopes, she veered abruptly away from the river and down a long narrow valley, walled on both sides by heavily forested slopes. All of this speed and motion did Rupert's britches and his sense of security no good whatsoever and he rapidly decided that he couldn't be responsible for everyone's welfare. When Grippeldice passed the next particularly abundantly leafed tree, he would drop the merchant into it and relieve some of the strain on his own midsection and trouser seat. The merchant would simply have to hope for the best.

He did not give up, after all, however, for his pants beat him to it. He cried out as he felt rather than heard the rip as cold air rushed against tender parts. The three of them dropped, dizzyingly, for half a heartbeat before dangling by the remaining strip of his belt. The invisible dragon sought to reduce altitude and potential injuries with all possible haste. When the belt gave way and the three of them were pitched to earth, it was blessedly not too far down and they rolled harmlessly onto the grass.

Rupert, having made sure that he rolled onto his back before collapsing, gave in to the searing pain in his arms and middle and to the generalized aching of his entire body. He sobbed.

Carole sat up and rubbed her head, a luxury she had had to forego while hanging on for dear life and being carried aloft. The ground cover between Rupert and her suddenly crushed itself flat and a piece of ragged double-woven woolen cloth spewed out of nowhere, drifting gently down to cover one of Rupert's ankles.

"Ptui," the dragon said in Pan-Elvin, then, more elegantly, "Will he live, the one who warms my heart?"

Carole examined the heartwarming party in question critically. "Barely, I think. He'll need some mending."

"Hist!" the dragon said. "Something's cooking."

The horse's wingbeats seemed light as a bird's after listening to the heavy drumming of the dragon's flight. High overhead it soared as its rider cautiously patrolled the valley, slowly circling, scouting. The merchant rolled his eyes back in his head and covered them with an arm. Rupert looked past caring. The horse was far beyond them when suddenly it reared, whinnying, and galloped upward, wings and hooves working double time to gain altitude. The rider hung on for dear life. Clearly the animal was running away from him. As the horse sailed over their heads, a curse echoed downward from the rider and a thunderbolt streaked from his hand into a low-hanging cloud, the impact crackling through the treetops.

Ominous rumbling followed close on the initial crack, clouds obediently gathered, the wind freshened and whipped the trees, the sky darkened even further, and soon icy rain slanted through the pervasive shadows.

"That is just what I dislike about Miragenians," the merchant complained. "No sense of fair play. His miserable companions could not find us, he could not find us, but does he give up and go away peacefully? No, he has to make things miserable for this whole valley, whether he thinks we're in it or not."

"We are, though," Carole grumbled argumentatively, not because she didn't agree with him but because being knocked out and dragged through the air was not the sort of thing that brought out the good side of her naturally uneven temperament.

"We might not have been," the merchant said stubbornly.

Carole sighed and stretched with her hands on the small of her aching back. Rupert groaned and she abruptly felt ashamed of herself and began to wonder if there wasn't something she could do about him. He was writhing, arching his spine and trying to rub it. Judging from her own soreness, which did not compel her to contort herself in nearly so extreme a fashion, Rupert's must be nearly unendurable. She turned to the merchant. "See if you can get that log of yours out of the rain and dry the river water off it somewhat, will you? As soon as the weather clears a little, we'll need to build a fire, which should be easy enough with Grippeldice here. I'll try to find some kindling."

She gathered the kindling by hand, trying to move quickly enough to keep warm, a process hindered by her protesting muscles. Ordinarily, had she been feeling lazy, she might have used her magic to save herself the physical effort but her music was spent from her efforts of the day and previous night. She shivered with the dank drizzle and marveled at the abrupt transition from searing Miragenian sunlight to this dim chill, but reminded herself that part of the abruptness was magically induced by the thunderbolt. The spell would probably wear off soon.

While she searched for kindling, she kept her eyes open for a certain flower from which a painkilling tea could be brewed for Rupert. She had had her doubts about him from time to time, true, but he quite literally hadn't let her down when she most needed him and clearly needed help in return now. She spied a cluster of the helpful bell-shaped white blossoms a ways further through the trees and started picking her way toward them.

The sticks she carried snagged in the trees as she passed, breaking and tumbling from her arms, scattering on the ground. Bending her aching back again to collect them, she felt like lying down beside them and crying. Slowly, she retrieved the wood, but decided emphatically that she could not juggle two things at once and returned to the spot where she had left her companions.

Rupert huddled into himself, shivering. The merchant, to Carole's surprise, was finally showing some concern for someone other than himself and was piling bits of his own sodden tatters on top of the moaning prince. Carole stashed her kindling with the log under a protecting bush and retraced her steps to find the flowers again.

They weren't there. The spot was the same one she had seen before. The trees were identical—a large elm with dead vine stalks weaving up the side opposite a shaggy-barked hickory with a broken branch hanging from its top creaking back and forth at right angles. But the little pool of blossoms that had nested between them was missing. Kneeling with less grace and agility than her Great-granny Brown, Carole examined the place where the flowers had been. Broken stems pricked up among the moss-beared tree roots, and one or two leaves remained to reassure her that indeed these were the remains of the flowers she sought.

She shivered and looked quickly around her, searching the gloom. She saw no one, either friend or foe, and half-shrugged, half-flexed her stiff shoulders. At any rate, she was fairly certain that the armed mercenaries on their winged steeds were unlikely to be her rival posy pickers. As her eyes scanned the trees, however, they lit on a refreshing patch of white. This time her effort was rewarded with success and she returned to her companions with her skirt cradling enough flowers to brew the tea.

The enchanted rain was short-lived, but so was the sunlight in the steep-sided valley, and by the time the one left, so had the other. Grippeldice lit a fire with only a minimum of delay caused by the need to dry the travel log. Rupert and the merchant huddled so near that their clothing smoldered. The dragon stayed close, her invisible tail whipping like a gale across the grass as she thrashed it anxiously, rumbling concern for her Prince.

Though Grippeldice had not had the foresight to drop them conveniently near a stream, every curled leaf and every knot hold on every fallen tree in the forest held water, so that was no impediment to making the tea. The dragon stopped rumbling concern for Rupert and started bellowing on her own behalf, however, when Carole said that all they needed was an implement in which to brew the tea and suggested to Grippeldice the only item she could think of with which they could improvise such an implement.

"One of my scales? That is not one of your hotter ideas, witch."

"Perhaps not, but there's nothing else available that's fire resistant. Don't be so selfish. Look at poor Rupert. He needs that tea."

A long silence. Rupert remained huddled, but looked up at his name and attempted a valiant smile, which didn't work out at all.

Near Carole's face a curl of smoke blossomed, a long sigh smelling of rotten eggs escaping with it. "I'm sure it will hurt quite a lot," the dragon said.

"I thought you said you loved him," Carole chided shamelessly. "What about all those noble deeds one hears involving great pain and sacrifice for love between dragons and knights?"

"Is that what they were about?" Grippeldice brightened a little. "I somehow never thought they went that way from the snatches I heard. Mummy said I was too young yet to be told. Do you know any?"

"I'm not much good at telling stories, but once the Prince is feeling better, no doubt he'll recall some he learned from the Archives when he was a boy. I'll be happy to translate."

"Well . . . oh, holy smokes, I suppose so. It won't have to be a very large scale though, will it?"

"Large enough for at least one cup of tea. I can reuse it to make enough for that other man and me."

The dragon snuffled and smoke boiled forth with enough volume to cause Carole to step backwards.

"This *is* an emergency, you know. I do wish you wouldn't be such a baby."

"I know, and I'm trying to be brave, but I *am* a baby," the dragon protested. "I'm still not quite a half a century old. That's extremely young for a dragon." She snuffled again. "Very well. You may take a scale. But try to take one of the ones low on my side, near my belly, where the ground and the air currents loosen them anyway."

Carole reached toward the voice till she touched the dragon, who guided her with rather finicky instructions until she worked her way down the invisible side to a scale sufficiently loose to suit its owner and sufficiently large for her own purposes. Gently but firmly, the witch gave a sharp tug and dislodged the scale. The dragon almost forgot herself and burned down the forest.

Rupert and the merchant found that in spite of their infirmities they could move with amazing speed when necessary. Carole hugged the ground with the scale shielding her head until Grippeldice regained her composure.

The three humans sat side by side on a fallen log, any garments that could be spared draped over twigs by the fire. Until the Prince was sufficiently convalescent to deliver the promised tales of love and valor about dragons and princes, the merchant regaled Grippeldice with an account of a journey he had once guided into the realm of the Queen of Dragons, with whom he claimed to be well acquainted. Carole applied a bone needle and a bit of yarn she had unwoven from Rupert's trouser leg to the seat of his pants while he sat bare-legged, his Miragenian robe wrapped demurely across his lap. He made ungrateful faces while sipping the first infusion of the hard-won tea.

Suddenly the wind whipped viciously across their fire, bending it low, whipping loose the twigs serving as clothes hangers and singeing the hem of Carole's cloak. A shadow fell across the crushed brush where Grippeldice invisibly curled. Behind it, shrouded in deeper shadow, something stood, eyes mirroring the flames.

"Interloper," it accused in a low, slightly nasal feminine voice throbbing with anger. "Defilers of magic. Ghouls who drink the very blood of universal wisdom—"

"You got us wrong, lady," the merchant said. "This is not blood, just a little herb tea. We are not what you say. These two are Argonians and me, I'm a traveling man."

"You are interlopers!" the voice said, its source shifting forward. The outline might have belonged to a smallish woman wearing a cloak with a stylish puffy hood, but Carole couldn't make out the details clearly.

"Just who do you think you are to come barging in as if you owned the place, calling people names?" Carole demanded. Rupert freed a hand from balancing the scale at his lips long enough to touch her arm restrainingly. Without thinking, he shifted the fingers of his left hand to support the rest of the puddle of tea suspended seemingly in midair above it.

"I am Effluvia, guardian of the valley, protectress of this sacred place and these sacred plants and their proper usage. I alone know how each magical aspect of this valley must be treated, nurtured, and cultivated to produce a power for wisdom and glory in its truest and purest form. You have dared to trample this ground, to ravish this valley for your own selfish ends. For that I will punish you, summoning the concentrated power of my own divine essence, loosing it· upon you so that—" The voice stopped and focused on Rupert, who still sat with his head lowered, sipping, trying to pretend he wasn't present. "You. Man. Dast you continue to commit your crime even as I confront you with its enormity?"

"Lady," Carole said wearily, hoping that her whistle had been restored enough by now to allow her to deal with this creature, "My cousin has had a very hard day. If you'll be so kind as to excuse us?"

The creature—for as it stepped forward into the firelight Carole could see it was not entirely a woman—did not respond well to firm courtesy. With a nasty snarl she stretched out her clawed hand and hurled a spell, something like a thunderbolt, but smaller and more to the point. The spell knocked the tea-filled invisible scale from Rupert's lips. Almost in the same motion the creature spun around in the light, so that her victims got a good look at what they were dealing with. Her face was long and pointed in the middle, her chin receding, her forehead and nose prominent, eyes small and shining hard and bright as arrowheads in the rain. Her waist-length hair was unbound and blacker than the shadows except for two broad white streaks like parallel lightning bolts shooting from her widow's peak to the beginning of what Carole had mistaken for a cloak. This last item had been curled around Effluvia's head and as it unfurled was revealed as a long, luxuriant tail of black fur. This she brandished at them like a banner, except of course that she had had to turn herself around backwards to do so.

"If you would smell my flowers, interlopers, smell this as well!" the Effluvia creature cried, and her tail tip jerked.

At the same time the brush between merchant and cousins and their assailant sprang up. "Knock my friends around and attack an unarmed injured man, will you? I'll cook your goose, skunk!" Grippeldice roared in Pan-Elvin. Her three former passengers were knocked off the log by her strong tail even as that other tail jerked and a dreadful stink of dragon-sized proportions assaulted the air from around an invisible but equally dragon-sized space in front of them.

Grippeldice roared and the woman shrieked, suddenly aware that these were not just any dragonless wayfarers she was tormenting. She spun back around, caught some of her own essence reflected from the invisible scales, and reeled backwards in a swoon. A great gust of wind swept between her and her intended victims as first the grass, then the tree tops flattened with the dragon's passing. A most unsavory odor floated back to settle over the spectators as the tree tops lashed back into place again.

The merchant was laughing, his eyes and nose running in unseemly chorus. Carole fanned the air rapidly with both hands while holding her breath and wondering if her magic could come up with a fume-dissipating song. Rupert struggled to his feet and approached the fallen skunk-woman, who had recovered enough to cough, a feat complicated by her attempts to hold her nose at the same time.

"Madam, I fear there has been some terrible mistake that has caused distress to us all. Pray let us help you clean yourself and we'll discuss this like civilized creatures," Rupert offered gallantly, though nasally, for he too was of necessity holding his nose.

She said nothing, too busy coughing to speak or even to hear him, and he turned, walked away a short distance, sighed deeply, squatted down, and very carefully began to pick up a handful of large wet leaves, with which he proceeded to wipe all exposed surfaces, save the fur of her tail, which he left strictly alone for reasons of prudence as well as propriety.

"Watch that tail or she'll have you for sure this time," Carole cautioned, but he shook his head.

"I don't think she's able. She's quite debilitated by her own—er—essence. But see here, cousin, her tail has caught most of the stink and she is a *lady* whatever. I don't suppose you would mind, uh. . . ?"

She rolled her eyes but obligingly gathered a fresh batch of leaves and, with Rupert supporting Effluvia's front end, brushed the fur of the creature's tail with them until she was unable to hold her breath any longer. She staggered away, breathed deeply for a moment, gathered fresh leaves, and started over again.

Effluvia still could barely speak. She looked up at Rupert

wonderingly, blinking rapidly as the tears coursed down her cheeks. Rupert patted her shoulder. "Maybe you can make magic with some of the other flowers you have here to improve the atmosphere."

Effluvia's lips moved, murmuring, "My God," it sounded like then, pettishly, "I have been shamed. You're trying to rub it in."

"We're trying to rub it off," Carole corrected her with exaggerated patience. "If you hadn't been so possessive about a few little flowers . . ."

"But I am the guardian of magic in this valley and the custodian of its use."

"Unless I missed something, those flowers were just flowers," Carole scolded. "They're not magic at all until you use them and anyone has a right to use wildflowers, for pity's sake. I've heard of game preserves where you can't chop wood or kill animals, but plucking wildflowers?"

"Standards must be maintained," the skunk-woman said, her long nose twitching but her beady eyes looking pleadingly at Rupert.

"In that case, lady, why did you not ask to taste my tea?" Rupert asked gently. "You could have told in that way that my cousin upholds the highest standards in her brewing. She sought only to ease my pain so that we might continue our quest to find my infant niece, who has been ruthlessly abducted."

"But surely *you* must understand that no one knows how to truly use the magic of this sacred valley but myself," Effluvia continued to plead, now whining slightly as she brushed the moisture from her pointed face with two hands still odiferous enough to cause her snoutish nose to wrinkle. "I must protect the wonders of this place against those who ride the flying horses. Those pimps of magic dwelling in Miragenia are not fit to step foot in this valley."

"I do understand," Prince Rupert said quickly, "and we

couldn't agree with you more, could we, Lady Carole? As our—er—native guide mentioned, we are Argonian ourselves, not Miragenian at all. He is, but—"

"I've been meaning to talk to you about that, Prince," the merchant said, raising a finger to draw attention to himself. He was standing as far from them as he could while still remaining as close to the ruined embers of the fire as possible.

"Later," the Prince said firmly.

"As His Highness pointed out, I think we've had a misunderstanding here, Effluvia," Carole said just as firmly. "I take it that you are a sorceress or a priestess of some sort, charged with protecting this valley. Yet we saw no signs posted, no wards against entering, no medicine bags in the trees, no guardian beasts. We had no way of knowing we were trespassing on your realm. I occupy a similar position to yours myself in my own village, so you see if anyone can understand your position, I can. And while I must say I still maintain that wildflowers are wild and should be free to anyone, we had no mind to offend you. Had you spoken to us first before just wading in and attacking Rupert, this could have all been settled without so much fuss. As it is, you made the dragon angry, spilt the tea and didn't do yourself any good either."

"Oh, I do see your point, and while I was only doing my appointed sacred duty to the greater glory of the Grand Prismatic, as I'm sure you'll understand"—this with an almost coy look at Rupert—"I accept your apology and ask you all to be my guests. You must tell me of your travail and let me show you the compassion and hospitality the valley can offer to those who would honor rather than defile it."

"We do appreciate that," Rupert said humbly.

"I must ask, of course, that you leave your own guardian beast outside," Effluvia said. "Whatever it was."

"A dragon," Carole enlightened her quickly. "A very protective and jealous dragon."

CHAPTER VII

By the time the group reached Effluvia's den, Effluvia had gone from trying to run them off to being effusively thrilled that they were honoring her humble hut with their presence—"they" meaning Rupert, of course.

Her den burrowed into a mountainside, with a front of slim branches and packed mud fronting on a shallow cave. A curtain of furs hung over the doorway. Their suddenly solicitous hostess wrapped everyone in furs from a pile that smelled faintly of skunk and poorly tanned hides.

To Rupert she said, "Your Highness, if you and your companions will divest yourselves of your wet and soiled garments, I will take them outside and wash them in a bath of herbs that will leave them clean and sweet-smelling."

As she expected, everyone was too stunned by her graciousness to object, and she gathered the clothing and departed with it without interference. Once outside her muzzle split in a wide toothy version of the human grin she had once been capable of displaying, her little eyes dancing with blissful wonder at the gift that the god had bestowed upon her in the guise of the Prince. After hugging his clothing to her until she reached a semblance of calmness, she dumped the entire pile in the hollowed log that served as a rain barrel. She was thankful that the magic many-hued tulip, whose mate bloomed within the great temple, was some distance away from her hut. If the Prince knew of the power of his sacred face, he was being very cagey about it. But he was not the only one who could be cagey. Though she had known him at once when he bent over her after what had seemed her ignominious defeat, she had kept her peace, waiting for a sign. When he maintained his pose of humility and ignorance, she maintained hers of loyal guardian who had to be won over by unintentional interlopers. But all the while, the knowledge burst in her breast that the god had jested with her. While pretending to send an opponent to defeat and disgrace her, the Great Polyhued had manifested himself in this amazing show of grace. She could hardly wait to tell His Brilliance. She would, though. The blessing was hers alone, and she of all of the god's servants knew best how to use it to its fullest advantage. Kneeling, she whispered the briefest possible message into the tulip's petals.

Rupert was nodding when she returned, without the clothing and with a smug expression on her snout. Effluvia brushed his face with the end of her tail, newly and more pleasantly scented. She was not prepared for them to sleep. Rupert, gratified by her apparent change of heart and curious to learn what caused it, was content to loll against the wall, a roll of skins supporting his bare back while the fur robe covered him from mid-chest to mid-shin. His lower legs and feet hung out. Effluvia tapped them with her tail from time to time, to emphasize certain things she had to say. This made him smile no matter how serious the subject. Fur tickled.

He told her without embellishment of unnecessary explanation why he and Carole sought Gorequartz. In her present friendly mood, perhaps she could help. On the other hand, he did not yet trust her and disliked volunteering any more information than absolutely essential to elicit a sympathetic response.

"I think what you wish to do is very noble," Effluvia

gushed when Rupert had finished. "But I doubt if the evil King will allow it. You'll need the help of the priests."

"You seem to know a great deal, madam, for a woman who sports a tail and lives in the woods," the merchant observed slyly from his cozy nest of skins.

"You seem to speak freely for one who has not even given his name," she countered.

"I am Timoteo, adventurer, raconteur, and traveler of great renown. I seek not to be rude, dear lady, merely to comment that your degree of erudition about matters in Gorequartz seems unusual for a person of such a rustic background."

"I have not always lived here nor have I always appeared as I do now. In part my current condition is due to that same evil King of whom I speak, he who holds your niece, my dear Prince." She paused dramatically. "For you see, your niece could not possibly be the firstborn daughter of this King. He had a daughter by his first wife, the true Queen of Gorequartz. I am that child."

"What race did you say these people *are*?" Carole whispered to the merchant.

"A superior and magical one," Effluvia said in a voice that overrode her.

"They would be," Carole muttered to herself.

"They slew the sorceress who ruled there, gave the backward denizens of the land productive employment in the crystal mines, and avenged the Rainbow God, the Grand Prismatic, the Many-Hued, serving him with devotion and sacrifice which he has handsomely repaid over the years by granting his favorites great prosperity and an elevated form of civilization."

"About your tail, though," Rupert prompted. "What about that? Do all of your people possess tails?"

"Of course not. No one else is so honored because no one else is guardian of this valley and particular handmaiden of the god. The tail is part of my present form, a gift spell placed upon me by my benefactor, the High Priest of the Grand Prismatic. My father would have had me slain but the High Priest, an admirer of my late mother, preserved me from death and gave me this form that I might serve the god with my life and essence until such a time that he called me to a higher, more public sort of task, fitted to the wisdom and grace I have obtained while performing my humble duty in exile."

"That was very decent of the High Priest," Rupert said, "But I don't understand why he needed to save you. If you're the King's daughter, and he wanted a daughter badly enough to convince the Miragenians it would be profitable to have my niece passed off for his own child, why did he try to kill you? Didn't your mother have anything to say about that?"

"She would have had, but, alas, for her, she did not say so quickly enough. The King is desperate for a male heir, someone suitable to take his place so that a secular person may sit upon the throne of Gorequartz, disputing the judgment of the divinely inspired priests. As the King has the army, the situation is very difficult for those who serve the god truly and lovingly. When my mother bore me, my father was greatly disappointed, and when by the time I was seven years of age she had no other issue, he was beside himself with rage. I was playing innocently in the garden one day when I overheard him telling his steward that he would either have to offer my mother up to the god, making it possible for him to take a new wife, or else my mother would have to agree to follow an old custom of my people, sacrificing the child of unsuitable sex so that the divine would know they had made a mistake and supply a more appropriate offspring.

"Naturally, this shattered my young life. I couldn't think what to do. I could not go to my mother, for surely my father would be there, speaking to her, and I was afraid for him. Mother and I had made many pleasant trips through a secret passage to the temple, however, where I played with the crystal prisms and blew bubbles on the rainbow pipes while Mother confided with the High Priest in his chambers. The High Priest had always been kind and good to me, more like a father than the King. In my distress, I ran through the secret passage and found the good man. I told him what my father had said, and that I knew my mother would want me to have his protection. He kept me hidden there in the temple until the day when he was called upon by the King to send Mother to join the god. Tender of my youthful sensibilities, he told me he had an important task for me and that he would use great magic to make me fit for it, child though I was. Thereafter he sent me here in this shape to guard this valley and here I have remained."

"But if the King doesn't want a girl baby, why didn't the new Queen import a son?" Rupert asked.

"I suppose none were available—especially none that look like the King. He's the kind of man who notices those things. If the new Queen is barren, someone else's daughter will at least give her a few years to bargain with until she can conceive a son—"

"Or sacrifice my niece to save her own life," Rupert said, shaking his head in disbelief at such barbarism.

"Unless your niece is as fast with her feet and tongue and as well-connected as Lady Effluvia here," the merchant said with admiration.

Carole said nothing, but stood, grasping her fur robe around her, and hobbled toward the door.

When she had been gone for some time, Rupert wrapped his own robe about him and ducked outside to look for her. She had found her still-damp clothing drying beside the hut and was pulling on her leggings.

"Where do you think you're going?" he asked in a low voice he hoped would not penetrate the skin hanging over the door.

"Anywhere, as long as it's away from here. Effluvia's furry

tail isn't the only one she has that stinks. Do you really think she'd help Bronwyn's child when she's as good as admitted she's already sacrificed her own mother?"

The skin slipped aside and Effluvia's snout poked out, sniffing. "That's easy enough for you to say. You obviously have no concept of higher responsibilities than mere family loyalty. I have my own destiny to fulfill, my own obligation to the god. Even at an early age I knew it transcended being a mere brood mare for the royal line, as my mother was, poor thing. And I do wish to help this niece of yours, dear Prince. I wish very much to help her escape the fate I almost fell prey to. Tomorrow I shall personally guide you all through my valley and to the temple where my benefactor, I'm sure, will aid you even as he has me."

On that note, she popped back inside, leaving Carole fuming and Rupert staring thoughtfully off into space. Carole couldn't tell whether or not he believed in Effluvia's self-proclaimed compassion, but she did not. It was out of character.

"That creature burns me up," a familiar voice said from atop a rocky ledge just above the roof of Effluvia's hut. "Who does she think she's fooling?" Carole looked up, hoping to see Grippeldice, since by now the hidebehind pill should have started to wear off. Instead the dragon, after her thorough bath in the river, resembled nothing more than a rain shower as her run-off pattered on the roof.

"Ah, Grippeldice," Rupert said cheerfully, speaking to the dripping ledge.

A stream of steam mixed with flames warmed his left side, boiling the vegetation behind him. "What's the matter with her?" Rupert asked, rubbing his face. The air was redolent of hot skunk.

"She's jealous and angry," Carole answered, "and tired of being invisible, no doubt." She scratched her head and regarded the ledge, frowning. "You don't suppose that hidebehind pill might have fermented after all these years and gotten stronger instead of weaker, do you? Surely not. Still, I must ask Rusty—"

"What's she jealous about?" Rupert asked, a hint of satisfaction marring the tone of innocent concern he strove to project.

"What? Why, that you've taken up with and—as nearly as I can tell—been taken in by Effluvia. Don't ask me to intervene, either. I agree with Grippeldice."

"I can explain it all, I promise you," he said, and gazed up at the dripping wind steaming and streaming around them in its aggrieved fashion. "But please tell my dragon everything is all right and that, if only she'll be patient and help us a while longer, we should be in Gorequartz tomorrow."

Carole translated, then shook her head. "She says not if Effluvia is going with us. Grippeldice will have nothing to do with that woman. You'll have to choose between them."

"Can't you reason with her?"

Carole shrugged. "I'd rather reason with you, since personally I feel that Grippeldice is the one showing sound judgment. You may not have noticed but those are skunk skins wrapped around you in such profusion. That woman has no compunctions about betraying anyone and has as good as bragged about it. What makes you think she's not going to buy her way back into her father's favor by seeing to it that if he sacrifices Bronwyn's baby, he can include us and make a family affair of it?"

"I think you're exaggerating," Rupert said stubbornly. "It doesn't sound to me as if he'd have her back on any terms. I agree that she may have something up her sleeve but if we keep our wits about us . . ." His voice trailed off, giving way to a discreet and supposedly crafty look.

"That's what I like. A definite plan," Carole said.

"Have you a better one?"

"Certainly. Let's climb aboard Grippeldice right now and have her take us to Gorequartz."

"I can't think how that would help, except to shorten the journey and to soothe Grippeldice's feelings. If Effluvia has the influence she claims, she can help us. If not, we will be in no worse straits in her company than we would be going as uninvited strangers into what I can only presume from its customs must be a rather hostile culture. If the priests oppose the King and realize that an impostor child has been substituted, it may well be to their benefit to help us, to let the baby return with us."

"I can't believe Effluvia is interested in helping anyone but herself."

"No, perhaps not, but, on the other hand, it probably matters little to her if, while helping herself, she helps someone else in the process. That, my dear cousin, is what diplomacy is all about. To convince the other party that one's own best interests serve them even better than oneself."

"Very well then. I'll let you explain that to the dragon," Carole said, and returned inside.

Without the dragon's cooperation, the walk through the valley took most of the next day, and Carole's spine itched every step of the way. She wished Grippeldice had remained in sight. The dragon's protective presence would have been a practical sort of comfort, but the beast had clearly departed ahead of them. Very sensible of her. Any witch with a modicum of self-respect would have done the same thing. Or better yet, persuaded the beast to take her aboard as a lone passenger and gone to fetch the baby without the rest of the tiresome party. Of course, Rupert *could* be right in his wishful thinking that Effluvia would somehow prove herself more help than hindrance, but, oddly, it was less the Prince's optimism than Carole's own dead-certain conviction that the skunk-woman was going to betray them that kept the witch pacing behind the others, starting at rustlings in the trees, peering into shadows, and listening closely to every change in conversational timbre that might indicate the moment had arrived to muster her own magic to their defense.

Because however muddle-headed her royal cousin might be at the moment, he was family and he had saved her life. He was, on the whole, a very decent young man. She was growing quite fond of him. Nevertheless, she felt he needed the benefit of a more suspicious nature to keep him from falling prey to wistful thinking and misplaced idealism. The merchant definitely had a suspicious nature, but would hardly fill the bill, since he was one of the very persons Carole felt Rupert needed to be suspicious of. Therefore, she could no more leave him to the mercies of the various unscrupulous parties with whom he was choosing to involve himself in this escapade than she could leave Bronwyn's baby to the tender mercies of her infanticide-prone foster parents.

Her resolve wavered badly at times, however, for the going was rough. The merchant insisted on rattling off lurid descriptions of the countryside at every other tree. She reminded him that he no longer had the so-called travel log and didn't need to keep up the accompanying prattle, but he shrugged and grinned at her infuriatingly and said he had gotten into the habit and who knew but what he might not find another log? He wouldn't want to be ill-prepared. But the worst thing was that Effluvia led them on a circuitous path through the valley, "protecting" various sites along the way with her nauseating scent.

The first of these was another innocent patch of the pain-killing flowers.

Rupert stepped gently over them but Effluvia made a disgusted sound in her throat. "Too bad that by the time I return they'll have died. I gathered for drying that other batch your little friend would have defiled yesterday, Prince, but I have no use for any more now. Oh well. The worst thing is that the Miragenian pigs should have them." And with that, before the merchant and Carole could step around the flowers,

Effluvia imperiously held her hand aloft, waved them aside, raised her tail, and proceeded to make it most expedient for them to circumvent the patch by a field's length. The flowers wilted on their stalks with barely a whisper of protest.

They were dead before Rupert could so much as open his mouth, but he looked back at the flowers with a stricken expression. "If you weren't going to use them, I don't see what difference it would have made to let them live a day or so more," he said.

"You have no idea how depraved some people are. They use such magic to relieve them of pain they've obviously brought on themselves. The most disgusting thing about the Miragenians is that they use absolutely no sense of discernment about their clientele. They'll sell to anyone who pays them, regardless of worth or station in life."

"I see," Rupert said politely, but he walked half a pace ahead of her and said little until they reached a rocky cliff. Here, too, Effluvia raised her tail.

"You will note on our immediate left and for some distance above us rock of the finest kind, with its stunning blue-gray striping casting long and sturdy shadows onto the leafy forest floor."

"Phew!" the merchant finished unceremoniously. He had failed to notice that the rock was about to be protected. When he could breathe again he asked, "Your pardon, lady, but why do you think anyone would want to steal any of this stupid rock, with or without your stinking it up?"

"Stinking it up, indeed! A lot you know," Effluvia told him. "That rock *you* so stupidly refer to as stupid will be chiseled into an entirely different formation by the time I return if I don't properly safeguard it. A small fragment of it in the pocket of a delegate to the god is enough to send the most cowardly and whining sacrifice staunchly to his death. Before I came to this valley there was a heavy black-market trade in pieces from this stone. I am proud to say I have successfully put an end to that. This cliff has not lost one chip since I arrived."

"It seems to me people who . . . practice a religion involving human—er—delegates to the gods . . . would prefer to have those delegates go calmly," Rupert said. He was trying very hard to be, or at least sound, broad-minded.

Effluvia gave him a small, knowing smile having all the charm of green mold on his breakfast toast. "You know nothing of our magic. True, the priests keep some few pieces of the rock on hand for specially favored prisoners. My mother may have been granted it as a boon in honor of her long friendship with the High Priest, for instance. But a sacrifice without fear and pain is really only half a sacrifice. To extract the most benefit, the delegate should feel the maximum amount of fear and mental chaos before the god sunders his body from his spirit. Fear and pain have great power, as does the fascination and dread they arouse in onlookers. Our priests are able to condense and use that power to the greater glory of the god and the magic of Gorequartz."

She spoke with a faraway look in her eye, her head tilted, the small smile growing vaguer, softer, as if she were remembering a particularly entertaining ball she had once attended, or an athletic event of some sort. Rupert shuddered.

Later that afternoon, Effluvia protected a spring whose water could inspire love, and the gemstones in it, which could ease grief. A mountain pasture, whose grasses could guarantee inner peace for as long as a blade could be chewed, was her next target. By the time she finished with the pasture, chewing its grasses would ease nothing but the necessity to chew anything the rest of one's life. By evening, the magical and wondrous places in the forest were cloaked in a miasma of bad odor. Effluvia looked heartily pleased with herself.

She graciously extended her protective powers to include them when they camped that night, halfway up a mountain pass. Before any of them could utter a word of protest, the skunk-woman paced around them, enclosing them in a circle of stench. Carole scooted closer to the clean smell of the campfire and tried not to inhale. Rupert hunkered beside her, making himself as small as he could. He shivered slightly in the cold, thin air. His nose twitched uncontrollably and he looked miserable.

"Enough to choke a horse, isn't it?" he asked.

"You'll notice we saw only magic things. No magic beasts," Carole replied with as little movement of her mouth as possible. "If she tried her nasty business on a unicorn, she'd be punctured in a thrice. Mum's friend Moonshine would never stand for her polluting any of the streams he cleanses with his horn. And you know what Grippeldice thinks of her."

"Yes," the Prince said. "Of course, she did have a hard childhood, still . . ."

The merchant Timoteo, already curled by the fire for sleep, opened his eyes long enough to look imploringly heavenward and then back to Carole, who nodded slightly, patted Rupert's forearm, and assumed her own sleeping position. Little space remained between her and Timoteo but Rupert squeezed himself into it, something Carole did not appreciate since he left no place for Effluvia but next to her, where the skunk-woman's unfragrant tail twitched ticklingly near the witch's nose all night.

Effluvia proved a more helpful companion the following day. They reached the bottom of the pass by noon, the river less than an hour later. They followed the river upstream around a sharp bend, beyond which it spilled from a sizable tunnel carved into the mountainside. A long, wooden boat was tied near the tunnel's entrance. Effluvia immediately climbed into it.

The merchant was the first to follow her, eyeing the length of the vessel warily. How very convenient that Effluvia should have a boat here just when she needed one. Even more convenient that it should be just the right size. But then, she did possess a certain magic—most of it less helpful than this. He shrugged.

Rupert followed him, looking upward one last time before boarding.

Once they entered the first tunnel, they were underground most of the way. Now and then the river slipped out of one hole and into the open before slipping into another, but mostly they rowed upstream in darkness. Rupert and the merchant took turns at the oars. Even when they had been rowing for some time, neither of them suggested aloud that Carole use her magic. Nonetheless, Carole hummed a soft song to the boat to ease its glide and let it cut through the water with minimal effort on the part of the oarsmen. This much she could do without Effluvia's knowledge, for the river roared in all their ears and no one could be heard without shouting.

All the rest of that day the men rowed, the river roared, and Carole sat in the dark humming. When they saw light again, it was twilight.

The boat bumped gently against a dock leading from the water into the nothingness of a thick mist. Behind them the tunnel was no longer a natural indentation in rock but a carefully carved arch over a long stretch of increasingly calm water. Ahead of them, boats and barges of all descriptions plied the smooth, shining expanse daubed pink with the setting sun. Above them rose an incredible edifice, the same Carole had seen in the stream in Mashkent's house, a conical tower of rising domes, walled with gold and roofed with clearest crystal, surrounded at the base by a bank of silvery mist.

"How strange," Effluvia mused as two massive men with manes of golden hair and arms as big around as Carole's thighs tugged the little boat to a mooring. "I grew up in the palace amidst wealth and luxury, it is true, but somehow it is only here in this simple holy place that I truly feel at home."

"My dear, I do understand," Carole could not resist saying. "I feel the same way every time I leave my father's hall to visit the seamstress's cousin, Sean the Shepherd, in his little hut in the hills."

CHAPTER VIII

The High Priest appeared nonplussed when Effluvia had herself announced and then pushed her way in before the lay brother guarding the door had time to finish the announcement.

"My . . . my dear, how you've changed," the man on the crystal throne said, his golden beard dropping an inch lower on the V of tanned chest bared by his suit woven of every shade, tint, and primary color in the spectrum.

"Oh, yes, Your Brilliance. I have. How long has it been, ten years? But the god blessed my vigil with success at last and I think that you will find that not only have I grown in stature but also that I have been transfigured by the experience of living in the woods, by the grace and wisdom of the god, protecting the tranquility and order of the growing things."

"You certainly have," the High Priest said. "Brother Bullcow, will you be so good as to swing that incense a bit closer? Ah, there, thank you."

"Furthermore, Your Brilliance, I think that you will agree that the fact that I have been chosen to be the custodian of the marvel I bring to you will demonstrate beyond my own admittedly ample abilities that the time has come when you should reverse the spell upon me, allow me to resume my residence and rightful place here, along with my more standard female appearance, and use this person I present to

123

you as an instrument to forever bring Gorequartz under the sway of those of us who are holier than the rest."

"No doubt I will agree, my dear child, but I think it necessary that first you show me this person."

She had been blocking the doorway, much to the annoyance of the brother serving as herald. Now she turned and, with a clash and a tinkle of crystal on crystal, swept aside the curtain of colored, tear-shaped beads which shielded the High Priest, even when the gilded wooden door was open, from the view of the secular not specifically admitted to his presence. Carole and the merchant sauntered in blinking at the sudden flood of light pouring down from the transparent ceiling and bouncing from the solid gold walls. Rupert, to Effluvia's annoyance, insisted on finishing explaining to the lay brother guarding the outer door what the device on his rowan shield meant. It took a cross look and an ominous hist from Effluvia to capture his attention.

Rupert ducked through the door to avoid bumping his head on the golden curlicues protruding from the arch. The High Priest's expression spawned a thin squirm of a smile on Effluvia's ungenerous mouth. His Brilliance was obviously trying very hard not to look startled, and was failing miserably. Nor did Carole feel that His Brilliance was simply unused to extremely tall people. He stared at Rupert's face in a fashion bordering on fascination.

Everyone continued to either stare at Rupert or stare at everyone else staring at Rupert for several moments.

"You see, Your Brilliance, that in no way did I misrepresent the importance of my blessing," Effluvia said, talking slowly, sure that she would not be interrupted by the High Priest, who sat with a smile dawning on his face, beaming rays of approval in her direction. "This gentleman is known as Rupert Rowan, a Prince of Argonia."

His Brilliance kept nodding but did so in Rupert's specific direction now, still smiling and staring.

Rupert, after a polite interval, said, "I take it then that you are the gentleman of whom Lady Effluvia has spoken? Very pleased to make your acquaintance, I'm sure. Perhaps I should explain why I asked this lady to escort us here. As a member of the Argonian Royal House, I have been designated diplomatic representative of my sister, Princess Consort of Ablemarle. These folk accompanying me are my staff, my cousin, the Honorable Lady Goodwitch Carole Songsmith Brown, a theologian like yourself, and Mr. . . . Timoteo, who has helped with our travel arrangements. We have come in regard to a misunderstanding which has occurred and with which the Lady Effluvia seems to feel you might be able to help us. We are quite willing to negotiate. I am widely known in my own lands as Rowan the Rational."

The High Priest continued to nod, evidently enjoying himself immensely.

Rupert smiled, too, and nodded. "I'm so glad you see it that way. Perhaps if I outline the problem for you. It goes back many years, to a time when the Miragenian firm of Mukbar, Mashkent, and Mirza had occasion to assist Princess Bronwyn and Lady Carole on a mission."

"Your Highness, please, I'm sure as you say that we can work out some arrangement which will be mutually satisfactory," the High Priest said, beaming at Rupert, something like awe still making his eyes round under his bushy dark gold brows. "You have traveled long, I know, and little of daylight remains, but there is something I would like to show you before darkness settles on us completely. Please, if you and your party will accompany Brother Bullcow, I will just arrange to have a little supper prepared for us to take aboard the barge while you are freshening up."

Brother Bullcow headed for the door, incense swinging. They all turned to follow him when the High Priest added, "Oh, Your Highness, our people are not used to visitors. It would be provident therefore if you and your staff would don the robes worn by our lay brothers prior to leaving the temple. Just for discretion's sake, you understand."

Rupert nodded gravely.

Effluvia stood by the High Priest's throne, looking after the others with a triumphant smile.

"My darling child," the High Priest said, "you showed great promise as a youngster, but you have now quite outdone yourself. Where did you find him?"

Effluvia lowered her eyes modestly, "It is as I told you, Father. The god sent him to me as a mark of favor. He literally fell from the sky. What do you suppose it means, Father? There I am, all alone in the valley, the outcast child of the secular Queen and the god's representative on earth, and all at once *he* drops from the sky?"

The High Priest frowned for a moment, then tenderly stroked the black crown of the skunk-woman's head. "Always plotting, eh, my dear? Even now. Well, it may very well be true, what you're thinking. It may indeed be the only way to use this miraculous gift." He shook his head, laughing silently. "The resemblance is absolutely astounding."

Two pikemen and five full-fledged priests herded Carole, Rupert, and Timoteo down several winding flights of stairs, across a floor larger than most of the village of Wormhaven, and down more steps. All three looked a great deal like the common conception of a spectre—dressed in long, white robes of loose and gauzy material complete with deep hoods that shadowed their faces. Underneath, they wore their original clothing. Each robe was ample enough to cover a very large person in full court costume under winter gear. Rupert's robe hit him at knee level, while Carole's and the merchant's dragged the ground.

The foot of the last staircase was swallowed by boiling silver mist. The priests walked through it as if it didn't exist and urged their guests to do the same. Carole kept expecting a trick, a hole to open under her feet, a monster to coil around an ankle. Instead, after a brief thickening, the mist parted to reveal a somewhat larger dock than the one at which they had landed, surrounded in deepening gloom relieved by a row of torches set in brackets along its length. At the end of the long wooden ramp, a barge awaited them.

On its open deck three golden steps led to a long couch upholstered in cloth of gold. The hull rose at either end in a graceful curl. Four men, two at each end, stood with long paddles, the blades shaped like a sun with waving rays. The priests surrounded Rupert and Timoteo as they seated themselves. Rupert slid four of them aside to make room for Carole between them. The High Priest himself boarded last. Hampers smelling of hot spices, bread, and chicken were placed on the deck beside the golden steps. To Carole's relief, Effluvia did not join them.

The river lay calm as glass between its banks. One of the priests explained that further ahead, a special barrier called a lock had been built to regulate the flow of water, so that the traffic of large vessels to and from the sea could be restricted. Lining the banks on each side were buildings rivaling the temple in magnificence. Each of the buildings was long and low, with a courtyard looking onto the river and steps leading to the water. Spires were set on either side of the steps and the openings were the by-now predictable pointed arches. What was not predictable, however, was the building material. For each edifice was constructed entirely of small squares of colored crystal, each square a different hue from the ones adjoining it. The dying light of day washed through these panes onto the water, giving it the appearance of one enormous, multi-faceted rainbow. Her face and those of her companions bathed in particolored light, Carole watched the buildings slip behind, while the long rainbow of river rinsed away beneath her. She was aware of an odd feeling of recognition that puzzled her until she realized that the buildings reminded her very much of the merchant's show-room window before she had removed the bottles containing the mists.

Several barges passed them further down the river, many more opulent and elaborate than the barge on which they traveled. The helmsmen of the richer vessels nonetheless bowed as they passed. From curtained alcoves, fingers swept dense velvets aside. Eyes peered out with bright curiosity. Where the passengers rode open to the air, they bowed low to the priests, eyeing the guests only covertly. Lay brother garb did not entirely conceal Rupert's unusual stature, and he kept pushing the hood back and twisting to see his surroundings.

"Perhaps we should have brought the screens, Your Brilliance," one of the priests suggested with a shrewd look at Rupert.

"Not at all. We may stimulate a few exciting rumors before our disclosure is made public, but no one except those we wish to know will be aware that our guests are other than newly appointed lay brothers. Relax, my child."

Carole watched her hosts warily and wished they would stop their mysterious chitchat. It made her nervous. For all of his apparent amiability, the High Priest did not strike her as being anyone who was going to be terribly interested in the plight of Bronwyn's baby—or her relatives for that matter. And no doubt it was easy to be pleasant when one knew that one had enough power to do whatever one chose whenever one got around to it.

The river looped to the right. Suddenly, dead ahead loomed a castle. Carole was sure it was a castle rather than a temple this time for the design was dedicated to fortification, with the proper towers and battlements she was used to seeing in Argonia. They were, however, gorgeous turrets and towers and battlements, all in rough stone through which glimmered raw crystals of amythest, agate, garnet, and sapphire. Not a good defensive design, of course. Far too easy to scale such walls even without a ladder. But awe-inspiring nonetheless.

The river turned left at the castle after filling a loop of moat separated from the main body of water by earthworks reinforced with stone topped with a wide paved foothpath. Armed guards stood at either end of the path, and greeted the priests with deference.

The High Priest muttered something to a lesser priest, who muttered something in turn to a boatman, who whispered to a guard. The guard spun a tidy about-face, unhooked a horn from his belt and blew a long, lowing note. A general scurrying ensued from the wall facing the moat. A short time later the chain clanked and weathered wood creaked and the huge slab of a drawbridge lowered ponderously into its slot on the far side of the footpath. Two other guards strolled forward, received and departed with a message, and in a short time a harried-looking herald issued forth, bowed low before the junior priest, nodded sharply three times and scuttled back across the bridge.

The High Priest nodded. His minions began arranging the hampers of food on the path, brilliant cloths spread upon the ground first, followed by the golden cushions from the divan on the barge, followed by an array of fruit, chicken, bread, and sweets, as well as crystal decanters of wine. The dishes were of etched gold. Carole was very glad she would not be responsible for cleaning them. She also wished they might have been able to have some of the chicken while it was hot, for the chill as the sun went down was seeping through her layers of clothing. Hot food would have helped.

Soon a great clamor arose from beyond the drawbridge, a horn blared, and a matched set of heralds announced, "All hail King Yagthra, Lion of Gorequartz, and Queen Egelina the Fair."

Carole did not believe she had ever seen a Queen look as twitchy as Egelina the Fair. Not even Amberwine when

Bronwyn was married. Egelina, like almost everyone else in Gorequartz, was indeed fair, with a tumbling corona of golden curls under her lacy crystal circlet, and blue eyes large and frightened. The rest of her was also large, the reason evident, for her eyes kept darting to the food throughout the conversation. The rest of the time they were fastened on Rupert, now and then jumping apprehensively to the snoozing bronze-haired infant carried by the third unliveried adult who trailed behind both King and Queen. This person kept her eyes modestly lowered, ostensibly observing her charge much more closely than babies really need to be observed, while casting quick, melancholy glances toward Rupert. Never once did the woman look at the High Priest, and only when she was addressed did she make eye contact with His or Her Majesty. Rupert, for his part, spent a great deal of time watching her and the baby, who could only be the kidnapped heiress to the Ablemarlonian throne.

King Yagthra might once have been handsome, but his face bore the ruddy sheen of someone who had been drinking far too much wine for far too long. His pores were large and coarse, his nose bulbous, his eyes veined and teary-looking. His aroma made Carole think that perhaps he had served as the inspiration for the High Priest when that individual had decided on the particular spell he used to "enhance" Effluvia's personal power. The High Priest did not stand when greeting Yagthra and Yagthra did not so much as incline his head to see what was on the menu.

"Greetings, Your Majesty," His Brilliance said, indicating the spread. "We have guests to honor and thought, who but the sovereigns of the city are worthy to make these particular people welcome? Therefore we had this repast made ready and sent forth the invitation to you and your lady and daughter to join us." Now he rose, offering his own cushion to the King, who, spotting Rupert, suddenly seemed barely able to stand. The High Priest nodded toward the nurse and child standing behind the Queen. "My, your new daughter is large for her age. And red of hair also. How very unusual."

The Queen sat down abruptly and began munching a plum. Rupert joined her immediately, to cover her breach of manners, and the High Priest, with some amusement, seated himself beside her, speared a chicken leg and used it to gesture with, saying, "Your Majesties, allow me to present our guests, Lady Carole, her cousin and guardian in our land, Prince Rupert, and their servant. Perhaps we could all dispense with our hoods now, Prince Rupert. It is the custom—"

"Of course," Rupert said, and tugged his down around his neck. The Queen gagged on her plum, the King turned redder, and the baby began to squall. The High Priest appeared vastly amused.

"Is this some sort of priest's trick, Jasper?"

"You wound me, brother," His Brilliance replied. "I merely wanted to share with you the special properties of these guests of ours. I wanted your opinion on how to best utilize their unique contributions in the upcoming festivities. Or perhaps your lady would be so kind as to give us her opinion. She seems to have a few tricks of her own," and he looked unmistakably, pointedly at the baby. Yagthra glared at the High Priest. Now that it had been mentioned, Carole could discern a family resemblance in the set of their jowls, the knobs on the ends of their noses. The King was not presently overcome with family feeling, however, and jerked his wife unceremoniously to her feet, while the nurse scurried ahead of them, throwing only a single last wondering glance back at Rupert.

His point made, the High Priest seemed to lose sight of the fact that his guests had still not actually had time to eat, and ordered the feast taken up again. Carole quickly snagged a chicken breast, a half loaf of bread, and a bunch of grapes, and climbed back on the boat. Regardless of whatever other dramas were taking place, there was really nothing so sordid as family jealousies.

Rupert chewed thoughtfully on a chicken bone as he boarded the barge, and paused before he sat down to stare after the departing royalty. Timoteo and Carole were behind him and the lesser priests, followed by the High Priest, who motioned them all ahead. Suddenly, Rupert let out a "whoof" and fell into his seat coughing and thumping his chest while everyone else strove to keep their balance. One of the priests pitched overboard and had to be plucked from the river. The High Priest took the disturbance placidly, boarding the boat only after it had ceased rocking maniacally to and fro. Not until he was comfortably settled and the boat was proceeding down river did they notice the missing place on the couch.

"Where is the scruffy fellow? What's his name? What became of him?" he asked. One of the priests made as if to look under a cushion but thought better of it.

The wet priest, now encased in one of the picnic cloths, said, "I didn't see him, Your Brilliance, but perhaps he, too, was thrown overboard."

"Find him," the High Priest commanded with much authority but little interest in the subject.

The boatmen poked along both sides of the canal with their oars and the priest who was already wet was lowered again on a rope to search but no trace of the merchant was found. Carole thought of diving to fetch him, but something held her back. The merchant had always been a noisy fellow when in jeopardy. If he was so quiet now, either he had reason to be or he was past reasoning. She had been watching the King's departure and the High Priest's preparations for leaving when Rupert overbalanced the boat, and had not actually noticed the merchant falling overboard. But it seemed to her that she did recall a release of pressure on the cushions beside her. She had heard not a splash, but a careful plop, as of something sliding deliberately into the water.

THE CHRISTENING QUEST

After their perfunctory initial search, the priests made no further effort to locate the merchant's body and at the High Priest's insistence continued instead past the palace, down the river, and through the lock.

The lock was well-named, resembling nothing so much as a giant door bar. Earth and stone jutted into the river for a cart length or so on either side, while between stretched a sheet of solid iron. Torchlight from the little hut atop the earthworks bounced off the iron, and the water slapped powerlessly against it. A man emerged from the hut, bowed, and at the High Priest's direction gave orders to one of the great, grey beasts Carole had seen in Miragenia. The beast lumbered forward, dragging a chain which powered a cogged wheel, thereby sliding the iron barrier back into the cliff rising on the eastern side of the lock. On the earthworks sheltered by the cliffs on the western side another beast rocked back and forth, dragging its chain, no doubt waiting orders to drag the barrier back into place. In fact, there were two of the barriers, with a little valley of water trapped between them. When those slid aside, the priests' barge rose on the flow of newly freed water and floated easily through the locks.

They saw no more palaces, temples, or even houses for the remainder of the short distance between the locks and the harbor. Craggy cliffs soared above them on either side, studded at regular intervals by torches whose light reached the water as little more than candle flame. Nevertheless, when they gained the bay, between the three-quarter moon and the torchlight Rupert and Carole were able to view clearly the thing they had been brought to see.

The sight of it wiped all thoughts of the priests, Effluvia, even Bronwyn's baby from Rupert's mind as he stared, his eyes rising slowly to take in the whole object. Carole whistled a low, unmagical exclamation of surprise. The priests looked from Rupert to the object, nodding and murmuring excitedly, and the High Priest looked even more pleased than he had when he first saw Rupert. And no wonder. There was more of Rupert to be pleased with—or at least, there was a larger edition of him. Rising from the waters was a duplicate of Rupert's head and face, about twice as large as the drawbridge at the castle and seemingly carved completely out of crystal. The sea lapped around its chin and earlobes, wetting the curls twining toward the throat. The expression was the same one Rupert wore when he concentrated hard on some knotty problem or the other. Except that when Rupert wore that look, it made one want to pat him like a puppy and tell him not to fret. Blown up, with its crystalline angles basking in moonlight and torchlight, the same expression on the image was stern and forbidding.

"So," Rupert said. "I'll be blessed. Now at last we know what became of Rowan the Recreant. How reassuring. I never did believe what they said about him."

"Who?" Carole asked. "What did they say about him?"

"It is appropriate to genuflect before the Rainbow God, woman," one of the junior priests told her, and pushed her firmly to the floor, forcing her to kneel, halfway facing Rupert, halfway facing the statue.

She started to whistle the clod into the sea but Rupert knelt rapidly beside her. "Never mind, cousin. It isn't important. I'll tell you later." He had scarcely bent his knee, however, when the High Priest caught his elbow and motioned him back onto his seat on the couch.

"Not you, dear boy," His Brilliance said. "You're the god reincarnate. Hereafter you do not bow, you are bowed to."

CHAPTER IX

"*There* you are," the furious collection of flying draperies accused the boatload of priests, witch, and newly appointed God as if they were a cart full of hoodlums. "Rupert, darling, will you be so kind as to tell these provincials who I am and what would become of their teeny little economy without the buying power of my firm?"

Rupert, who had been uncommonly quiet all the way back to the temple, still bore a stunned look, as if someone had separated his brains from his face by means of a hearty blow from a mace. He stared rather stupidly for a moment at the raven-haired lady clad in scarlet and silver, hands on hips and arms akimbo, clearly waiting for something. The witch at his side elbowed him in the waist.

"Isn't that the Mukbar woman? What in the name of the Mother's sweet earth is she doing here?"

The High Priest overheard and swept in front of Rupert. "Illustrious mademoiselle, to what do we owe the honor of this unusual, and may I say unprecedented, visit?"

"I have come to reclaim company assets," she replied, looking straight at Rupert.

"Could this not have been handled in some other fashion? Our agreement with your firm, mademoiselle, is that all transactions are to take place in Miragenia."

"And who are you to quote me trade agreements?" she asked.

The brother in charge of patrolling the mist ended his measured rounds in a skittering run. "Your Brilliance, forgive me. This accursed woman has been braying at the door all evening. I told her to go away, and tried to force her to depart, but she flew out of reach on her wretched rug."

"I want that man fired for incompetence, and his pay docked," Alireza demanded, pointing a dramatic, long, carmined fingernail at the offending person. "I did not fly through duststorms and rain, pursued by your inadequately controlled demons, to endure idiots when I've come to speak with someone in authority. I take it, sir, that you *are* someone in authority?"

The High Priest flushed; he momentarily bore a striking resemblance to his brother. "You might say that. I am Jaspar the Deep-Veined, High Priest of the Grand Prismatic, Spiritual Father of Gorequartz."

Alireza took in the title with a satisfied gleam under her curling lashes and a little lick at her full upper lip before saying, "Ah, forgive me, Your Brilliance. I had no idea . . ."

His Brilliance took in the seductive look and savored it, forgetting the less savory insult. "Of course not. We have never met. I last visited Miragenia before your dear, departed father joined his gods. Though I must say, I recognized you at once. The legends of your beauty and business acumen rampant among those of us who trade with your firm have not been exaggerated. We are honored. Please, please, come inside."

Effluvia was much less charmed by the new visitor, and didn't hesitate to say so. Her tail rose to half mast almost involuntarily, and the High Priest, standing beside her, stroked her back quickly in an attempt to soothe her. When Carole left Rupert to the mercy of the embattled women and the priests, he was looking rather dazed. For once she was more than happy to be overlooked.

The room in which she had been installed was grand and spacious, with the moon shining in from the crystal dome as well as a bed with an optional canopy to shield those who preferred the security of a properly enclosed sleeping space to the grandeur of the natural spectacle above them.

She did not mind that her magic was so little regarded that the lock which snapped shut behind her as she entered was neither iron nor apparently warded against her, but the absence of wash water and a bit of stiff grass with which to clean her teeth did impress her as sloppy. Perhaps while everybody was entertaining themselves watching the High Priest and his powerful female associates torment poor Rupert, she could slip out and find some, and lock her door back behind her with no one the wiser. Later that night she intended to slip out again and find a clear spot from which she would be visible. There she hoped to be spotted by Grippeldice. She would feel much better about the whole situation once the dragon knew where they were.

The lock gave easily after she hummed two bars. She peered out into the hall, wondering where the water containers were kept. In the kitchen, no doubt, but where was that? She watched for wandering members of the household, glad for the protective coloring of the hooded robe. Rounding a corner, she saw a flash of white as a lay brother slapped barefooted down the hall ahead of her. He left behind him an open door and she walked toward it, praying he had been returning from a late snack.

He had not. Reaching the room's open door, she saw that it was another bedroom, but an extremely luxurious one, with crystal bedposts and a canopy colored like the rainbow, golden walls, and a fountain, which at least solved the water problem. Then she spied Rupert's cloak draped over a chest in the corner and realized the brother had been readying the room for the temple's most illustrious guest. Well, Rupert wouldn't mind if she washed up and borrowed a bit of water. She would do her washing here and tote a basinful back to her own room for use in the morning. She would need to look fresh if she spent most of the night waiting for the dragon to appear.

She washed quickly in Rupert's basin, dumped the water back in the pool, and held the bowl under the fountain. That was when the quartz-studded wall behind the pool creaked open and a woman peeked around the corner. Seeing Carole she started to retreat again, but Carole whistled her to a shrill stop and slowly jigged her forward.

When the woman had done a little bransle step around the edge of the fountain and was standing in the center of the room, the witch confronted her.

"I beg your pardon, mistress," the girl said, her feet still shuffling in the dance and her face full of guilty confusion. "I knew not that this was your place. I was looking for the god."

"The god is out right now," Carole said, patiently. "Perhaps I could take a message?"

"That won't be necessary," the girl said, drawing herself up a little and trying unsuccessfully to stare Carole in the eye. "The god is all-knowing."

"In that case I don't see why you need to be sneaking around through fountains to find him." The girl lowered her eyes, more confused than ever, and Carole recognized her. "You're the nurse to the Queen's daughter, aren't you?"

"I—no, I mean—who are you? You were with him and the priests, weren't you?"

"I hardly thought you noticed."

"Are you his handmaiden?"

"Not if I can help it," Carole muttered.

"What?"

"Nothing. I said, I suppose you could say that I am. Are you quite sure I can't help you?"

"Perhaps. It's about the Princess."

Carole kept quiet and tried not to appear to be holding her breath.

"Well," the girl said, shifting her weight from one foot to the other. "It's just not fair. I know the god is all-knowing but probably he wouldn't even think to question Her Majesty if she chooses to claim a baby is hers. But the Princess isn't, you know. She's not even from Gorequartz."

"No!" Carole said. "You don't say."

"Oh, yes," the girl said. "You see, the Queen sent me to fetch her from the Miragenians."

"All alone?"

"One of the priests went with me."

"Really? Then they knew about the exchange."

"Certainly. There's nothing goes on in this city they don't know about—and arrange."

"But the High Priest seemed only to be suspicious of the Queen this evening—"

"He was just twisting the knife," the girl said. "I wish you would speak to the god about him. He's not a nice man at all and I don't think he's truly dedicated. When the Queen first married His Majesty, His Brilliance sent for her. I know. She had me come with her, through the secret passages, which is how I learned of them. His Brilliance doesn't know I know because I stayed hidden. But I heard him propose that she betray the King with him. She never really refused him but after that she started eating heavily and not letting her hair be brushed except once a day. I think she was just frightened. If she betrayed the King and he found out, she was doomed, and if she didn't accept the High Priest, she was also doomed; she made herself undesirable so she would not need to choose. It worked well except that she never conceived a child. His Brilliance proposed the plan to her, told her that there would soon be a baby available."

"And she accepted?" Carole asked, her anger rising. "Knowing that the baby would eventually be killed?"

"Not necessarily," the girl defended her mistress." Normally she would have until the girl is seven years old to bear the King a boy. Should that happen, she and both children would be safe. However, I fear His Brilliance only proposed the plot to expose it, to get revenge on her for depriving him of enjoying her beauty." Even with such a euphemistic finish, the girl lowered her lashes again, no doubt blushing, if only the light were sufficient to register it.

"Well, it seems she fell for it, didn't she? I still don't understand your part in all this however. Why should you care what happens to the child?"

"Oh, mistress, I am her nurse. She feeds at my breast. How can I not care? Perhaps it is wrong of me, but I feel that the god sent her to me for taking my own little one, the one I lost these three months past at the summer's-end sacrifice, when my beloved Selig was mur . . . was chosen as delegate to the god. Seeing the god today, I knew I must be right, for he is not so stern as his image, but kindly in appearance, and caring. I know now that my Selig is eternally happy with him, that he has had compassion for my loss and will help me to preserve the little one he sent to comfort me."

"My, you do have a lot of faith, don't you?" Carole said.

"I never did before I saw him today with my own eyes. I thought he was as hard and cruel as his priests but—"

Her worshipful look as her eyes lingered on her memory of Rupert was almost embarrassing. "I do see," Carole said quickly. "And you are absolutely right. The god is a very pleasant sort of deity and I am positive he'll be glad to help you with this matter but—"

A scuffling noise overrode her voice from the hallway beyond, followed by the slapping of feet.

"Is there room in there for me, too?" Carole asked.

"It's very narrow here, I—" the girl began.

"Never mind then. Back in you go, quickly." She had long since released the spell, but the girl's movements were swifter than any dance step as she disappeared back into the wall. Just in time, too, for the slapping footsteps reached the room and a lay brother scowled at Carole from the doorway.

"What are you doing here?"

"Looking for my cousin," she said innocently.

"He's still with His Brilliance," the brother said. "And I think it would be a good idea if you were, too." With that, he waited with stiff spine and stern countenance until she meekly stepped around him and allowed him to forcibly escort her where she wished to go anyway.

Rupert almost wished he were the god everybody felt he resembled. Then he could smite the lot of them and be done with it. Both of the women seemed to feel that they had some claim to him. In the case of Alireza Mukbar, he was not surprised, since he had allowed her to seduce him and believe that he endorsed her plans for their so-called future together in order to extract necessary information from her. But Effluvia's counterclaim both baffled and repulsed him. The High Priest's proud look in the skunk-woman's direction bothered him even more.

Moreover, the High Priest positively gloated over the venomous darts shooting between the women and the outrageous things they said to each other. He stroked Effluvia as if she were a house cat, only partially to keep her tail under control. The rest of the motivation for the petting seemed to Rupert rather unwholesome. Meanwhile, the High Priest's eyes drank in Alireza's heaving bosom and gesticulating limbs, his fingers fondling Effluvia's hair.

Rupert did have to admire one thing about Alireza, however. Impassioned as her speech and gestures were, she was not totally out of control. She pointed out that Rupert had a prior commitment to her and her firm and that arrangements could still be made for the people of Gorequartz to lease his services. She also pointed out that any attempt to try to retain him would cancel out a rather large debt still owed by the Miragenians for the last shipment of crystal bottles.

"Speaking of the bottles, your quality control is way out of line these days. That abominable witch who attached herself to my fiance was able to loosened practically the entire last shipment. The bazaar is still in an uproar and my uncle has taken to his bed. If the *creature* who has the audacity to claim that she is entitled to any consideration where His Highness is concerned had been doing her proper job as a guardian, the witch would never have escaped us. I demand her return."

"My dear, dear young lady," the High Priest said, droplets of spittle forming at the sides of his mouth with the strength of his sincerity. "We can do better than that. We will use her in the dedication ceremony, two days hence. Several significant delegates will be sent forth. I am sure the recent conversation we had with Her Majesty may bring some bearing on her decision of what gesture is needed to provide her with more appropriate offspring—"

Rupert again forgot his diplomatic training in the face of his moral outrage. "See here, Your Brilliance. If you have any notion of indiscriminately disposing of a member of my staff and an innocent infant in your vile rites of human sacrifice—"

"My dear young man, what utter nonsense! Indiscriminate? Vile rites? Wherever did you get such an idea?"

"Is it not true then?" Rupert asked hopefully, the heat and color draining a bit from his face.

"Certainly not."

"I am so pleased to hear it. Of course, I felt all along that it was rubbish to suppose that one of the world's greatest exporters of magic practiced human sacrifice. . . ."

"Now that part *is* true," His Brilliance admitted as if modestly acknowledging a compliment. "How could it be otherwise? All greatness among men is the result of human sacrifice of one sort or the other—for one to gain, another must be deprived. It's only natural—or, as in the case of the Great Polyhued—supernatural. But I can assure you that there is nothing vile or indiscriminate about our rites. They are exceedingly tasteful and have a wealth of socially significant factors surrounding them and are celebrated most discriminatingly at specific times of the year."

"Ah," Rupert said. "And what times are those?"

"Oh, there are a great many. I'll be happy to see that you are provided with a calendar to memorize. All that need concern you right now is the one taking place just before sundown tomorrow. Right now the preparations are being made for the ceremony later tonight at which we will arrange for the appropriate conditions. I wish I could invite you to witness it, but that really would spoil the surprise."

"Naturally, we can't have the surprise spoiled," Rupert said, barely keeping the sarcasm out of his voice. "Tell me, who else do you intend to kill this time?"

"Kill? We kill no one. We send our delegates living into the mouth of the god, who regurgitates them as magical entities, empowered to serve in a far more fascinating and useful fashion than they did formerly. You understand that unlike many of the more primitive peoples who pathetically ape our worship, we do not generally sacrifice our best contributing members: beautiful virgins, good-looking heroes, those sorts of people. Only in extraordinary circumstances, and extenuating ones at that, does an unusually able and attractive individual go to the god. No, we send those who are in some way unable in their present form to making their greatest contribution: thieves, you see, dissidents, unfit spouses, children of the wrong sex—"

"You mean daughters," Carole said from the doorway, through which she preceded her keeper, her entrance sudden and dramatic amid the chiming of crystal beads. Effluvia and Alireza, who had stopped their wrangling long enough to listen to the man they were fighting over gain instruction from the one able to grant him to either female contestant, glared in unison at the outside interruption.

"Of course," His Brilliance replied, beckoning the two

newcomers in without missing a beat. "What else would I mean? Though you understand, not only the children but all of the delegates are marked by the god for his transformation by their very unsuitability to move among the rest of our people. As for the transformation itself, the god in his glory manifests that. We priests are merely donors of the delegates, and are personally responsible for nothing save donating, and collecting the resulting product, and seeing that it is properly packaged and utilized. Other than that, we serve only to distribute the credits due from the sacrifice to the proper sources and thereby increase the gross national magical byproduct."

"Hmm," Carole said. "I wonder if my great-grandmother who enhanced her magic by eating children looked at it that way."

"That's something else entirely!" the lay brother beside her said, making a determined effort to tower menacingly above her.

Effluvia spoke up, her tail rising behind her more ominously than ever. "Was there some reason for this impertinent interruption? I was under the impression the underlings had been secured already, Your Brilliance."

"I found her in the god's room," the burly lay brother explained to the High Priest. "And that after I saw Brother Bullcow lock her in her room as sure as I see her standing here now."

"I needed to have a private word with His Highness," Carole explained with smiling patience, quite enjoying the discomfiture of the others.

"I'm afraid that's impossible," Alireza said, linking her arm in Rupert's. "His Highness is vital to this discussion."

Rupert's chin firmed and his eyes flashed for a moment, as he firmly and with very deliberate gentleness disentangled himself. "Surely you can spare me a moment to consult with my staff," he said.

The High Priest intervened. "A moment only, Your Highness. There is much you need to understand, much to learn, and much to settle among us before your introduction to our people, and precious little time. That must take up all of tomorrow. You must be well rested so that you thoroughly comprehend what you are told. I can spare only a moment more in clarifying this situation for Mademoiselle Mukbar and then I must hasten to perform my offices at tonight's ceremony. The only thing of interest your staff member can possibly add to this discussion is an explanation of how she came to be here. All guest quarters are locked automatically. Is this in some way connected with her magic power?"

"You might say that," Rupert replied quickly.

"Indeed I might. I just did as a matter of fact. Please do me the favor of elucidating. Outside magic is always of great interest. One learns even from the humblest of sources."

"Ah, yes. Well, you see, my cousin just happens to be a very special sort of witch. She is a great sorceress of doors. They find her powers irresistable."

"Remarkable," the High Priest said. "Just how does this power work?"

"Goodness knows," Rupert said, smiling innocently. When the High Priest began tapping his nails on the arm of his crystal throne, the Prince added quickly and in what he hoped was an erudite and knowledgeable tone, "You see, magical power is, for the Argonian witch, frequently a matter of ancestral inheritance. My cousin was related to a wood nymph on her father's side. The wood in the doors still recognizes her as a relative. Because of that bond it refuses to bind her in other, more customary manners, or to cooperate with others who would do so."

"My, that *is* remarkable," Alireza said, fanning her eyelashes up at him. "I don't believe I've ever heard that particular type of power explained so well before."

Brother Bullcow rushed in before Rupert succumbed to

the temptation to make the explanation yet more interesting. The brother's spindly legs pumped beneath his gold-colored, diaper-like temple garment. His lofty forehead was dotted with sweat. "Your Brilliance, your indulgence please, but I must interrupt. A messenger has just arrived from the palace. The Queen says—"

"Not in public, you fool," His Brilliance snapped. "Gentle ladies, Your Highness, I fear we must delay this discussion until later. Brother Erng, please see that Lady Carole is placed behind her friendly door once more, only this time please add a lay brother to keep the door from being so easily swayed by her charms. Mademoiselle Mukbar, it grieves me to leave you but—"

"I do understand."

"Effluvia, my dear, if you would linger for a moment. Remember, Your Highness, your instruction begins early."

Rupert gave him a curt nod and followed Carole and Brother Erng, who closed the door on Carole and posted the guard before Rupert was able to learn what had caused her to seek him out. Behind the door to his own pleasant quarters, he paced for a moment, worrying a thumbnail and staring distractedly at the fountain. Presently he heard a faint creaking. Something in the fountain stared shyly back.

He circled the fountain slowly. Just as slowly she stepped out, still staring, taking him in with eyelids still half lowered, long hair, not the yellow-blonde shade common in Gorequartz but a pale caramel strung with gold shadowing her face. He gave her his hand to guide her around the fountain. She amazed him by falling to her knees, hair sweeping over her head as she pressed face and arms to the floor.

"My dear lady," he said, kneeling beside her, "are you ill?"

"No, Precious Polyhued. I come in worship and supplication. I bespoke your handmaiden and pray you will be merciful and grant my plea."

"Yes, and what was that?" Rupert asked. "My . . . hand-

146

maiden was unavoidably detained before she could discuss this with me."

"My Lord, I ask that you spare my little Princess, my baby. Take me instead if you must, but spare her. She is so small and helpless and she is not truly the daughter of the Queen."

"Sweet lady, no project could be dearer to my heart. But how can I do so?"

She was taken aback. "How can you? But . . . ah, I see. This is a test, isn't it? You're testing my faith. But I do believe in you, which you must understand, even though you may see into my heart and know that I find your priests abominably cruel, your image forbidding. Your person, on the other hand, is all I could wish for in a god." She gazed wonderingly into his eyes as she said this, and he found he was stroking her cheek and brushing back her hair as she spoke. "You are so warm, and I know you are kind—you are the god. You have only to spare her, do you not?"

He stopped stroking and looked at the floor.

"Well, do you not? Oh, no, was I wrong? Is your gentle countenance a jest crueller than the fists of your priests?"

"Believe me, I'm not jesting," he replied, looking up quickly and gaining courage from her desperation, her very helplessness. "I want to help the child but to do so I must thwart those very evil priests you so bravely denounce in your adorably valiant way."

She sighed and smiled slightly, the suspicion abating from her expression. "But could you not deny them the rainbows they seek tonight, and thereby thwart them?"

"It isn't that easy," he said. He wanted badly to tell her that he wasn't a god, but doubted she would believe him. Besides, it was as the god she wanted his help for Bronwyn's child. "You see, in this incarnation, a lot of my powers have been hidden from me. My cousin, the one you call my handmaiden, knows a great deal. She's sort of a minor goddess herself." He was rather proud of that. Why should he bear the burden of deification alone after all? And Carole was better equipped to play the part than he. "Give me a chance to talk to her."

"When?"

"I'm afraid it can't be until tomorrow. She's locked in her room again and this time with a guard."

"But that is no problem for you, Grand Prismatic!"

"Isn't it?" he asked.

"No, for you have shown *me* the way to help you. You need only use the secret passage and guide her through it."

"Now why didn't I think of that? So I have. And the guards will probably be distracted anyway, what with the ceremony and the hoopla at the palace Brother Bullcow came rushing into the audience chamber about."

"At the palace?" she asked suddenly, springing to her feet. "There is trouble at the palace? What sort of trouble?"

"I don't know. The Queen wanted to send a message to the priest about something—"

"Oh, no. I should not have stayed so long. They will discover I am gone and have left my child alone. Oh, please, grant my wish. Deliver my child."

"I have a better idea," he said. "Why don't you deliver the child to me? Then my handmaiden and I can take you both somewhere safe. To tell you the truth, that is why I've come among your people this time."

"Truly?" Her voice was so faint he thought she would drop to the floor before he could help her back into the passage.

"Truly. But you must help us. We can't have you bringing the baby here. Where is a safe place?"

"Until tomorrow night, the safest place in all Gorequartz is that most sacred to you, most taboo to all others. Your image in the harbor."

"Wonderful. You fetch the baby. I'll fetch Carole and we'll

meet there and—I'm sorry, I'm afraid I don't even know your name."

"Jushia," she said.

"Oh, yes. Jushia, of course. It would be," he said, remembering belatedly that he was supposed to be omnipotent. "Jushia, don't worry."

"Oh, no, my lord. With you on my side, never. To do so would be heresy."

"There's my girl," he beamed, and patted her fanny as she fled ahead of him into the passage.

He had one foot on the threshold when there was the slightest of taps on his door; a scraping as someone pushed it open. He shut the secret door on his sleeve and was still trying to extricate it when Alireza Mukbar slithered into the room.

"Rupert, darling. I'm here. Sorry I'm late but it took me a little time to bribe the wretched guards. I *told* them their god would be ever so disappointed, but the fellows haven't a jot of romance in their souls. Come to me, my lo . . . just what is it that you're doing there?"

"Washing a spot from my coat," he said, splashing a little in the fountain while still furtively tugging to loose the sleeve without tearing it.

"With you still in it? Silly boy. Men are such babies. What do you think servants are for?" She undulated toward him and as he turned to shield the door from her view, his sleeve, or most of it, pulled free.

"Ah, that's better," he said, tucking the telltale arm behind his back. "Now then, what can I do for you?"

"What can *you* do for *me*? Darling, don't be ridiculous. When you know you've been dying to see me. Rupert, you *have* been dying to see me, haven't you? Surely you can't be taking that hideous skunk creature seriously?"

Her delectable lower lip trembled, but Rupert was too distracted to be interested. What if she heard the scraping noises issuing from the walls.

"Alireza, you are an extremely beautiful and desirable woman," he said in a voice a bit too loud to be intimate.

"Yes, of course," she said, her eyes widening, startled.

"Well, I think I have been taking advantage of you. No, no, don't protest so sweetly. I'm very smooth when I want to be. You probably just haven't caught on yet."

"Not caught on? Do you think I'm a fool? I knew you would come here. I—"

"Yes, but did you know I'd release those smoky things? Eh? I doubt that occurred to you."

"Really, Rupert, that *was* inconsiderate of you. Why, they've done three times your weight in gold pieces in damage to the city. Not even the shrewdest of Profit prophets can foresee what will happen if they decide to wreak their vengeance elsewhere. Don't you care that they might have hurt *me*? They chased my carpet until I cleared the city walls."

"One can't blame them really," he said. "I would have chased you myself."

"You're too gallant," she said, giving him a look as hot as the desert from which her power base sprang.

"No, that's not what I mean. I simply can't blame the bottled things for being angry about being kept slaves."

"Darling, you're a bit confused. *People* are slaves. Magical entities are just there. If they're a useful commodity, one uses them but—"

"Without their consent?"

"I admit one never thinks to ask them."

"There, you see. You admit it."

"Admit what? Why are you trying to tell me how to run my business all of a sudden? I came here to—"

"Shhh," he said, muffling her face against his chest before shoving her towards the door. "You've had a long trip and you're becoming overwrought. I think we should talk about this later. Goodnight now. I'll see you tomorrow."

She had unlocked his door upon entering and as he

pushed her out, he fastened the bar that locked it from the inside.

He was allowing himself a sigh of relief that diplomatic training included how to start a fight as well as prevent one. A resounding clamor echoed from within the walls and the passage door popped open again, spilling Carole into the fountain.

She sputtered and dripped as she climbed out onto the carpet while Rupert looked on with a mixture of consternation and wonder. "I knew that opening had to be around here somewhere," she said, nodding at it in an emphatic and victorious gesture. "But where is that woman? Did she find you?"

"Which woman?" he asked a little plaintively. "You're the third who's been here since I left the audience chamber."

"Poor thing. I mean the baby's nurse. Or was she among your admirers tonight?"

"Cousin, sarcasm ill befits your role as priestess."

"Perhaps you'd rather I'd sacrifice people instead?"

"Never mind. In answer to your question, yes, Jushia found me. If you'll just pop back into that passage before we're detained again, I'll tell you all about it as we go."

Timoteo the travel logger shivered in his soaked robes and wished his accomplices had thought to leave him a change of clothes. He felt like a fish baking in wet leaves as he huddled in the tiny secret room beneath the footpath separating the moat from the canal. He would have to dry off before he executed his plan or he would leave big muddy footprints all over the palace floors.

He thought weeks had passed instead of only hours since the priests stopped splashing around looking for him and the drawbridge was finally raised. He was glad the entrance had been where his accomplices said it would be, and well marked with the shell-tied ribbon he pulled inside after him. He had always been a bit squeamish about jumping into rivers, though the terror with which he had so thoroughly impressed the Prince and the witch in preparation for this moment had been more or less feigned. They were both, he could be sure, thoroughly convinced that he had drowned, and since they were convinced, the priests would also be convinced. His hiding place would remain a secret, as it had been since it was clandestinely built into the footpath by the ancestors of his friends when their slave labor constructed the path. Its admittedly modest secret was passed from father to son, mother to daughter, and had proved useful for slipping past the guards at either end of the footpath and onto the drawbridge when lowered for heavy traffic. The use of the little room provided his friends with a way to evade inconvenient questions, prevented them from having to construct untruthful excuses for their comings and goings when truthful explanations would assuredly have pleased neither the guards nor Their Majesties.

He heard the groan of iron and timbers and the stone-enforced walls of the little chamber quivered slightly as the drawbridge thunked down onto the path above him. He did not use the entrance through which he had come. Instead, he used the one on the opposite side of the path. It opened under the bridge, just above water level in the moat, which was lower than that of the canal. The guards customarily faced out, his allies assured him, and with the ponderous bridge in position, his exit would be unobserved.

Footsteps were overlayed by the low murmur of voices soberly conversing in tones suitable to the religious occasion drawing them forth. When the clamor overhead reached what Timoteo judged a prudently crowded level, he swung himself up onto the bridge, landing acrobatically upright. Most of the traffic was concentrated near the center of the bridge, but enough people strayed near the edges to conceal him. No one gave him a second glance, each person intent upon his own business which, judging from the expressions on their faces, was not cheerful.

Timoteo scowled and marched briskly against the tide of people, his expression arranged to say to all who saw him that he was a busy, important man who had been accidentally drenched and who needed urgently to return to his chambers in the palace for a change of clothing before rejoining the crowd bustling off to the ceremony. He kept within the throng until he was inside the palace. His allies had drawn him a floor plan, which he had memorized, and now he had no trouble locating the privy tower, where he secreted himself in darkness almost as overpoweringly smelly as the skunk-woman. To pass the time until the castle would be clear enough of inhabitants, he recalled his recent travels in four different countries and went back over the instructions he had received from the relatives of the allies he had met in one of them. He hoped his contacts had stayed on friendly terms with their kin, and that the prearranged signal would have indeed been prearranged on this end as well. If not . . .

With that foray into futile worry, he decided that the atmosphere of his hiding place was depressing him. Slipping out into the torchlit hall, he turned left at one of the bedchambers, dried his feet and legs, and regretted that he could not borrow an item or two of dry clothing without providing clues to his identity. He used the front staircase to reach the second floor, and the main hallways rather than the back ways, reasoning that for the ceremony of which he had been told, a lesser servant or two was more likely than his or her betters to be running loose, unconsoled by religion. He fully expected, on reaching the nursery, that the nurse and her charge would both be absent, tending to their spiritual needs.

He opened the door to the nursery as if he had come bearing a message for the nurse. As he expected, however, she was not there. The room was dark and gently redolent of baby oil, powder, and the faintest lingering scent of soiled diaper.

The nurse's cot was flat and tidy, the blanket pulled up over the pillow. Outside the narrow window thunder crashed and lightning crackled across the pane. From the cradle beside the window a thin and plaintive cry arose. Smiling, Timoteo knelt and scooped up his quarry, quieting her with the extravagant promises he made to all females of any age.

Now came the difficult part, the part with which he needed help. Suddenly he felt sure that it would not be there, that his allies in the city would not be alert for his signal. Though the plans had been set for the night of the ceremony from the beginning, he had not had time to contact anyone after his arrival and make them aware of his presence. The barge's proximity to the little room had been a fortunate happenstance that was supposed to take place in a more deliberate fashion, and would have, had he not been under guard with the witch and Prince. Still, his allies were exceptionally well-informed of activities in and around both temple and palace. He had to trust that his predicament had been noted. If so, they should be watching.

He lifted a torch from its sconce outside the doorway and carried it back into the darkened room. With the baby snuggled in the crook of one arm, he carried the torch to the window, raising and lowering it in a deliberate pattern, slowly and precisely, so that it would not be confused with lightning.

The baby slept against his chest and he folded his wet robe over her blanket as he carried her through the hallways and down the steps to the delivery entrance. No sooner had he reached the door than another lightning flash revealed a rope writhing down across the wall, atop which a man stood with outstretched arms.

Timoteo handed him the child and scaled the rope without further encouragement. Vast relief expanded within him as the man handed the child to a woman standing in a small craft on the other side of the wall. The woman cradled the baby against her breast. The men joined her, and silently they rowed across to the opposite shore.

Timoteo had to hand it to these Gorequartz kinfolk of his friends. They knew how to steal a child. There was still much more to be done, of course, but the hard part was over. They could work the rest of it out later, when it was safe to talk.

CHAPTER X

Rupert would have liked to lead the way, but was daunted despite all of his best intentions. The passage, just large enough for any average-to-smallish size person, took considerable contortions and acrobatics on his part to accommodate his great stature. These were made no easier by the inflexibility of the rowan shield still strapped to his back. It insisted on catching on the walls at every twist and turn, but he dare not leave it behind. The explanations and instructions he had planned to issue had to wait until he and Carole entered a wide spot, a central downward staircase with the narrower corridors branching off of it in two directions at each level.

He told her the bare bones of Jushia's message, ending with the caution that they would be making their way to the godhead in the midst of what had been referred to as the Ceremony of the Midnight Rainbow.

"Hmph," Carole said. "Sounds like a lodge meeting for old trappers' wives or something to me. Still, I suppose it will keep everyone too preoccupied to follow us for a while."

"I suggest we keep moving unless you wish to return to languish in your dungeon again. I can handle this alone, you know."

"I wouldn't dream of it. Once we have the child, I see nothing to stop us from just continuing on until we're back in

Argonia. And I'm afraid if we're caught again I'll have to languish somewhere other than the very nice room I have so cleverly escaped this time. One gets awfully good service associating with a God."

"I'm not a God," he said testily.

"Yes, well, I think we should both try to bear that in mind, eh?" They were descending the staircase as they talked and suddenly found it ended in a blank wall. Although they felt along it and Rupert went so far as to put his shoulder to it, it offered no egress. Carole softly hummed several religious-sounding hymns before recalling that the chief function of the passage seemed to be to expedite trysts. Thereafter she hummed one of her father's favorite ballads about illicit love, cuckholded husbands, and indiscreet horse grooms who came to especially gruesome ends. The wall swung inward with barely a whisper, nearly knocking them both flat before they could scramble around it and out into the mist.

The mist had changed. Instead of the dense, obscuring silver-white of earlier in the evening, it now surrounded them in a glowing kaleidoscope of pearlized color, lit from without and dancing with shadows. They walked cautiously through it, listening for the pacing of the sentry, the slish of canal water against the banks. They heard nothing but a vague disturbance, then, as they stepped forward, a subdued chanting rising on the swirls of color, falling in a hushed murmur to the docks where it hissed like the inhalation of some great monster, muffled by mist and distance.

Carole sidled forward and Rupert lost sight of the tail of her skirt in the mist until her hand reached back for him, fingers wiggling at him to follow. He did. He didn't need the warning gesture of those same fingers at her lips. He stayed perfectly quiet of his own volition, his breath deserting him as he surveyed the scene before him.

The lights of moon, stars, torches and candles shone through the crystal panes of the shrines lining the banks.

Bubbles of irridescence skimmed the breeze across the canal, illuminating the water, collecting the reflections from the brightly lit shrines and casting them into the canal as dark, moist replicas of their daylight manifestations. Elongated shadows swayed somewhere in the midst of the light behind the dazzling panes, intoning a song as regular and monotonous as a drumbeat. The river nearest the temple dock, shadowed by the great edifice, was dark. With a meaningful glance back at Rupert, Carole lowered herself carefully into the river. Rupert paused long enough to adjust the strap of the shield so it wouldn't unduly hinder his movements then pulled off his boots and let them fill with water and sink before joining Carole. The water was warm and fragrant with the freshness of a storm-bearing wind.

"Are you a strong enough swimmer to reach the harbor?" she asked.

"I was strong enough to save you," he reminded her.

"I know, but that was a short ways. This is quite long."

"Yes, in fact, you know, I believe that perhaps while I wear the comb it may give me a certain advantage in the water. I seemed to have no problem breathing that other time—"

"Fine. We can swim above water most of the time so that we'll spot the nurse, should we pass her, but we may need to stay submerged for some time to hide."

He nodded and they set out, Carole leading, side-stroking with their faces to the shrines illuminating one bank.

During their previous twilit ride, they had failed to notice the rectangular pools connecting the shrines along each bank to each other. But now the beaming colors danced off the pools and the water cast bright snakes of light and shadow across the countenances of those who chanted beside the pools, staring upward with eyes full of prayer and terror. Very far away, thunder boomed. The moon and stars simmered in a cloudy stew.

Carole and Rupert stroked past three more of the shrines.

The same scene was repeated over and over, as if they kept swimming past the same place. Far away, lightning first blanketed the sky with light, then pierced it through with blazing forks.

As the lightning sizzled closer, the chanting increased in volume, the swaying of the worshippers echoed in the clawing limbs and whipping trunks of the trees framing the shrines and pools. Carole stopped stroking and rested, floating with her hands grasping the bank, her chin on her knuckles, watching. Rupert had been watching her rather than the shrine, so when the first bolt actually struck the spires, he missed all but the flash. Beside him, Carole's breath stopped sharply and her eyelids flew wide.

"Wha—" he began. She lay a finger on his hand and pointed.

In Gorequartz, lightning was not only striking twice in the same place, it was striking repeatedly through the spires and into the shrine pools, the forks aiming themselves with the accuracy of catspaws. In the pool they faced, the High Priest stood ankle deep, clad now in a black-cowled robe with a multicolored hem that stretched above him in a semicircle as he lifted his arms to pray. Upon his chest was a long prismatic stone that sang with a light of its own. When the lightning struck the spires, it channeled through the pool and into the stone, which gathered the light in a great shining star and dispersed it through the High Priest, who jerked spasmodically. Then, his rigid form bowed backward, and all of him disappeared—cowl, robe, flesh, muscle, tissue, and organs snuffed out by pulsing jolts. Only the bones were left, spine arched, jawbone rising and falling with the chant, empty eye sockets beseeching the sky.

The lightning died. Once more the High Priest stood whole, clothed in his robes, his arms still raised, prayers interrupted. Rupert shivered, neck hairs bristling. He watched fascinated while the chanting priest was flayed twice more by the lightning and reclothed in flesh and vestments as the spires collected and transmitted the deadly light. Then Carole tugged at Rupert's hand and they swam again, now carefully avoiding catching sight of the spires.

They had all but lingered too long. As the lightning receded, the chanting dribbled to a mournful thread. The worshippers filed away, one by one, from the river back to the secular reaches of the city. The swimmers reached the castle just as several richly clad folk arrived, dripping water from elaborate headgear that kept most of the precipitation from their fine garments. They hurried across the lowered drawbridge back into the palace. A fleeting, graceful shape, bareheaded, with hair dark and shining, caught Rupert's eye and he nodded silently to his cousin.

Carole pitched her hum deep and made it slow enough that the girl did a gentle two-step toward them that looked rather as if she was undecided between returning to bed or singing in the rain.

Seeing Rupert, albeit a bedraggled and drenched Rupert, the girl's face suffused with alarm. "Grand Prismatic! Forgive me but I was delayed. The Midnight Rainbow began before I reached the castle. I could not but stay."

"Perfectly all right," Rupert reassured her. "We just wanted to be sure everything was well with you and the baby—"

Jushia bit her lip and her feet kept wanting to two-step back toward the drawbridge. "I don't know yet, Precious Polyhued. But I shall know more when I can row her to you at dawn, when the locks open."

"Fair enough," Rupert said, "We'll be waiting." And as she left he said to Carole, "Sorry, old girl, but it looks as if we're in for a damp night." But the mer-descended witch was already stroking ahead of him, into the concealing shadows and away from the torch glare of the lights left burning on the castle walls for returning worshippers.

Around the bend the locks loomed, outlined by shimmies of dimming sheet lightning. The great beasts stood at either end, heads lowered, extra tails swinging gently. The hut was alight with the flicker of a single candle. An occasional snort of laughter or a quarrelsome burst of conversation carried across the water.

"We must go over, for we can't go through. Unless you can whistle the locks open, that is?" Rupert's voice was half-mocking, half-hopeful.

Carole shook the water from her hair and blew her nose clear. "You may not have noticed but the locks are made of iron. My magic won't budge them."

"Then over it is. I'd like it better if those chaps up there were sleeping on the job, I must admit. Why is it only in repressive societies that one can get decent help?"

"Perhaps they'll be too taken with their own pastimes to notice us. After all, they're just supposed to accommodate nighttime barges and things. I don't imagine they're used to guarding *against* anyone. We'll see soon enough, I suppose."

The stones embedded in the earthen portion of the locks were slick with water and weed and deadly cold, but they were also irregular and provided good handholds and footholds. Carole's feet were small enough that she was easily able to haul herself belly down onto the flat cottage-wide surface atop the lock. Rupert's much larger foot slipped, skinning his bare toes and instep. He bellowed—not a very intelligible or human sounding bellow, but a definite noise. The chatter inside the hut silenced abruptly. The whites of Rupert's eyes looked big as hen's eggs. Carole swallowed. The great beast on the end of the lock nearest them rocked restlessly against the chain confining one of its heavy, wrinkled legs and turned its head almost fearfully in the direction of the newcomers.

Carole took a deep breath and hummed quietly to the beast, but in a compelling, forcefully driving rhythm that set it rocking harder, straining the clanking chain, then tearing the stake from the ground before trudging tunefully toward the hut.

The swimmers dashed for the other side of the lock while the occupants of the hut dashed away from it. The clamor they made stampeding to the opposite end of the lock while the beast trampled their hut and its counterpart across the river cheered it on, trumpeting from its front tail, was quite enough to conceal any slight sound Carole and Rupert made scrambling down the far wall and back into the river.

The torches on the ridge top flickered in the rain, many of them darkened and half-hidden by the smoke of the others. The swimmers steered away from the stripes of light cast by the torches, clinging instead to the darkness near the cliff walls. Swimming was rougher where the river dumped into a sea whipped into waves by the last of the storm winds. Rupert had to abandon the side stroke and swim as strongly as he could to keep from being swamped. The comb might be protecting him and it might not, but he would prefer to test it at some later time, when he—or it—could afford to fail.

The godhead was unguarded and unlighted, alone, frowning sternly in the middle of the harbor. Carole made a sudden porpoise-like leap and grabbed the lower lip with both hands, hoisting herself easily onto the shelf between lip and teeth. Rupert jumped up after her, his extra height helping him achieve what his lesser buoyancy would not.

The mouth was open to form a quizzical snarl, the tongue a wide, curving platform where the sacrifices were dashed to death. Rupert couldn't see how at first, but holding on to the roof of the mouth he made his way carefully to the back of the tongue. A tentative hello fell endlessly down the throat and echoed back to him.

"I don't like it here," he said. "One . . . one can't see clearly from here, and it's the first place the priests will look. They make their sacrifices here, you know."

"I didn't," Carole said. "I wish you hadn't told me." She

leaned backwards across the teeth, bracing herself with her hands, and stared up the nostrils. "I can't believe the detail in this thing. Will you look at those little crystal hairs? They've gone to incredible trouble to make this idol look like a real person."

"Oh, I doubt very much that anyone made him look like anything," Rupert replied somewhat absently, for he was studying the distance between the corner of the mouth and the earlobe and wondering if the dimple in between would provide sufficient handhold until he could set foot on the end of the curl jutting out along the chin. "The family resemblance is proof enough to me that they left him entirely authentic."

"Left him? Whatever are you talking about?"

"Rowan the Recreant, of course. This poor fellow we're standing in. Mother help him, I always had a feeling that the stories were wrong. Cowardliness just isn't a family trait. I had supposed they just made him up as a cautionary tale, but apparently not." Carole continued to look puzzled and a shade annoyed. "He was one of my ancestors—one of the great frost giants from before we Rowans came to Argonia. Father told me about all of them, way back, as soon as I was able to recite the family chain. Not much about him, you understand, because he was a disgrace, left Great-great-etc-grandmother Adelheit alone with a whole passle of gigantic Rowans. But Sir Cyril took an interest in him and did a bit of research among other tellers of tales for the archives, to add to the chronicles of the Royal Family. I used to spend a great deal of time with Sir Cyril before I was sent to Wasimarkan. Splendid fellow. It must have been that shape-shifting enchantress who did him in."

"Sir Cyril?"

"Rowan the Recreant. There are stories about the enchantress elsewhere in the family chronicles, and a descendant or two later in the lines who supposedly was attributable to her. She was very powerful—much more powerful than anyone we know today. She was thought to be immortal, though since she's not around now she couldn't have been, could she? And she could change her size at will, which was the aspect that I imagine attracted the forefathers. Ladies of their own stature in foreign lands must have been hard to come by for a fellow as big as this one." He patted Rowan the Recreant's upper lip sympathetically.

"I suppose it's not unlikely, considering that she was able to shift her own shape and also considering the wealth of crystal in this country, that she might have been able to change him into crystal, too. The way I would reconstruct the story, going on what was told to me already, was that after that first fling—the one that's in the family chronicles—where he outsmarted the enchantress and escaped her land with all those jewels that he took back to give to Adelheit's father to win her hand, he must have had second thoughts. The next time the ship was passing by, he decided to give the enchantress another lookover. Perhaps Grandmother Adelheit wasn't that easy to live with. Perhaps the enchantress had more to offer than jewels. Who knows? But apparently she was not the sort of lady who took kindly to being left to pursue her own career while her lover ran off with the proceeds. Perhaps, who knows, those descendants that were hers were also his, unbeknownst to Grandmother Adelheit. At any rate, I think this is absolute proof that when he jumped that ship, he never intended to desert his lord, but was merely taking a little detour to see an old friend who proved not so friendly. Clearly, he was never again able to leave this harbor."

"Uck," Carole said, "You mean to say that we're *in* him?"

"Yes, isn't it intriguing? I shall have to speak to Father and to Sir Cyril about clearing up his reputation when we return home."

"Do that," Carole said, "I'm sure they'll be relieved to hear that he's come up in the world from being a berserking coward to being worshipped as a god." She yawned and shivered in her wet clothing.

"Well, yes, I suppose legend might choose to see it that way. I hope you won't make too much of the resemblance though, when we tell them about it. I confess I find it rather embarrassing."

"Convenient though."

Rupert couldn't argue that, but nevertheless he felt a twinge of guilt for making use of the situation. He wondered what he would do if they were somehow unable to make good their escape and he was forced to continue in the role in which the priests had cast him.

"Rupert?" Carole asked.

"Yes?" He was busy inspecting the ear again.

"What do you suppose that Midnight Rainbow ceremony really does? Besides scare everyone with the power of the priests?"

"Eh? What? Oh, I haven't the foggiest idea about that. You're the magician here. Look, I'm going to climb to the top of Grandpa's curls and keep a lookout, what do you think?"

"You could stay here and rest where it's dry, but I agree that one of us should go up there. That way if Grippeldice passes by she'll be sure to see us. It would be wonderful to have her on hand as soon as the nurse and the baby arrive. But we could always take turns. Dawn is still a long time off."

"I know," he said, "But I'm so tired that if I fall asleep here I probably won't wake in time to relieve you. Up there the light will waken me."

"Suit yourself," she said. "But I could go as easily."

He shook her shoulder in a friendly grasp, like a mother dog mouthing a pup. "I have a better disguise than you do in this situation, cousin. If I am spotted, nothing very dire will happen to me. What could be more natural than a god perching on his own likeness? I'd be able to warn you, so you could jump into the sea. The other way wouldn't work nearly as well. Wait. Here. . . . " With a certain amount of fumbling and genteel cursing, he unslung the shield from his back and handed it to her. Shortly thereafter the mer comb clattered down upon it. "The christening gifts should all be in one place, with you, where they can be bestowed as soon as possible. Even though we'll have to carry the gifts for her later, the bestowing will give her some protection. Now you stay here and rest up so your magic will be ready to use when we need it."

With that he hooked his fingers over the sharp crystalline edge of the famous Rowan dimple, crawled along the Rowan cheek until he could place a large foot on the tip of the Rowan curl, and grasped the Rowan earlobe to pull himself up into the ear. He had little problem maintaining a grip on the slippery crystal surface—Rowan the Recreant had large pores. The giant's stony curls proved easy to climb. Rupert found a flattened place at the crown, probably where the giant's helmet usually rested, since Rowans had never had to worry about baldness.

For her part, Carole made herself as comfortable as possible, curled up against the giant's gums, her head resting on the curve of the shield. The comb she tucked safely in her medicine pouch. She knew, despite Rupert's gallantry, that she would never be able to manage sleep under such circumstances, but she did.

Rupert slept sitting up amidst the crystal curls, his head drooping against his chest. The scrape of wood on stone just before dawn was not as loud as the pounding of the waves, but it was a different sound, and woke him at once. It came from behind him instead of in front of him, however, and he peered over the back of the giant's head to see the nurse sitting in her little boat, wringing hands stung red and raw by the salt water. Naturally, he realized, she would bring the boat in at the idol's rear, where she would not be so easily observed. Utilizing the many good gripping places offered by the giant's coiffure, he scrambled down to meet her.

Though Jushia looked as charmingly fragile as ever, with a hint of wildness added by her blowing hair and red-rimmed eyes, Rupert noted at once that something was conspicuously missing. "Where's the child?" he asked, lowering himself into the boat beside her while keeping it moored with a grip on one of Rowan the Recreant's stray tendrils.

She apparently noticed the same thing about him that he had noticed about her at about the same time. "You don't know?" she said, wailing slightly, which was fortunate for he could barely hear her over the pounding of the surf.

"Of course not. You were going to bring her here, remember?"

She pressed her face into her hands before looking up at him again, eyes wet with more than sea water. "Oh, dear. I thought perhaps you were testing me after all and had transported her here in some divine fashion." Her head craned slightly sideways, as if he might be concealing a child behind his back. "You really don't have her?" She saw without a reply that he did not.

He touched her shoulder reassuringly. "Maybe she woke up crying while you were gone and one of the other ladies fetched her to give her something to eat. Have you asked?"

"I looked in the quarters of Lady Fanya and Lady Aseneth. Both were alone and sleeping. I was afraid to raise a general alarm for fear you were testing me, you see. Now I must. Be gentle when they sacrifice me tomorrow."

"Now, now. Let's not be hasty. The child has to be around somewhere. There are only so many things you can do—er—" He stopped, deciding not to go into what things could be done with a helpless baby. "We'll return to the castle and search it as well as we can without rousing anyone before you raise the general alarm. I'm sure that we'll probably find the baby tucked away in the corner of the kitchen in the care of a kindly maid or something. You'll see."

He took the oars and pushed off with a kick from his large bare foot, cutting it slightly on the sharp-edged hair of his forebearer. His feet were so numb with cold that he hardly noticed. It occurred to him that perhaps he should wake Carole and apprise her of the new developments, but there was little she could actually do until they had found the child. She was much safer staying where she was and guarding the christening gifts. And should he and Jushia not find the baby, he would need to return through the secret passage to the temple. If the child caught between the powers that ruled Gorequartz was not with the King and Queen there was only one other logical place she might be—with the priests.

CHAPTER XI

Carole dozed off with the pounding of the surf vibrating against the giant's teeth, shaking her and, at the same time, lulling her with its rhythm. She became aware that the sound had quieted in the middle of a dream. She rolled fitfully over, so that her other cheek would rest against the carved rowan leaf on the shield. Her body had been clenched tight as a fist. She ached all over from cold, even as she slept. She heard the familiar Rowan rumble as she turned in her sleep. Rupert stood over her. His voice came and went with the waves and he gazed down at her, his face curiously altered. While she somehow did not find it strange that he should be glowing with his own light, she did wonder that he should have found a change of clothing: sandals of a design she had never seen and a sort of breechclout made of bearskin, which would have made her a very welcome blanket. Furthermore, the whole ensemble—bearskin, sandals, glow and all—was distinctly see-throughish. Rupert's expression was anguished and vaguely hostile as he looked down at her.

She raised herself on one elbow to ask what he wanted, but sank back down again as if her limbs were made of noodles.

"Morag, how come ye back?" the voice asked. It was at once softer and deeper than Rupert's. It gonged in the back of her mind rather than falling on her ears. He continued to look at her. She realized he had mistaken her for someone else.

171

"Come, lass, would you mock me, to lay here in your small size upon the rowan shield and look as innocent as if you had never doomed me to this?" He flung his arms up and shook his head helplessly at the crystal interior of his own mouth. Carole was not unacquainted with ghosts. Argonia was lousy with them. She just hadn't been prepared for this one in this place. She could not quite wake up but she did manage to gather her thoughts, to pull them in from the woolly world of other dreams so that she could focus. Someone needed to have their wits about them. The giant's ghost had obviously mistaken her for his old mistress and nemesis, the shape-shifting enchantress. Did she, Carole, resemble this Morag then? Perhaps the woman was an ancient Brown ancestress . . . but surely not. The giant was far older than Argonia and the whole line of Browns.

"Did you know what you did to me, Morag? Did you know it all? That I would stand here forever and never feeling with my body but feeling all the same? That I would stand for years in the sea, looking for you, that I would watch you die at the hands of the newcomers and never be able to save you any more than I could slay you?" He sighed and looked at her with infinite sadness. "Oh, girl, if you had to die, why did you not join me? I could have done you as I've learned to do those other poor sods those crazy religious fanatics stuff down me throat. Oh, Morag, I only wanted to see you again. Was this any way to treat the man you loved?"

He turned his face to the side where the tears slid off his nose while his shoulders and chest heaved and collapsed like the waves rolling against his stone body. Carole pitied him and also hoped he didn't grow so distraught he stepped on her. While in one sense she felt he was no larger than Rupert, in another she felt herself to be very much smaller. The matter of size seemed rather confused. Now, for instance, his face hung very high above her and his tears splashed toward her like washtubs full of water that never quite hit.

Carole sighed softly and somewhere inside of her another Carole stood to meet the giant. "Brace up," the dream self said, slapping the giant encouragingly on the ankle, which was all the farther she could reach. "Just look at you. You're a mess. What sort of God blubbers like this? Hundreds of people are sacrificed in your name and you stand about feeling sorry for yourself? What would your worshippers think? Aren't you supposed to be setting an example?"

"How can you speak to me so, Morag?"

"Not Morag, just a simple village witch and a priestess who knows good and well the responsibilities a deity has to its followers. And speaking of your followers, what do you *mean* allowing people to be sacrificed to you? That's the most repulsive, tyrannical, barbaric thing I've ever heard of, even from a giant barbarian!"

The giant mopped his eyes with one hairy arm and blew his nose rather disgustingly, but the danger of enormous hysterics or a towering rage resulting in rampage and destruction to Carole's sleeping person seemed delayed if not permanently abated. He bent and lifted the Carole dream-self in one hand, eyeing her suspiciously. "You're not Morag, eh? You do sound like her."

She assured him she was not, nevertheless. "Morag is long dead as you yourself just told me. What I'd like to know is why you aren't. Do the sacrifices your priests bring you give their lives to sustain yours?"

He snuffled and mumbled. She looked up at him sharply. Like a child guilty of overturning the milk pail he looked quickly down at her with his eyes the size of a cart and away again. "I said no. It's not like that. Not like you think. I've no wish for what those fanatics do to folk hereabouts in my name. Twas a fine thing to slay in the heat of battle with the blood rising in me, but to stand here forever cold and forever wet and forever alone, and have fools push people to death down my throat as if I were a man-eater of some kind, arragh, no. I never wished it. I would die and crumble and line the sea with these clear stone bones of mine if I could, but the stone preserves what was me, you see. I watch and listen and feel and never am able to stay a hand to those who would murder and cast the blame on me. I do all I can. When the bodies break inside me like cracked nuts I save the part that was human, the part that was that person, and before they can be trapped as I am, I belch 'em out quick as I can, and that much I can save. There are advantages for the disembodied who are not bound as I am, you know. A body who knows how can trick time and space, can enjoy anything. If only I were free of this crystal prison, I could do that."

"Just be careful if you ever leave *this* crystal prison that your faithful devotees don't snap you up as they do those poor souls you belch and put you and all of your wonderful otherworldly advantages in a shiny new crystal bottle to sell to anyone who wants to enjoy the benefits of both worlds."

"They do so? In truth?" His voice swelled like the tide and his right fist clenched and unclenched. Suddenly Carole saw the dream-self fall, but she couldn't tell if the height was great or small, or whether the moaning giant was growing or diminishing or if she was. In the middle of pondering the question she found that it wasn't the least bit important, since she was quite alone after all.

When Rupert joined Jushia in embarking upon the search of the castle for Bronwyn's baby on what would later be referred to as the Morning of the Divine Visitation, he learned one thing that had not previously impressed him about castles: Quite a few infants dwelt in one and each of those infants was prone to crying long before any sensible adult would consider arising.

He and Jushia separated to save time, she taking the west wing occupied by the royal family and the central portion containing the offices, meeting and court halls, and the kitchen. Rupert took the east wing, containing the quarters for the other nobles and the seaward extension that housed the servants. He realized almost at once that the search would have worked better the other way around. Jushia would have been far less conspicuous than he amidst the families and servants, he far more at home among the castle's administrative offices. He prided himself on his regal appearance, even in bare feet and wet trouser legs.

He did not search every room, of course, only the ones where he heard babies crying. That accounted for approximately every other room. Rupert was not shy about popping his head in, holding aloft the one of a series of guttering torches he borrowed from the hall sconces long enough to ascertain if the child in the room was the one he sought, which it invariably was not. Where the crying child was already tended by a woman or girl, he simply smiled and nodded amiably, checked the child, and headed for the next room emitting youthful howling. With babes in arms, some of the women followed him to the door and into the hallway, while others sank to their knees in awe and terror. Still others continued their tasks and wondered if the nice-looking, tallish fellow ever found his way to the privy tower after all.

It was not until Rupert left, disappointed in his quest and having seen a good many more of the offspring of Gorequartz than he cared to, that the women in the hall consulted with the women praying in their rooms and those gawking at the doorways and concluded that they and their children had been specially blessed by the God that morning. They then proceeded to try to decide what, if anything, the visit portended. Vociferous interpretations quite drowned out the cries of the babies.

Jushia was not in the linen storeroom where she had promised to meet him. With the castle stirring, he grew nervous waiting, twice having to hide behind bales of sheets and diapers to avoid detection when the maids and other nurses arrived to gather their supplies for the morning.

When the first of the bustle was over, Rupert peeked out. Finding the corridor temporarily clear, he left his sanctuary and strode importantly into the great hall, as if he belonged there. He hoped to find Jushia consulting with someone on the problem of the missing child, if indeed she hadn't already recovered the baby and was delayed by the need to fuss over it. He didn't seriously think anything was very wrong. Except for the theft of Bronwyn's child, which had given him an excellent excuse to have an adventure, nothing had ever gone very wrong in Rupert's life. His rank and personal charm, while not causing him to be unduly spoiled or callous, had nonetheless isolated him from the worst rigors of the lives of those less amply blessed.

So when he saw the priests proceeding from the King's audience chamber, he was not overly alarmed, but nonetheless took the reasonable precaution of stepping back into the shadows and watching.

Unfortunately, one of the passing court ladies had spent the wee hours of the morning nursing her sick child and spotted at once the god who had, as she later claimed, miraculously cured her little one just by looking in on him, showing a love and concern hitherto not identified with the Grand Prismatic.

"He's here! The Precious Polyhued is here, descended to join us!" she cried, and from all over the palace other worshippers began to flock, babbling supplication and adoration and a lot of other things impossible to make out.

The priests, who disliked the idea of anyone overwhelming the populace without their supervision, dispersed the worshippers by swinging the incense holder like a sling and uttering threats and imprecations. Rupert found to his surprise that he was almost glad to see them, particularly when he recognized one of the prostrate worshippers as the Queen, asking him to send her a son quickly, and offering up her person as an implement to be used for divine inspiration if he chose. Feeling a little queasy, Rupert patted her on the crown as he joined the priests.

The High Priest waited until they were all discreetly behind temple walls again to remonstrate with his god. Alireza Mashkent lounged possessively near the crystal throne and burly lay brothers guarded the exit through the beaded curtain.

"Now then," the High Priest said, "Suppose you explain to us, Your Highness, just what you were doing in the palace alone and without our per . . . protection."

"Since when does a god need protection?" Rupert asked innocently.

"You never know when some crazed iconoclast who lost a relative as last ceremony's delegate might try to test your divinity," the High Priest said. "It could even be arranged that one would do so."

Rupert nodded and stared, waiting. The High Priest stared back. Rupert was a good starer but the High Priest was better. He had had more experience, besides which his control of his followers was subtly magically enhanced. While in possession of the shield, Rupert had not felt the High Priest's power. Whether it was that power or his sleepless night that made the Prince feel slightly dizzy, he couldn't say. He *did* know that if he stood for a moment longer silent and stiff-kneed he was likely to keel over.

"So," he said coolly, "no doubt you were wondering why I was in the palace. I was searching for my niece."

"Your niece? The young woman with you? I thought she was your cousin," His Brilliance said. "I'm afraid I must have missed something vital in this conversation."

"Then perhaps Mlle. Mukbar can enlighten you. The Miragenians have lent my niece, the Crown Princess of Wasimarkan, tentatively named Magda Xenobia Amberwine

Ethel Ermintrude the First, Duchess of Millpond, Countess of Cedar Grove, Marquisa of three prime blocks of real estate in Queenston, Lady of Unicorn Bayou and Honorary City Assemblywoman of Fort Iceworm, Northern Territories, to your monarch's wife to impersonate her firstborn child until such time as she can produce one. The Miragenians are obligated to return the child to her parents in its fifteenth year under the terms of an agreement forged by Queen Bronwyn and themselves in the Year of the Great War in Argonia. If you sacrifice the baby first, it is clearly a breach of all agreements."

"*Fas*cinating," His Brilliance said, steepling his fingers in a judicious manner. "Well, then, if this is all done by some agreement or other I see no harm in accommodating you, though I must say it's highly irregular. An agreement is—"

"We've been told," the Prince said drily. "But Mlle. Mukbar's firm was a bit hasty in removing the child from her home and birthright—and her birth rite for that matter. They took the child before she could be christened. Therefore, I shall not only need to see her, but to see to it that she is christened in the religion of our native land by my cousin, who is a duly qualified representative of our faith."

"Christened?" His Brilliance asked as if Rupert had said "cooked."

"It's a name day and much more," Rupert said.

"It sounded to me from your recitation as if the child had quite enough names. I fail to see why she needs a special ceremony."

"The names aren't actually hers unless given to her at the ceremony along with the gifts and blessings of her people and the Mother—"

"These gifts, are they valuable?" Alireza asked.

"Only to the child. In a royal child especially, they form the basis for the character and personality of the adult."

"I see. Yours must have been extremely interesting."

Rupert ignored the lascivious smile accompanying the

Miragenian woman's last remark and waited for the High Priest to say something.

His Brilliance shrugged. "I see no reason why she shouldn't have this christening then, if it pleases you. You are the God reincarnate after all. But we could have had the child brought here. There was no need for you to roam about the palace alone, spoiling the impact of your appearance at the ceremony this evening."

"I beg your pardon," Rupert said. "But I believe it was necessary. As it happened, I did not find the child. Perhaps you will tell me where she is?"

"Alas, I fear we are unable to do that, though if you wish we can put her abductor to the question. So near to a ceremony, the usual procedure with any criminal is to sacrifice them, but I think we could make an exception if—"

"Excuse me," Rupert interrupted. "What abductor?"

"Her nurse was captured this morning trying to escape after having collaborated in the child's kidnapping. We were consoling and consulting with the parents—or should I say the foster parents—of the baby when we encountered you."

The beaded curtain tinkled and Brother Bullcow entered at a gallop, slid to a halt, and genuflected. "Your Brilliance, I beg your indulgence for interrupting, but I must report to you that the foreign witch is missing from her quarters again, despite the guard on the door."

"How sad," the High Priest said, his cold blue eyes on Rupert's face. "My, what a lot of disappearances there are today. Your Highness, do you know anything of this?"

"Nothing. I'm sure it is coincidence that two people you only casually mentioned you intended to honor so murderously on my behalf should disappear before you have the opportunity to do so."

"Heroically spoken," Alireza said. She descended from her place beside His Brilliance to twine herself around Rupert's arm. Rupert did not shake her off but neither did he change his posture except to stiffen slightly. "I think, Your Brilliance, that you should give your god a theology lesson. He's a nobleman, a diplomat. Surely he can be made to understand the interdependence of economy and religion, and why at times paltry personal considerations must be secondary to the good of government."

"Strange that *you* should be the one to make such a statement," Effluvia said, making a grand entrance by sweeping aside the curtain with a flash of her tail, "for I have come to report that by making such a fool of yourself as to follow the god from Miragenia, you have led the unbound entities here. They descended upon the quarrymen last evening. The miserable fellows fled for their lives, the oxen drawing the carts bolted, and the entire load of crystal for that day was lost."

"How very costly for you," Alireza said in a civilized tone.

The High Priest brushed his hand across his eyes and for the first time Rupert noticed that the man looked tired and ill. His skin bore a waxen sheen and his teeth were accompanied by more pale gum than usual. His voice lost its bantering superior quality as he spoke this time. "Enough of this infernal bickering. Mlle Mukbar, you have foolishly blundered, as Princess Effluvia so aptly pointed out, and thereby have canceled any claim you may have on my sympathy in your cause. Your company must decide to do without you, I'm afraid."

"This is outrageous! I demand a better deal! His Highness is mine."

"Not at all. His Highness is the very image of our god and more valuable to us than your entire firm. The Princess Effluvia is widely known as the daughter of the King. Their marriage will once and for all unite Gorequartz under a single holy figurehead, though I, of course, will continue to supervise until I expire. By that time, the union should have produced offspring: a boy fit to be my successor."

Rupert was stunned. He hardly approved of having his future disposed of in such a manner, but schooled himself to proffer only the mild comment that a youthful-looking man such as His Brilliance surely should not need to think of succession for some time, but could reign himself if he so desired without the help of Rupert, Effluvia, or any child of theirs—perish the thought, the Prince added to himself. He cringed at the idea of a fair-haired and dimpled daughter with a long black tail. He cringed even more at the thought of what would be required of him in the begetting of such a child.

The High Priest sighed deeply and pinched his nose between his thumb and forefinger. On some people it would have looked noble. "In that I fear you are wrong. You are still unfamiliar with our ceremony of the Midnight Rainbow, but it is my duty, as your earthly representative, to prepare for the sacrifices and the bounty collected thereafter. Look upward and tell me what you see."

Rupert looked. Above the crystal dome the iron-gray clouds tumbled, some of them edged with the pulsating bronze of lightning.

"To sacrifice to the god, to collect that which we require from the sacrifice, it is necessary to first draw upon the power of the storm. To do this I must wear the sacred pendant that directs the lightning through me, making of me a fit vessel for the work of the god. But vessels break with much use, you see, and more's the pity, so shall I. The High Priest traditionally lives but half a hundred years. That is one reason the central power of rulership has been vested in a secular King. If the King and High Priest were one man, himself of divine descent, there would be no need for him to personally undergo the rigors of the ceremony to maintain control. Lesser brothers could perform the more rigorous rites without loss of prestige to the ruler."

"I can see why you would find it of great Profit to thus thwart me, Your Brilliance," Alireza said with a confident sweep of her thick, dark lashes that in no way betrayed she was worried about being flung down the throat of a crystal idol. "His Highness is indeed worth a great deal to you. However, I am not without value. If harm befalls me, the firm of Mukbar, Mashkent, and Mirza will never buy another piece of goods from you."

"Madam, it is precisely for the commission of such follies as the trade agreement that commits Gorequartz to dealing exclusively with your firm that the present King should be deposed. Our wares are truly priceless. We should not be restricted to selling them at your price. And I think that you may be able to observe from your bottle later that your uncles will be no less eager to serve their Profit without you than they were under your directorship."

"If I agree to this plan," Rupert said, "you must allow my niece, my cousin, and Mlle. Mukbar to return to their homes. I will not play your part otherwise."

"No?" the High Priest smiled a weary and almost tender smile and snapped his fingers. Before Rupert understood quite what was happening, Brother Merryhue lit a candle from an assortment on a tray beside the wall and stuck it under the Prince's nose. Rupert suddenly realized that his own attitude was highly unreasonable. The High Priest naturally had the best interests of all concerned at heart. Having borne the rowan shield his whole life, Rupert had seldom been victimized by magic. The experience was novel. He was without resistance to it. He gazed at the priest with more trust than he had ever bestowed upon his own father, and, when Effluvia glided forward to take his hand, he beamed at her. Alireza Mukbar made choking sounds as the brothers hauled her away.

CHAPTER XII

Carole woke steaming. Her woolen clothing smoldered smotheringly against her sweating flesh, while beneath her head the smell of kindling ready to ignite rose from the rowan shield. She felt these changes but saw none of them, for when she tried to open her eyes, they were assailed by light of searing brilliance. She squeezed them tightly shut again and hoped she was not already blinded. While she lay still, the crystal beneath her, shadowed by her body, was bearable, but when she flung out her arm it burned. She allowed herself one or two heat-accelerated heartbeats to wonder what had happened and what to do about it before humping herself, hands and knees together, onto the shield.

Tugging the sleeves of her tunic down to cover her knuckles, she used them to push her and the shield forward, until she could peer out across the giant's teeth. Above a pounding sea, a hot wind seethed through turgid clouds, which in no way diminished the blaze of an oppressive orange sun dominating a full third of the eastern sky. Its fire flashed off every facet of Rowan the Recreant's face. Carole thought that on truly sunny days the frost giant must provide a traffic hazard quite as dangerous as mermaids to passing ships, if indeed any ships ever passed.

Balancing the shield on the Recreant's left molar, Carole flung herself over the tooth and lip and into the cool blue-green sea. The water was warm. When her hands and shoulders broke the surface, the saltiness was soothing as an herb bath to her lightly broiled skin. She dove deep, opening her eyes gratefully to an undersea terrain far more brightly lit than any place she had seen in the company of Cordelia and Lorelei. Still, the ferocious light was softened by the shadows of fish and seaweed and skipping waves. Long, green tendrils furled from the enormous bulk of the giant's submerged body. Carole swam in a tight, brief circle, orienting herself, noting the giant's position so that she wouldn't inadvertently swim headlong into his outstretched arm, half raised as if to protect himself. Rowans must have been less wary in those days, it occurred to her, for surely the famous shield would have protected the giant from the fatally magical aspects of the enchantress's wrath.

Thinking of Rowans and wrathful women reminded her that Rupert would still be waiting for her. He must still be asleep. How was he managing not to fry atop the head of his ancestor? Kicking upward, she saw Rupert's own shield bobbing just below the cleft in the giant's chin and she surfaced beneath it and tucked it under her arm.

With her hand shadowing her eyes, she searched the great head for her cousin. Pure and brilliant slabs of dancing light sculpted the nose and brow while the blinded eyes stared disbelievingly toward the cliffs, shadowed deeply in places while in others it was lit with rainbows on the sea and in the air and reflecting from the cliffsides, which winked with mirrored veins of icy-bright stone. No wonder the place was sacred and the hapless Rowan the Recreant had been named God of Rainbows. His former lady friend had certainly dressed him in the part.

All of that Carole saw clearly. What she did not see was Rupert, either perched or poached on the giant's pate, nor did she see boat, nurse, or child. She thought perhaps Rupert might have taken a swim but saw him nowhere near, and, besides, he was keeping lookout. Surely he would not have abandoned his post without alerting her. Several other possibilities presented themselves. Having examined and abandoned them all, Carole next dove to the bottom to satisfy herself that the most immediately dire fate she could imagine had not yet befallen him. While there were a few bones clothed in seaweed and barnacles instead of flesh, they were too old. Carole didn't bother to prod them. Instead, she swam upward again, under the giant's arm, toward the cliffs.

The cliff wall rose sheer and sharp. Any seaward invader would have to have good scaling ladders and tough boots. As she had neither, Carole dove again and surveyed the bottom, the topography of which was largely defined by the giant's huge feet, which met the cliffside on either side of the harbor. The right foot disappeared as far as the arch into the hill. Rowan the Recreant must have given a great kick, she thought, trying to get a leg up before the sorceress stiffened him for good. Fish swam in and out under his heel, toward and away from the toes, which made her curious. She dove a bit deeper and peered under his heel. The cliffside had crumbled away under his toe, forming a small cave. She wriggled closer, tucking her wet skirts up to free her legs and keep the cloth from tangling in the crystal.

The cave was not as dark as it appeared from the outside. She pushed her arms against her sides and bobbed up, seeking its roof. Her head broke water, and salty, wet, but perfectly breathable air filled her mouth and nostrils. She was in a grotto, pillared with crystal, dappled with wavery light. A beach of sharp quartz and clear white sand surrounded the pool. She scrambled up onto it, scratching herself on the sand. Beyond the pillars the grotto opened into narrow rooms, and she pressed back toward one of them.

Having seen nothing but temple, shrines, and castle, Carole had no idea where she was in relation to other areas of Gorequartz. When she heard the mumble of voices and the ring of metal on stone coming from somewhere above and in front of her, she was relieved to know she was near something that presumably had a landward exit. The only question was how would she get past the people behind the voices to reach it. Her wet clothing and the direction from which she came would, at the very least, present her with a somewhat unconventional appearance. The only way to avoid answering awkward questions would be to avoid the people who might ask them, so she was cautious as she felt her way upward, keeping to the wall and listening, trying to place where the voices were.

What she *heard* did not ultimately help as much as what fell on her. When a shower of sharp and shining sand spattered down on her scalp and shoulders, she realized that the voices, and the feet responsible for loosening the sand, were directly above her. The floor of the tunnel soon confirmed this when it took a goat-challenging slant upwards. She hoped the noise the workers were making would disguise the rattling of sand and the rasp of her breathing as she climbed. She had to sling the shield across her back to free her hands. The crystal pushed through the earth here, cool but cutting, and the sand stuck miserably to her wet skin. She slipped repeatedly, coating herself in grit. When her hands found a spot that no longer sloped away from her, she dragged the rest of herself up and stared blindly into the space before her while her breath evened and her pulse slowed. The pinpoints of light in the gloom ahead of her failed at first to register as anything but part of the random pattern of stars dancing inside her own eyes.

By the time her eyes had adjusted so that she was aware that the lights were moving, the men behind them had spotted her.

"See there! See there!" an excited voice hissed. A finger pointed past the light, eerily disembodied and importantly accusing. "I told you! Ears like a pachyderm's I've got and I told you there was someone back here but—"

"Hush. You'll bring the hill down on our ears. You there, come out here." He crunched towards her and she saw his white and shining face, lit from below, great holes around his eyes, which looked both frightened and belligerent about being frightened.

"Oh, Riz, it ain't a person," the other voice breathed.

Riz looked back into the darkness, then at Carole again. "It is so. What else would it be?"

"*Her*. The old one from before. Maybe a statue of her, put back here. What would an ordinary lady be doing in these caves?"

"No good, I say. And statues don't move."

"No one saw any woman before. And this section was blocked off till this morning. Mark me. This is *their* doings, them from before."

"You're daft, Ancher. That's superstition. Don't let the priests hear you."

Unable to impersonate a statue any longer, Carole very slowly raised a spectrally white arm and glided forward, as much as one could glide on sand.

One of the lights jumped backwards. "Oh, I told you, I told you. We'll be paying now for taking the crystal. The ghosts of them old ones is back. Them colored things that got the evening shift . . . ghosts, I tell you, and this is—"

"That's heresy, man. Do you fancy gagging the giant your own self?"

"Hey there!" a voice hailed from the back. "Riz! Ancher! What's going on back there?"

"Ancher's seen a ghost."

"What? Another one? What color?"

"White and shiny, like us."

"Ghosts ain't white and shiny they're—" A third light

joined the first two. "My-dear-old-mother-in-law-gone-to-give-the-god-the-bellyache, who the thunder is she?"

More lights confronted Carole, casting a sinister pattern of light and shadow on the staring faces. Carole had rather fancied having her turn at playing goddess, but couldn't wait for them to talk each other out of or into the notion. She started to whistle them a jig to dance them from her path.

"Who ever heard of a whistling ghost?" Riz asked. "Take her!"

She was still struggling for the strap that bound the rowan shield to her back when they seized her and dragged her out of the mine.

Their overseer didn't seem to be under any delusions about her mortality or lack of it, but was nonetheless delighted to see her for reasons of his own. With the shield strapped to her, she could whistle and hum all day to no particular effect, so she stood quietly while the man inspected her.

"Anyone know who she is?"

"Ancher'n Riz say a spook."

"She will be soon if she ain't already. I reckon the warder at the dungeon will be agreeable to taking her for the ceremony instead of my ma. That damned pious brother-in-law of mine thought he'd get rid of her, but the priests'll take a substitute. You three bring her along and keep her quiet. I want no husband or father come looking for her before she's locked away safe and ready to be decked with pretty posies.

They loaded her in an ore cart with a freshly mended side and wheel.

"Ooo, didn't they do a lovely job?" Riz asked. "I saw this last night, after the oxen wrecked it, and I never thought to see it roll again."

Though not so influential with priests as his brother-in-law, the overseer was a man of no mean influence himself, and the gold pieces he slipped the warder readily persuaded the official to bring forth the missing mother and take Carole in her stead. All of this was done with the nonchalance of an everyday business transaction. Carole could see where it might be. The edicts and rites of officialdom often needed to be modified by ordinary people and the bureaucrats responsible for carrying out the attendant procedures. One man's detested and expendable mother-in-law was another's beloved mother, after all. The position of warder must be a coveted one. The man was plump and affluent-looking with a magnificent silver beard and a number of gold and crystal rings augmenting his spotless black uniform.

"Well now," he said when the miners and the overseer's mother had left. "You'll need a bath. Can't have you going dirty like that to the god, now can we? Makes a poor appearance. Spoils the ceremony and musses the flowers. You're in luck, my girl. We have plenty of water around here and one of your fellow delegates is a real ladies' maid formerly in the employ of the Princess herself. Boys, take this woman to the holding tank for the delegates, will you?" Meaty hands clamped on her arms and led her firmly away before she could extricate herself from the shield's restraining influence. If only they had been efficient at their jobs instead of so lazy and corrupt they would have had the sense to take a shield from her at least long enough to see if she had a weapon. They did not, however, and when she was able to take it off, she saw that it was so crusted with crystal sand they probably had simply failed to notice that it wasn't part of her clothing.

The holding tank was not a dingy cell but a room with a view of the moat—through iron bars—a southern exposure, and comfortable low couches. The floor was of scrubbed wood. The walls were painted with inspirational pictures of the temple and the godhead. Three other people occupied the room.

"That water's coming right up, miss, and a spot of lunch as well," the guard said, sounding more like an innkeeper. "Two of the ladies ate before they arrived but the King's chef sent down some very tasty victuals for the other young lady on non-volunteer status." He indicated a woman huddled in a cloak that looked smothering, then shoved Carole almost gently down beside her, saying, "I heard the conversation out there and I just want you to know that we custodians of the delegates here at the dungeon don't think less of you for being an exchange. Your sacrifice is greatly appreciated by us, I can say for me and all the others, and I don't want you to be concerned about being pleasing to the god. I'm sure you'll wash up fine."

She stared after him for a moment.

"Don't look so stunned, my dear," said the comfortable-looking matron sitting across from her. "Naturally he's grateful. Those of us making the ultimate sacrifice enrich our land and loved ones by doing so."

"Not to mention that if we go, he doesn't have to, nor any of his relatives," a thin, dark man added, smiling wolfishly.

Carole shook her head back and forth once and began skinning out of the rowan shield. The strap caught on her elbow. She cursed and turned her back to the cloaked figure next to her. "D'you mind?" she asked. Trembling fingers complied. Divested of the object, Carole turned to thank the woman, and the nurse Jushia's face looked miserably up at her.

"What are you doing here?" Carole asked. "Where's Rupert?"

"I beg your pardon?" the girl said, dusting off the sand Carole shed with every movement.

"Rupert. Where is he? Did he meet you?"

By that time enough sand had fallen from her face that the girl blinked with recognition and gasped slightly. "Milady, your pardon. I didn't realize it was you. As to the God, I know not. I left him searching to halls for the Princess." She explained about the Princess's disappearance and her subsequent meeting with Rupert and added sadly, "He didn't even materialize to vent his wrath on those who persecuted me. Do you suppose I proved unworthy?"

"I doubt it," Carole said, brushing the worst of the sand from her, liberally sprinkling the floor and the nurse in the process. She wished she could stay for the bath the warder had promised her, but she needed to pounce with an appropriate song the minute the iron-bound door opened again. "I could use your help," she told Jushia.

"Anything, milady. Though as handmaiden to the god you—"

"Do forget that for now, won't you? It's a misunderstanding. Rupert—the god—isn't free to do as he chooses."

"He explained all that," the girl said. "About how he was reincarnated without the powers befitting his station. And how his evil advisors seek to take advantage of him."

"Good. Then you'll help?"

The girl nodded, although she looked almost as frightened of Carole as she was of imminent death.

"It's very easy. All you have to do is hold onto this shield and follow me carrying it. You will find it quite serviceable in case matters should become complicated, and, in addition, it will protect you from spells."

Though their conversation was carried on in murmurs, the other occupants of the room watched them closely. The matron pursed her lips and whuffed with disapproval. The thin, dark man uncurled himself, stretched, and sauntered over to them.

"You breaking out of here, are you?" he asked Carole. "I am better help than she is."

Jushia hugged the god's shield and stared balkily up at him.

"You're free to come along if you like," Carole said. "But don't get in the way."

"Who, me? Get in the way? Lady, had I not been fingered by jealous rivals I would still be the slickest thief in Gorequartz. I disappear like a shadow in the night, you mark me. Just get the door open."

191

That was done for them in short order by the sympathetic guard, who found himself engaged in the acrobatic chore of doing a series of high-speed pirouettes away from the door while twirling the water basin above his head. Carole whistled until the others, safely lined up behind the rowan shield, filed out behind her. Only the matron remained.

"Fancy not wanting to do your part," the woman said. "It'll go hard on you for your selfishness." What could be harder than being sacrificed to a crystal idol she didn't get a chance to explain, for they quickly left her alone with her good opinion of herself.

The warder soon joined his men in the dance. Carole stopped whistling when the escapees reached the courtyard. The others scattered while she and Jushia followed the thief. Carole was rather hoping that in this backward part of the world they might not have heard of a portcullis yet, but her hopes were in vain. The thief ran straight up to the portcullis and stopped, looking momentarily puzzled before snapping his fingers, dodging across the portcullis to dash up the steps leading to the castle wall, and plunging himself into the moat. The nurse hesitated only a moment before diving in after him and Carole followed.

By the time the pair of guards stationed on either side of the drawbridge ran to investigate all the splashing, the thief had led the other two back of the crystal shrines, into a warren of houses and small tributary ditches leading to the central canal. He slunk like an eel along the pathways and alleys, leading them at last to a street where people sat earnestly weaving flowers into garlands and swags, across a tributary that smelled like a sewer, and through a crack in the far wall, to a rickety ladder that dropped into a dark hole smelling of urine, mold, and stale smoke.

A torch flared as they descended. A grizzled face examined them, and questioned the thief sharply. The thief's reply must have been satisfactory. Other torches flared up and revealed a group of raggedy people lounging beside racks of dusty bottles. All but three of the group were men. From the corner a child cried. Jushia sprang down the last rung, dropped the shield, and leaped forward, to be hauled back by the laughing thief.

From the shadows behind a rack of bottles stepped a familiar figure, smoking a thin roll of weeds stuck in the side of his mouth, while with a certain competent grace that was not at all unmasculine he bounced a redhaired baby over one shoulder. Pulling the roll from his lips with his free hand, he nodded approval to the thief. "Excellent, my friend, excellent."

The thief took a flourishing bow then broke into a wide, foolish grin. "We pulled it off, Timoteo! We did well, eh?" The thief said this with such joy that it was evident his ventures did not always go so smoothly.

The man Carole had known as a merchant did not indulge in such a crude display of pleasure but allowed himself instead a small, restrained smile, its effect spoiled only slightly when he chucked the baby under the chin before turning her to face Carole. Despite the chucking, the royal chin trembled with impending howls.

Carole felt a rush of absolutely maternal affection for this small relative. Despite all the trouble she had been through on behalf of the little scamp, she had been thinking of her as more of a goal than a person. The sight of the largish human infant with the chubby wet fingers and dissatisfied pout, lying absolutely trustingly, if not happily, in the arms of the disreputable Timoteo, made the witch feel that even if she had not been bored out of her mind at Wormroost she would willingly undertake the quest again. Between the Miragenians, the Gorequartz throne, the priests, and now Timoteo, the child was being tossed around as if she was a ball.

"Priestess, I believe your side of the family delegated you to christen this child. Please do so now. Our side of the family will stand witness. It is too bad Prince Rupert cannot be with us on this occasion, since I am sure he believes this whole snatch to be of his devising. Still, he will have the satisfaction, should he survive the devotion of his worshippers, of knowing he has created a most excellent diversion."

"Master Timoteo, excuse me if I seem a little puzzled. Are you claiming kinship with this child? There is no Miragenian blood in her lineage of which I am aware."

The merchant smiled sweetly at her. "Cute," he said and to the motley group behind him, "Isn't she cute? I never knew witches were so cute. I always thought they were serious, dour women. You mean to say you did not realize by this time, seeing us all together here, that we are gypsies, the family of Xenobia and Prince Jack? Kinswoman-much-removed, you wound me. I am Timoteo, also grandson of Xenobia, she who is twice a Queen. She regrets that she cannot be here herself, that my grandfather, my Uncle Davey, and my cousin Jack could not personally attend this important event, but that would appear too outwardly a breach of the famous deal, would it not? That so stupid deal made by my cousin, who can hardly call himself a gypsy now, without the consent of his Queen, the great-grandmother of this child. Unfortunately, she is not only Queen of the Gypsies but also Queen of Wasimarkan, so matters had to be handled delicately. But I assure you, never once from the time this baby was taken by those dogs of merchants, did we intend to tolerate it. No one, but no one, steals a child from the gypsies. It is always and has always been quite the other way around. A matter of honor, you see?"

Carole couldn't decide whether to dance or faint. What with talking to long-dead giant gods, fretting over the absence of princes who weren't gods, being captured and imprisoned for sacrifice and just as precipitously escaping, she had had rather a lot to take in that day. To find the baby safe with the paternal side of the family, the quest all but over, was a bit more than she could assimilate. So, as the representative of the maternal side of the family, she merely nodded. Actually, she only caught snatches of what Timoteo was saying. The baby had not been considerate enough to wait until her rescuer finished his speech but had commenced howling in the middle of it. Carole jerked a thumb in the direction of the nurse and covered an ear with her free hand. The gypsy took the hint and unceremoniously deposited the child in her nurse's arms. The nurse repaired to the corner occupied by two of the gypsy women.

Carole sighed with relief at the reduction in the noise level and at the fortuitous turn of events. She smiled at Timoteo with deliberately open admiration. "I must say your disguise was worthy of the famous Wizard Raspberry. I never guessed you were other than a real Miragenian merchant and I could have sworn all along there was no band of gypsies accompanying you."

"Oh, as to that: I was always alone but wore the disguise so that I would not be so obvious as your very large cousin, the Prince. One can be more useful that way. In fact, I found it possible to be of aid to you before I met you in Miragenia—there on the river bank in Frostingdung, where I frightened away the Miragenian who set his mist upon you. These people here had nothing to do with that. They are relatives of a tribe allied to us by marriage and other little favors, and they have traveled all through these lands and worked the Gorequartz area extensively, though very carefully. We gypsies are widely connected. They were honor bound to help us, for it is not possible for any gypsy to tolerate the insult of outsiders stealing a gypsy child."

Carole scanned the swarthy faces. None of them was as well-to-do as the gypsies she had seen, certainly none as well-fed as Jack had been in his boyhood. As she watched them, their eyes slipped from hers. They did not trust her and did not like her presence. Gypsy honor or no, their cooperation in Timoteo's scheme could cost them dearly.

"We'll need mud," she told Timoteo. "And I'm afraid the mud of this city won't do. It's tainted and unsuitable. I suppose it's not possible to get good Argonian soil already consecrated, but soil from the farmlands here would be close enough."

The thief spread his hands expansively. "But that is very easy. The flowers were carted in this morning from the country in their own dirt to keep them fresh. There are barrows of leftover dirt sitting nearby. The garland makers will be only too happy to have us remove it. Choomia, you go," he said to one of the women. "Miri, help her. It's honest work. Not fit for a man."

The women returned in a short time, the topmost of the several tattered skirts each wore bulging from the arms of its wearer with a load of rich brown dirt.

"And water," Carole said apologetically. "River water is best. The sea water is too polluted for our purposes by being dedicated, however mistakenly, to that crystallized frost giant in the bay, and the canal is as bad."

"Fortunately, lady, the highborns agree with you, though for different reasons. They import river water for washing and drinking," the thief said. "This is work more to my taste." And he swung gaily up the ladder, to return shortly bearing the water in a pitcher of silver set with cut gems. No one had said that he should be the only one in Gorequartz not to profit from a religious occasion.

They poured the dirt into a pile which Carole then spread out on the top of a splintered piece of an old door. She blessed it, strewed it with cleansing herbs, and added to it the ashes from the small parchment rolls bearing the gifts of distant well-wishers, Rusty Killgilles and those early donors whose gifts Bronwyn had entrusted to Rupert earlier and which he had in turn entrusted to Carole shortly after she agreed to accompany him. All of these she had kept dry, rolling them in fish bladders. The bladders fit readily in her pouch for just such purposes—they also made excellent balloons should an occasion turn festive.

One by one she burned the rune-covered bits of parchment, letting the ashes mingle freely with the dirt. The runes endowed clear-sightedness from her seeress Aunt Sybil, a good ear from her own father, Colin Songsmith, and a few other gifts that were more on the order of well wishes than magical bestowments. Wasimarkan was too far to send anything very potent. It was a good thing for this child that a few extra things had been added between home and here.

Using the special priestess grip she had learned at the seminar in Little Darlingham, she smeared the baby totally with mud while getting practically none of it on herself. When the child resembled a mud pie, Carole held her aloft, saying, as Rupert had instructed her, "In the name of the Mother we who are gathered today name you Magda Xenobia Amberwine Ethel Ermintrude the—!"

"Wait," Timoteo said. "She cannot be called that. There are already people in her family with those names."

"That is the idea," Carole said. "To honor those people—"

"It is not a good idea. We cannot have two Xenobias. One is quite enough. You must give her her own name. A name suitable for a gypsy girl. Call her Romany also."

The interruption in the ceremony and last-minute addition of a name was highly irregular, of course, and Carole gave Timoteo a stern look to let him know she knew. On the other hand, the whole situation was highly irregular, and what difference could one name more or less possibly make? "Very well," she said, "Magda Xenobia Amberwine Ethel Ermintrude Romany it is. So you are christened. So shall you be called—though not all of it all of the time, of course."

She used the remainder of the river water to wipe off the mud before handing the child back to Jushia.

"Good," Timoteo said. "Now we feast."

Carole was mildly surprised at that, but Timoteo drew

forth a dagger and someone else pulled a loaf of bread from the belly of his tunic. There were even a few berries and a great deal of wine, which had been stored in the dusty crystal bottles.

The gypsies were universally drunk by the time Carole decided that if she was going to give the child the remaining gifts, she had better do so while they were only seeing one child. Retrieving the baby from Jushia, she pressed the mermaid's comb into the little fist. She explained to the gypsies and the nurse what the gifts were for, since they might need to help her use them. The comb she tied around the baby's neck with a sandal lace. Jushia regarded it with frightened eyes but cocked her head at it attentively, as if its magic were speaking to her.

The shield was used as a cradle, the child deposited in the middle of it while Jushia rocked it back and forth with her thumb. Then, one by one, the gypsies stepped forward to bestow their own gifts: a ring to give the child lightness of finger, a pair of ankle bracelets to bestow fleetness of foot for dancing and running, a colorful flowered scarf to wrap around her head and conceal her true thoughts from her enemies, an embroidered sash to tighten around her middle so her belly wouldn't hurt when it was empty, a pair of earrings that would enable her always to hear what was to her advantage, the promise of a tamborine to fill with music and money. Timoteo presented her with the last gift: a twig, he said, from the travel log, which would always show her the surest and most interesting ways to wander.

The gypsies toasted solemnly if not soberly, then Timoteo stepped forward and picked up shield, baby and all. "I will keep these things for her, priestess. Romany will live with us."

"Nonsense," Carole said. "If we can get her out of this alive she will be returned to her parents."

"They do not deserve her. Besides, the Miragenians would be able to steal her from you again and send her back.

How would you prevent that, eh? With us she will be disguised and safe. I want your word as a priestess you will tell no one and will not try to find the child."

"I can't promise that. Rupert and the baby's parents will be frantic about her. Don't be unreasonable. There's no longer any question of a "deal" since the Miragenians have negated it by sending her somewhere to be killed. They're not entitled to her so-called services any longer, and we can make war on them if they try to take her now."

"Ah, a very sensible solution. Why do we simple gypsies never think with such admirable clarity? Nevertheless, the baby goes with us. Your word, priestess. You may let the relatives know she is safe. We will give you escort back to your land."

"And that's all?"

"There is nothing else."

"What of Prince Rupert? He saved your life as well as mine. Are we to leave him here?"

"Why not? He is a god here. You can send the dragon back for him later, perhaps, but he may not wish to go."

"I fail to believe that. If the priests start demanding that he allow people to be sacrificed to him, I imagine he will place himself in danger in short order."

The gypsy shook his head sadly and placed his hand on Carole's shoulder. "You are a nice lady, witch, but you don't understand noblemen as I do. My own kinsman, once he became noble, conspired with your kinswoman to sacrifice this child before she was born. It is the way of noblemen to sacrifice people for their own safety, the way of the rich to sacrifice the poor, the way of the poor to sacrifice each other not to be poor any more. In this place they take it to extremes, it is true, but I think the adjustment will be less for your prince than you imagine. Come with us, or you may make all of our cleverness on your behalf come to nothing."

"That was clever? That your friend would have been

slaughtered if I hadn't happened to be captured and managed to free him?"

"We knew you would show up at the dungeon eventually. Your guide was a plant, he was waiting for you. I know your true powers, and knew also that you would free him when you freed yourself. We had, of course, an alternate plan if you did not."

"Which was?"

"Once you had christened the child, trade you back for him. What else?" He grinned broadly at her. "But I knew you would save him. You're a nice lady."

"Your confidence in me is touching," she replied. "But if I'm to maintain your high opinion of me, not to mention mine, I simply must find a way to desanctify Prince Rupert so we can both be quit of this Mother-forsaken place. I'm very happy that you'll be taking the child now. But can't someone please stay here just a while longer to lead us to the rest of you? I know a secret passage. I should be able to bring him straight back, or perhaps meet you somewhere safer."

The gypsy shook his head again, this time fiercely, all trace of tolerance or humor purged from his face. "Too dangerous."

She glared at him, then spun on her heel and headed for the ladder. "Thank you for helping me escape. Good luck"

The kindness was back in his face, along with a hint of reluctant shame as he said, "Murdo, Pietro, blindfold her and lead her to the alley near the shrines, where she can see the temple without attracting the priests' guards. You know the way, so that she won't find this place again." She drew back and pursed her lips to whistle, but he leaned forward and clamped his hand over her mouth, his other hand against the back of her head while his companions did as they were bid. "You don't understand, nice lady. You are not a gypsy able to find your way to us without giving us away. Anyone sent to meet you would be likely to end up making nasty little clouds for the priests to put in bottles and sell to the merchants. Probably along with the rest of us. Gypsies do many things better than other people, but being killed is not one of them. That is why we know so well how not to get caught. And why we trust no one but our own. And please do not worry if they manage to make you tell how you were brought here. You would never possibly find it again. But just in case you do, try to avoid getting recaptured as long as possible, eh?"

He released her and she resisted a childish impulse to spit at him, and said instead, as she was being led away, "Noblemen aren't the only ones who sacrifice other people to their own ends, are they?"

"Stop right there." He jerked the blindfold loose and stared her in the eye. "Priestess, witch lady, what are you doing? You trying to appeal to a gypsy's chivalry? Because if you are, dear lady, I can tell you, we don't have anything like that. We can't afford it. I want it very clear in your mind that you are going out there, probably to die, because you are being stubborn about a fellow who is having a very nice time and probably even now does not care about you or me at all. I appreciate that he saved my skin when he thought I was a worthless merchant. And I am saving him the aggravation of doing what he set out to do and saving the child for him so he can continue to have a very nice time. You could come, too, but you won't. So no more back talk, eh?"

A very weak cough broke the tension between them. Jushia stepped timidly forward, her chin extended a little as if waiting for a blow. "Excuse me, but I must know: Rupert, the Prince, is he not truly the god?"

"Having just seen me consecrate a child to the Mother of all creation, how do you suppose I'm going to answer that?" Carole snapped, as angry at the interruption as she was at the gypsy.

"He is a minor nobleman with a fortunate face that will provide for him the rest of his life," Timoteo answered more politely.

"However long that is," Carole added.

Jushia looked as if she might cry. She reached across Timoteo to stroke the baby's red curls and stood staring at the child rather than at either of them as she said, "If he is not a god, then he is a very good man who has willingly endangered himself on behalf of my little one. Your Choomia has milk enough for two, she says, Master Timoteo, and I feel sure you will get my Princess away if anyone can. So blindfold me, too. I know things that may help this lady save her kinsman."

Timoteo signaled and the nurse was blindfolded along with Carole. The two of them were led away.

When they were gone he turned abruptly from the ladder and bounced the baby so fiercely she started crying. "Women," he spat.

When at last their guides deserted them, Carole and Jushia tugged off their blindfolds and gratefully leaned against the nearest building. The streets were noisy and teaming with shouting, screaming people and the crash of things breaking, the scent of flowers and dung. The gypsies had not led them through the throngs, but along the byways. Nevertheless, the agitation and the smell of fear was as tangible as the rain that drizzled steadily down all day. The atmosphere felt shrill and jumpy. The gypsies had whispered agitatedly between themselves and stopped and backtracked along another route two or three times, and on several occasions someone had bolted past them running in the opposite direction.

As promised, their guides had left the women within a quick sprint of the mist at the temple's base. The guard's sandals smacking the wooden dock on the far side of the temple reassured them that they still had time to locate the secret passage. Jushia groped for the passage for a time, unable to locate it. Carole softly hummed the ribald ballad, and the door wall slid away two handspans down from her. Both women stole quickly inside, leaning upon the wall until it closed. Carole found to her surprise that the inside was not so dark in the daytime as she had imagined it would be. Where the crystal dome met the inner wall, a thin strip of light brightened the passage. Jushia led her directly to the central staircase, and proceeded to climb. Carole followed her up two twisting flights, to the level of the audience chamber and the rooms where she and Rupert had been kept.

Carole hesitated, but Jushia touched her arm and gestured upward. Down one of the narrow passages, Carole thought she heard Rupert's familiar rumbling voice, but Jushia was already three steps ahead of her so she followed. They reached the top of the stairs only to face a blank wall.

"Now what?" Carole asked, but Jushia was already fumbling with the wall. When she had fumbled for several moments, Carole grew impatient and hummed the song that had opened the lower door. Nothing happened.

"Why are we here?" she asked.

"The pendant," Jushia said. "The pendant of the Midnight Rainbow, the one that empowers the priests to collect spirits in bottles. It is kept here. If we take that, if we can destroy it, the priests will be unable to make a profit from the sacrifices, to give lives to the god only to rob him again."

"Good thinking," Carole said, and began humming what she could recall of the chant from the ceremony. The door swung open almost at once.

Jushia made no move to enter, but looked at Carole expectantly. "Do you think you can conjure the guardian of the pendant as you did the door?" she asked.

"What guardian? You didn't mention a guardian."

"There. See, beneath the altar. That must be it. I've heard tales." As Jushia spoke the molding beneath the altar, which was the only furnishing of the small, crystal-domed room, raised all seven of its heads and hissed at them. Carole hummed to it softly and skirted the altar to one side. The heads followed her movement. Jushia, her face white and her hands trembling, circled around to the other side and snatched the treasure from its pedestal. A brief flash in the sunlight and it disappeared in Jushia's mouth while the snake swayed to Carole's tune.

The nurse backed out into the passage again. Carole followed, still humming. Once through she tugged at the door with all her might to close it behind her.

The two of them fled back down the stairs to the level Carole had wanted to stop at originally. Carole panted for a moment, looking back up behind her. "That was very easy," she said. "You'd think they'd have more of a guard."

"That serpent would be a deadly guard to anyone else," Jushia remarked, when she had spit the pendant into the palm of her hand. "The priests are unused to anyone else possessing magic here, and have guarded only against their own sort of powers. I suppose they protect against the regular kind of heroes, warriors, you know. No doubt the snake has the power to grow three heads for every one cleaved from it."

"How about that? Good for me," Carole said. "And if we have that pendant the priests can't perform the ceremony?"

"Not the ceremony of the Midnight Rainbow, which empowers them to collect the spirits after the sacrifice. But I'm afraid they have already performed it this time. They will be able to take ours. But perhaps with this we can bargain. Otherwise, I intend to take it to my death, if need be."

"Let's hope that won't be necessary."

Another rumbling query from Rupert lured them down the side passage. The tone of his voice was aggrieved. The women rushed as quickly and quietly as they could. They were not so quiet, however, that they failed to mask the swish and thump of a seven-headed body negotiating the staircase above them.

Two crystal goblets stood on a quartz table between Rupert and the High Priest. The table was a huge slab of stone, rough rock on the outside, clear crystal with hints of purple in the center.

His Brilliance held a crystal decanter, from which he poured each of them another draught of honey-colored fluid. Lifting a goblet by its stem, he proposed a toast. "To the growth of your faith in you."

Rupert smiled, both to be courteous and because he was in a pleasantly mellow frame of mind. "As you say. But what is this drink? It's excellent."

"Elixir of the gods, shall we say?" His Brilliance chuckled benignly. "You qualify. Enjoy it."

It was sweet and rather oily and went down smoothly. "Nice," Rupert said. "Lovely goblets. Lots of nice glasswork in this region." He had dozed fitfully for three hours in this room waiting for the High Priest. During that time, Brother Merryhue had kept the incense burning near his couch, which helped him relax, feel less upset about the situation, more willing to see the viewpoint of his hosts. He realized he had been rather selfish previously, insisting on having his own way. If it helped these people to worship him, who was he to deny them? On the other hand, part of him wasn't willing to make any such concessions but wanted only to demand, "Just who and how many of your devotees am I supposed to sacrifice to myself?"

"Crystal," His Brilliance was saying. "We don't make glass. We mine and carve crystal. It is useful for . . . holding things. And amplifying them."

"Amplifying?" Rupert asked, sipping.

The High Priest shifted slightly in his seat, his half smile deepening into a sort of patriarchal contentment at being the holder and dispenser of wisdom. "How much magic have you practiced, my son?" he asked. It was neither an accusation nor an expression of awe, doubt, or fear. It was asked more in the tone of an innkeeper inquiring of another how many customers he had served.

"Very little," Rupert said. "My family has not, at least on my father's side, bred magicians."

That caused the High Priest's smile to deepen even more, which suited Rupert, who was beginning to think ever more highly of the man, of what an attractive person he was, of how comfortable this room was, this temple. All those nice little arched windows with the breeze from the river, the tinkle of chimes, the coolness of uncarpeted stone, the quartz tables, all very gracious, very distinctive.

"You mustn't apologize," His Brilliance said. Rupert hadn't realized he sounded apologetic. He hadn't intended to. "I ask only to point out to you that you needn't be anything more than you are to practice almost any sort of magic worth doing. Why, you could enchant rings around that slovenly girl you brought with you using the proper incantations, mordants, and agents."

Rupert's head buzzed. He took another draught of the liquid to clear it. "Wait now. Incantations I've heard of. But mordants? Agents?"

"You've encountered the agents already. They are the entities we will collect at the ceremony tonight for exportation. But first, in a separate set of bottles, we siphon the energy of the crowd—the fear, the anger, the blood lust, all of those wonderfully powerful feelings that, when bottled, add power to any incantation, any spell, making even the most minor of magicians able to work truly potent magic. Yes, indeed, it is the mordants and agents provided for us by the god you represent that bring us the prosperity and plenty we here in Gorequartz enjoy for the very nominal sacrifice of a few misfits and malcontents."

"Ah, prosperity and plenty. That is why the people don't mind, eh?" Rupert slid down in his chair, most of him contented and wanting to smother with sleep the part that clamored against the inertia of his body, the lethargy of his spirit that made him listen so contentedly.

"Why, they more than tolerate it, my son. They embrace it! My children love their God of Rainbows, his bounteous gifts of rain and sunlight that make the food grow, the mining easy, and the gold flow in from afar. The sacrifices add a little zest to life. Enjoy it while you can, you might be next, you see? And our system of selection does get rid of all of the scolds and rebels, the officious but inefficient official, the extra daughter, the unwanted relative. What other system does so much? Our ancestors, having a smaller population, were able to utilize the inferior folk they conquered in this region. Can you imagine a people so ignorant that they ignored the god in the bay, did not go near him? Instead, they worshipped some dingy woods goddess, a deity totally inappropriate to the climate and terrain, whom they credited with creating the crystal. The fools never even connected the rainbows or the crystal with the god, who was after all *made* of the stuff.

"But we, who had for ages sacrificed to our battle god, Utur, saw him at once in the head in the harbor and embraced him. We decked him with flowers and fed him our enemies. He rewarded us, when we had discovered the secret of the pendant captured from the heathen witch, not only with victory, as your ordinary battle god might, but with an ongoing means of establishing a solid and flourishing economy, which is much rarer. No, no, my son, these people are not apt to return to the ways of darkness and dissidence for the sake of an unwanted relative or two. And the ceremonies themselves are such marvelous affairs. With your presence they'll be that much more so. Why, using our enlightened process of collecting that wondrous energy obtainable only from those who die, not in battle or honorably or of old age, but deliberately, helplessly at the hands of their leaders under the eyes of their fellows, makes our ceremonies so much more fulfilling than they were. They were not so exciting before we discovered the use of the pendant and how it can be used to gather power in the person of the priest by channeling the storm's power into him that he in turn may use it to set up the proper vibration in the bottles for sucking the spirits from the air, that he may meld them shut and seal them with the seal that binds them to service.

"Now we can capture the screams, the pure elemental terror of the sacrificial delegate and use it productively to facilitate all manner of curses, spells, and enchantments, lending them power and weight not to be obtained in other times. I used just such a mordant to effect the spell on my dear Effluvia. I will use a similar mordant to release it, restoring her to her former beauty and grace. But you can see, it is a process to be proud of and one you may well feel privileged to be a part of. Why, the survivors of the delegates have often remarked to me what a comfort it is to know that no tiny portion of their contributing member's Ultimate Ecstasy is going to waste."

Overhead the clouds had turned black and suddenly a bolt of lightning cracked against the dome, flashing through the chamber with pure dazzling light before sheets of rain began rolling off the dome. The small part of Rupert that was not trained, not ensorcelled, not drunk, and no longer shielded from the force of the evil around him, stopped cowering for that flashing instant and cried out in protest, overturning the table and sending Rupert lurching for the door. At that moment, someone called his name and a piece of the wall swung forward.

The High Priest lunged for the door ahead of Rupert, but it opened before he reached it, and three lay brothers tumbled in. "Your pardon, Your Brilliance, but we had to report—"

Carole and Jushia crowded at the entrance in the wall, beckoning frantically to Rupert, who tried to reverse course and stumble toward them.

"We had to report that while trying to contain an outbreak of the marauding entities on the edge of the city, a group of palace guardsmen captured a band of thieves with the Princess in their possession. They have been taken to the holding tank for—"

Carole ran into the room and grabbed Rupert's arm,

dragging him toward the secret exit while whistling a dance tune at the guards and the High Priest. Jushia pranced in the entrance, unable to resist the song. She dare not enter the room or be trapped but she was able to turn to try to set her dancing feet in the direction they wanted to go, to take herself out of Carole's and Rupert's way. She screamed, the pendant falling from her mouth to lodge in the scooped neckline of her gown.

Carole and Rupert reached the exit just in time for Carole to switch her whistle back to the one that had tamed the monster originally. Slowly it uncoiled, swayed, and slithered back up the passageway. But too late. The High Priest and the lay brothers had freed themselves of the spell. It took only two of the brothers to subdue the drunkenly befuddled Rupert, while the High Priest sagely clapped a hand over Carole's mouth, and the remaining brother caught Jushia with an arm around her neck.

CHAPTER XIII

The High Priest was aglow with the satisfaction of a day well spent. Despite the sloppy job that had been done of garlanding the barges due to the interference of the escaped entities, this was sure to be one of the finest sacrificial ceremonies he had ever conducted. True, he would not be as prominent a figure as he usually was, but he felt that the splendor of the occasion was not entirely due to the presence of the young buffoon who so resembled the god. Effluvia cut a wonderfully awe-inspiring figure with the black cloak covering her hair and tail, blood-red roses crowning her as she stood beside the white and gold figure of the living god, who was duly propped up with an oar at his back.

Though these two made a splendid spectacle, they were scarcely the most spectacular part of the ceremony. What the people who lined the rain-drenched rock of the cliffs had come to see was the parade of delegates, more than had ever been sent to the god at once since ancient times, when Gorequartz first was conquered. The bay was choked with boats and barges filled to the danger point with the privileged who paid for the honor of contributing to the mordant. Four barges besides the one containing the High Priest, Effluvia, the god, and the three women prisoners were filled with priests. Three more barges were crammed with delegates. The captive thieves alone filled two barges. The King and Queen rode in yet

211

another, the baby cradled in the Queen's plump arms. Overhead, the angry skies had given way—as the High Priest had compelled them to do when his magically charged presence passed between the spires and pools of the shrines—to dark blue sky, a brilliant if waning sun, and a rainbow of unsurpassed vibrance and clarity. In the bay, the rainbow crowned the crystal head with a halo of color reflected in every facet of the huge frowning face. The rainbow's beauty was echoed in the barge filled with crystal bottles ready to collect the rich mordant that would come of this ceremony, much enhanced by the gang of thieves who would multiply the benefits of each death with a multitude of grieving. Another barge contained the bottles for collecting the agents that would be belched forth by the god.

The crowds were gabbling with excitement and fear, for the escaped entities had been hard at work, systematically wrecking house after house, concentrating on only the nicest places. They were unable to touch the crystal, of course, but there were many fine articles made of other substances that had been lost forever. The High Priest had little fear that the entities would disrupt the ceremony itself, although the Mukbar bitch watched the occasional explosions of color spiraling above the rooftops with a smirk, her eyes narrowing vindictively at him if he caught her at it. Actually, he wished there were some way to lure the apparitions close enough. He knew they could be recaptured, if only they were not so afraid of being swallowed again by the god.

While the lay brothers, clad in their golden ceremonial robes, rowed forward in their barge full of mordanting bottles and carefully began placing them on all but three of the god's lower teeth and inside his mouth, between his tongue and teeth, His Brilliance debated about the order of sacrifices. In his sure-handed way, he decided after only brief deliberation that the witch should go first. For one thing, her own contribution to the mordanting would be small, since she was gagged and the only person who might presumably care about her was well-nigh oblivious to everything. Besides, who knew the full extent of her powers? Best dispose of her quickly, before she could cause more trouble.

And though it was usual to take the men first, since they generally died less sensationally and without that lovely surge of lust that added such a fine edge to the mordant, he thought the Mukbar woman should go next. What if her relatives came sailing in on rugs to rescue her and spoil the story he planned that she had in fact never reached Gorequartz. After her, the male thieves. Sometime in the interim the Queen would respond to the bait in his opening speech by offering up the baby and he would expose her and break up the monotony of the long string of males by sending the god that particularly fat and regal morsel. Then the nurse and baby, perhaps. When the sacrifices were done, the Prince could make another little speech thanking everyone on behalf of the god. Now then, if only he would look properly impressive while His Brilliance introduced him to the buzzing populace, along with Effluvia, just to get people used to them as a pair, Gorequartz would have a rite unlike any it had ever seen before.

Rupert felt violently ill. What in the name of the Mother's right nipple had they given him to drink anyway? Whatever it was, it was wearing off at just the wrong time, while he was being rocked into queasiness in the middle of the bay. No doubt the effects were meant to last longer, but His Brilliance had not reckoned with Rupert's sheer size—or maybe the High Priest just hadn't had time to get enough of the cursed stuff down him before all the interruptions. It took a bit more than that to fell a Rowan, as a rule.

As Rupert tried desperately to keep from embarrassing himself in front of all of Gorequartz, his relative sobriety was a mixed blessing. With no sword or shield or magical talent, what could he do to help anyone amidst this mass of hostile humanity? He wasn't yet sure he could stand up properly. Still, he knew he would have to die trying. The entreaty in Jushia's dark eyes unnerved him completely, as did the utter dejection in Carole's when he caught her looking at him over the puffiness of cheeks constricted by the gag, her flower garland slipping down over her angry eyes. On the barge adjoining theirs sat that merchant who was supposed to be dead, and the fellow all but snarled at him.

Inside the stone-bound body of his ancestor, the priests finished arranging the bottles, and Carole was plucked from the boat, hauled up to the giant mouth, and marched to the back of the tongue. The High Priest nodded. He and Effluvia took hold of Rupert on either side and helped him mount the wide ladder extending from the bow of the barge to the lower half of the crystal jaw. Rupert wobbled more than necessary, deciding it would not hurt to allow them to think him still under the influence of the drugged drink.

As he faced the crowd, the chant which had begun in the background rose to a crescendo, mingled with gasps and an occasional cheer. He felt their fear and anger, their pulsing excitement as if it were his own. It surged through him, and past, stirring some deep response within him he could have done without just then. He felt naked without his shield. Where was it now? Not doing the child any good, that was for sure. The poor little tyke writhed below in her false mother's arms. But he failed to see the shield.

The crowd blurred before him. He turned to look at Carole. She was on her knees, looking down the giant's throat. Already he felt her fear coursing toward him, passing him, through the High Priest, toward the bottles. Funny. He had not gained the impression that the mordanting emotions were so tangible, but he felt each of them, strong as his own pulse, Carole's the strongest now. Fear, yes, and dread, but dismay and regret at her failure to save anything, to spare even the child, her despair at having to die so futilely after so much effort. On all sides, the crowd throbbed with movement, the bay brimmed with chanting bodies.

214

The High Priest held his hand straight up, and stillness dropped over the crowd. "My children, the god has come among us again. He has been attended by enemies and ill-wishers and these he would have slain to his glory. He has been attended by liars, imposters so evil they lie even before they can speak, by women so debased as to pass off the get of foreigners for their own royal children, by witches and by thieves, but all of these shall be purified and utilized in his name to the greater prosperity of his people."

Though this was meant to be but a preview of events to come, it was spoiled by the King, who was gray with nervousness, and shoved the Queen and her baby forward, where they were handed along from man to man to the foot of the ladder as if they were no more than a child's ball. "Hear me, Grand Prismatic!" the King cried. "The faithless woman was my wife, the brat no kin to me. Take them both and use them, for they are worthless as they are."

The Queen shrieked as she was hauled aloft and almost dropped the baby. "It was that wretched nurse! I am innocent! She took my son because I sent her lover to the god and she gave me this girl-child instead. I am innocent!"

That gave the crowd something else to chant about, and Jushia was pushed forward, too. Rupert groaned as she was roughly hauled up the ladder and pushed down beside Carole. The High Priest groaned also. His predetermined order was being rent asunder by the untidy demands of the crowd. Still, they were generating the sort of excitement necessary for proper mordanting. He gestured. The tops of the giant's teeth and the cavity between teeth and tongue where the first row of bottles sat was filled with water. He stepped into the mouth with his bare feet. The Queen was being bound hand and foot by one of the priests, the baby thrust into the arms of Effluvia, who held it out from her as if it were a snake.

The High Priest would commence the mordant transferral at once, which would bind the crowd to his will again. He stood in the water, raised both hands and chanted, feeling the energy he had gathered join with that still flooding his veins from the ritual of the previous night. All before his eyes faded into one glorious prism of color and light and in his ears was a single roaring until everything had drained from him, into the bottle. But where was the rest of it? More of the raw mordanting emotion should be bleeding from the delegates, filling him from the crowd, but it was not. He opened his eyes and saw that the rainbow above him was hidden, the sky boiling with flashing clouds again. The crowd stirred and murmured as lightning forked closer.

The King was the first to pick up on the disturbance. "Is something amiss, Your Brilliance? Have your incantations gone wrong? Or perhaps they displease the living God?"

"Your Brilliance!" the lay brother whose duty it was to shove the delegates to their destiny cried. "Your Brilliance! The royal nurse—she has the pendant in her teeth."

At that the priest hopped, dripping from the water. Effluvia and Rupert were ahead of him, Effluvia holding onto the baby with one hand while clutching at the stone with the other. The nurse hung precariously over the back of the tongue, the chain of the pendant in her teeth, the long stone shimmering with movement and whining slightly. The High Priest felt his own excitement flow out of him and into the stone. The nurse's face was grim, her teeth clenched, eyes shut, sweat standing out on her brow as the pendant swung back and forth over the dark hole.

"Evil, vengeful woman," His Brilliance cried in a voice that echoed off the back of the giant's throat. "It will do you no good to destroy the sacred stone. You are doomed and all who are with you are doomed." But the time for threats or bargaining had passed. Effluvia grabbed for the stone. Rupert grabbed for the child with one arm, for Jushia's foot with the other. Jushia dropped the pendant.

It swung wide and shattered on the far side of the giant's

throat, its shards like shooting stars. The baby squirmed against Rupert's elbow and let out a great squalling cry as its blood spurted onto his hand. He saw that one of the shards had hit the baby's forehead, lodging just above her nose, but even as he looked the wound sealed and the bleeding stopped. Behind him he felt the crowd pushing forward, thrusting through the sea and over the boats, into the mouth of the giant. It would soon push them all into the gaping throat.

But the excitement was too much for Effluvia. For so many years, she had had but one response to threats of any kind that it was automatic now. Her tail flew up, her essence striking His Brilliance squarely on the belly of his rainbow-hued robe, filling the mouth of the giant with a cloud of putrid noxiousness and driving the crowd back into the sea, driving His Brilliance, the priests, and Rupert—still holding onto Jushia and the crying child—back toward the giant's teeth, panting for air.

The mordanting bottles were overturned, and many were broken. In the bay, people coughed spasmodically, some hanging onto the sides of boats where they had been knocked in the scuffle. His Brilliance, himself wracked with coughing, gave the sign that the mordanting bottles were to be disposed of, the agent-collecting ones set up.

The priests in charge of this procedure stalled a little, taking their time gathering the bottles together, hoping the brisk wind that had risen would cleanse some of the stink from the giant's mouth.

"NOW!" His Brilliance roared, and the bottles were set in place in the giant's mouth so fast none of the priests had need to draw breath again until safely back in the empty barge.

"Get that slut of a nurse off the God and throw her down the hole!" the High Priest commanded, turning away from the mob of worshippers. The words were not out of his mouth before a scream erupted from the bay. More screams were followed by thrashing, splashing, and the splintering of wood

217

as boats wrecked upon each other in their haste to escape the streaking bands of color descending vengefully upon the crowd.

"That's my property!" Alireza screeched, her voice roaring over the tumult of the crowd. She realized her mistake almost at once as the bands of light converged upon her in a single whirling mass. She dove overboard.

Everywhere people followed her example. Rupert thrust the baby into Jushia's arms, pulled Carole away from the hole, and began untying her hands.

In the bay Timoteo leapt from boat to boat, shield in one hand, knife in the other, cutting the bonds of his fellow gypsies and sending them into the sea. He somehow managed to avoid the streaking entities. He was scaling the ladder to the lower lip when the High Priest regained control, arms lifting, body swaying, chant rising high as the rainbow streaks abandoned their assault on Alireza Mukbar and whirled angrily toward the mouth of the giant.

The High Priest exalted as the entities flew toward him, but his exaltation wavered and died as they converged—he was not drawing them, they were attacking. He fell upon the bottles in the gutter of the giant's mouth and was enveloped in a buzzing blizzard of color. Another blizzard knocked Effluvia against the teeth. Still others went for the minor priests and the prisoners.

Carole jerked the gag from her mouth and blew a piercing whistle that escalated into a wild reeling song. Timoteo landed in front of Jushia and the child before the first note, covering them with the shield. The entities gathered themselves into an angry cloud, leaving behind the prostrate bodies of the priests and Effluvia, and danced out to sea just beyond range of the whistle, where they hovered like a cloud of wasps. The High Priest crawled to his feet, unharmed and infuriated. The priests from the boats swarmed up the ladder, pikes at the ready. Timoteo struggled with the first one, but his knife was knocked from his hand with the pikestaff.

The High Priest seized the baby away from Jushia again and held it aloft. To Carole he said, "You may live if you keep the wild agents away from us. But the sacrifice must go on. This child has caused much trouble. She shall be the first."

Carole wasn't listening. Her whistle had died on her lips even before the entities had departed. She turned to look at Rupert. Unshielded, he nevertheless was not dancing. Instead he stood near the back of the mouth where he had rushed to save her. He alone remained still in the midst of the turmoil. A glow emanated from his body. It brightened the longer he stood there.

Her first thought was that one of the entities had harmed him in some way, but when the High Priest carried the child Romany to the back of the cave, Rupert spread his arms and walked forward, driving the High Priest before him.

"What are you doing to me, man?" Rupert demanded in a voice as great as if it indeed came from the crystal head his own calm face resembled. "Go away. Send these people home. Give that baby back to its mother. Do you think I want you to murder little children? Fah! You don't think me a god, you think me a monster. Leave off then and be gone with you. You're giving me a headache."

"The Grand Prismatic has spoken!" the crowd cried. But while he was speaking, Carole was not whistling, and the streaking entities attacked again, flying toward the giant's nostrils this time. Carole tried to pucker, but the giant's tongue slipped out from under her and she fell. The crystal head quivered, as if in pain, and a long crack opened in one cheek.

"Quickly, go," Timoteo said, handing Jushia down to Murdo, who waited with a boat whose former occupants now inhabited the sea.

"The Princess!" she cried, but the colored streaks dived at them, knocking her to the deck and Timoteo into the sea.

Carole grabbed for him, but the head quaked again and a cavern split it from chin to nostril. Carole rolled to avoid it. Rupert grabbed the baby from the High Priest just as the entities shoved him off the back of the tongue, to fall screaming down the giant's craw. Another rent and the skull cracked apart. The entities did a jackknife turn in midair and swooped down upon Rupert. He dropped the baby into Carole's arms. "Swim!" he yelled.

She stayed for a moment and tried to whistle them away again, but by now the din was too loud for her to be heard. Before the crack that split the crystal head ear to ear and dumped her into the sea, she saw the jewel embedded in the child's forehead, as harmless-seeming as a pasted ornament. Taking up the shell comb, she managed to comb the fine red locks just two short strokes before they were forced to dive.

They had to dive deep because wreckage and bodies were everywhere, but finally Carole found a place to surface: near the boat containing Timoteo, Jushia, Murdo, and several other bedraggled gypsies. She tried to hand the baby to Jushia but the child flipped her tail and jumped like a porpoise from between Carole's hands. Jushia squealed and fished for her. Romany leapt up into her lap. Carole caught the glitter of the crystal above the baby's nose once more before diving again.

The giant calved like a glacier, pieces of his crystal shell crashing into the sea, exploding tons of water upon the remainder of his hapless worshippers. On a portion of lower jaw, Rupert fought the entities, flailing at them while his own mighty blows threatened to unbalance him as they struck through nothingness.

Damn, Carole thought. She should have taken the rowan shield from Timoteo. She tried to swim and whistle at the same time, but the water was boiling now. The rest of the giant began disintegrating. The part beneath Rupert trembled. The colored rainbows regrouped for a final assault.

A wave threw Carole backwards and swept over her.

When she looked up, the sky was black, with something shooting down from it. At first she thought it was another bolt of lightning, but then she heard the roar of the dragon, mightier than all other sounds, and saw that it was Grippeldice, who knocked the entities aside.

"Desist, nasty things!" she cried, "I told you to find him, not kill him. Haven't you any manners? Now depart before I turn you all into steam!" And with that she swooped down to retrieve Rupert, who flung himself gratefully onto her neck just as the last piece of Rowan the Recreant crumbled away beneath him.

In the dragon's wake, a great streak of white light rose from the sea, to join the scattering entities. Winding around them like a ribbon, it gathered them together and rose with them toward the clouds. Thunder rolled a black cloud across them and when the lightning next flashed, they were gone.

The storm cleared remarkably soon. From Grippeldice's back, Rupert and Carole hunted among those still left in the bay, searching for some sign of the gypsies, Jushia, and their small charge. Overhead a brilliant rainbow decorated the sky as if a disaster had not just occurred within its arch.

Carole dived repeatedly but was unable to go near the center of the bay because of the vast disturbance created by the destruction of the giant.

The rainbow had fled by the time Carole slung herself across the back of the floating dragon one last time. Rupert reached down and finished hauling her upright. She collapsed with her back against his chest and he almost collapsed under her weight. He was not in appreciably better shape than she was. Both were exhausted, shaken, and bitterly disappointed at having come so far and undergone so much for the sake of the child only to lose her again. Grippeldice alone was cheerful. She growled at them in what was meant to be a comforting fashion and rose, circling the bay again.

From the rocky precipice where hundreds of spectators

had stood a single arm waved slowly back and forth. Grippel-dice swooped towards it.

Timoteo basked in twilight as if it were the sun of noon and smiled at them. "Welcome, friends. I trust you had a pleasant swim."

"Where's the child?" Carole asked. "Where's Romany?"

"Safe," he said. "At her nurse's breast and well away from this wretched country under the protection of many fine fellows almost as splendid as me."

Rupert snorted most undiplomatically.

"Prince!" Timoteo sounded wounded. "Was that nice? You doubt I am a splendid fellow? I am such a splendid fellow I came back to let you and the witch lady know the little baby Romany is safe, so you should not worry, so her mama should not worry. And this is the thanks I get?"

"Timoteo, we're really not very concerned with your feelings right now, if you'll pardon me for saying so," Carole told him. "The child was wearing a fish tail and had a head wound when I entrusted her to you. It's a bit difficult for me to blandly accept your assurance that she is safe."

"You will take us to her now," Rupert said bluntly, "or I will instruct this dragon to burn you to a crisp."

Timoteo bobbed his head and scratched his whiskers in a meditative manner. "Yes, I thought of that. I said to myself, 'Timoteo, if you are a good fellow and go back there, that royal gentleman is apt to set his dragon on you. But then, if he does, he will have lost himself a very good friend, the only person in all the tribes who might let him know something about the child from time to time.' I would feel so sorry for you if that happened, Prince. And then, I am a brave kind of man, you know, so I decide to risk your dragon."

"You can't mean to keep her," Carole said flatly. "She's a Princess, entitled to a good education, a permanent home, good food—"

"Ah, lady, there is no education as good as the road. Nothing so enlightening as lacking occasionally for good food. As for a permanent home, have I not been telling you that travel is broadening?"

"She was wounded," Carole insisted. "And half fish."

"Lady, you told us yourself that the comb only makes her a fish while she is in water. As soon as she dried off, two little pink girl legs again, poof, just like that. As for the piece of crystal in her head, it doesn't seem to be hurting her. She acts no different than she did before. And it's kind of pretty. Gypsy girls like jewelry."

"That particular piece of jewelry was the one that the priests used to attract lightning to them, to harness its power for trapping souls," she said. "I have a hard time believing that it hasn't harmed her in some way."

Rupert kneaded her shoulder in a restraining way and said, "At any rate, she'll need special watching during thunderstorms. The piece that hit her is only a fragment of the original crystal, but who knows how much power may still be in it, or how it may have changed? She really should be back with her family where it can be studied and she can be properly protected."

"Protected as she was protected when the Miragenian soul-slavers stole her right out from under your nose, Prince? She is safe with her family now, with the part of her family who saved her. And that piece of stuff in her head is better hidden by her kerchief when among nobility than studied and prodded. Your nobility, Prince, would make her feel like a freak, a bear to be baited. With us she will be raised as one of our own, her little extra eye of no more interest than a cauliflower ear or a gold tooth."

"Timoteo," Carole said, her voice grating with reluctant menace, "I don't want to have to give you dancing lessons. Tell us where the child is."

"Witch, I love to dance, especially with such a pretty lady

to call the tune. I will not tell you. If I tell you you will use your dancing and your dragon and take her away from us. That would not be good for her and probably not so good for us either. You I will not tell at all because always you will have the unfair advantage of your magic power and could steal her away while making us all look like fools. The Prince here, though, he and I might work out a deal."

"What sort of deal?" Rupert asked. "The right is clearly on our side. The child belongs with her mother. Her mother wants her back."

"Her mother agreed to give her away for fifteen years to people who weren't even related to her. You weren't even supposed to get her back, just to get her christened. She's christened, she's with family. Her mother can pretend she's fostering. At least she will know little Romany is not being a slave."

"And just how is she supposed to know that?" Carole asked. "We have only your word and pardon me but—"

"Don't be insulting, lady. My word is good enough. But I know mothers. I know how difficult married sisters are. I know you and the Prince are going to have some time explaining this, that it may cause you trouble. And you are good people. So I tell you what. You don't talk to me any more about having dragons burn me up or dancing me into the ground and I promise, once a year, on the baby's birthday, I'll let you, Prince, see the child. You can visit her, see that she's safe. Tell her mama she's safe. But you must let us come for you. You must come blindfolded and not try to find us again. And you can't confuse the girl by telling her about her mama and papa or about being a princess. She'll be happier just thinking she's a gypsy girl. When she's fifteen and old enough to decide for herself what she wants, then she can know, she can choose. Fair enough?"

"I have no more right to make that kind of deal with you

than you say Bronwyn and Jack did to deal with the Miragenians in the first place."

"You also have no choice. It's the best offer you've had so far. What do you say?"

"Bronwyn will send armies, spies."

"She would be foolish to do so. Xenobia will explain it to her. But she can do whatever she likes. The deal is between you and me. You may act as her emissary to the baby as long as you don't interfere and meet my terms. Answer me now, give me your word, or nobody's going to see her or hear from her again until we're good and ready. And we may not ever *be* good and ready. She's a very nice little girl."

Rupert deliberated for a moment. If the gypsies were so confident they could keep the baby secreted from her mother and all the might of the combined Wasimarkanian and Argonian thrones, then perhaps she truly would be safer from the Miragenians with them. He stared into the gypsy's shrewd brown eyes, which met his steadily. And slowly he knew. The man was telling the truth. He was overextending himself in fact, going beyond the bounds of what the tribe wanted, risking his own prestige, despite his nonchalant air, to ensure that the child would have her heritage when it was safe for her to do so. The Prince was shocked to realize also that the gypsy man, for all his mocking ways, admired Rupert more than he envied him, had been surprised at a nobleman who declined to be a god, and felt that perhaps such a man could be trusted even by a gypsy.

"Very well. I accept your terms," Rupert said.

"Good. Then give me a ride on your dragon to the skunk-woman's woods and I will contact you in a year."

Bronwyn's reaction to their news, while less violent than some might have expected, was hardly calm. Still bedfast, she blanched even whiter than the knuckles of her clenched fists, then turned red as her hair, her blue eyes snapping as if about to explode from her face. To the maid who fidgeted beside her pillow she said, "Send me the captain of the guard, the commander of the army, and Her Majesty Queen Xenobia at once."

The maid tripped over her curtsy and escaped as quickly as possible, leaving Carole and Rupert to face her mistress's wrath alone.

"Now then," Bronwyn said, "let me get this straight. You found my baby, you christened her, you delivered her from murdering priests to whom the Miragenians sold her, thereby breaking our agreement—"

"The gypsies saved her, actually," Carole corrected, somewhat timidly in the face of Bronwyn's anger. "I only christened her as you requested."

"And you left her with them? And agreed that Rupert should see her once a year while I cannot? What sort of an agreement is that? Who gave you the right—"

"They're good people, Bronwyn, really. They'll look after her," Carole said placatingly.

"I know they're good people, you double-crossing witch! I married one of them, didn't I? But she's *my* daughter, and, since the Miragenians have broken their word—"

Rupert did not respond to her words, but held her hand tightly, feeling the guilt behind them as well as the anger, the fear and the anguish and the disappointment. Bronwyn tried to break away from him and slapped at him, but his arms were long enough. He easily kept well out of her reach while still retaining her hand. Finally she let out a huge breath, leaned back against her pillow, and stared at them. A single forlorn tear slid unnoticed through the freckles on her cheek.

"She had a fish tail when you saw her," Bronwyn continued bitterly. "And a piece of glass in her head. How safe can she be?"

"I know you don't like the mermaids, Bronwyn, but the ability to turn mer when necessary is a very practical gift in any circumstances. Timoteo said she was perfectly normal again as soon as she was dry," Carole said.

"Timoteo! Timoteo! He'll taste my blade if I ever find him, this Timoteo! He's stolen my little girl. And she's injured. That piece of glass—"

Rupert stroked her hand with his thumb and after a moment said, "It was crystal, Bronwyn. Magic crystal. And I don't feel that it was an accident that it struck the baby where and when it did. The giant—our ancestor—I think he meant it as his christening gift. It has powers that may protect her. He was so sorry for all the horror committed in his name, so appalled. I think the crystal shard embedding itself in her forehead was not a chance injury at all, but a deliberate benediction, a mark of favor to guard her. She'll need guarding, Bronwyn. The gypsies are right about that."

"That we are," Xenobia said, sweeping majestically into the room and facing her grandson's wife with the same imperial air with which she had always faced everything. "You think you can keep her safe? How well have you done so for, eh?"

"You had no right—" Bronwyn began, trying to climb out of bed. Rupert used his great strength as gently as possible to keep her there.

"And you had no right to put her in jeopardy in the first place, giving her to strangers as if she was a stray dog."

Rupert faced the gypsy woman angrily. "Have you learned nothing as Queen? Do you think she wanted to let the Miragenians have her baby? I was there. We had no choice. Their magic was powerful. Even if they had never made a bargain with Bronwyn, the Miragenians could have taken that child at any time."

Xenobia looked long into his face. Then, surprisingly, she dropped her gaze. Her elbows, crooked aggressively at her sides, relaxed. "I know. I know. That is why I sent Timoteo. That is why the child must not come back here." Her eyes met Bronwyn's and held them. "Forgive me. I have blamed you for the child's destiny. I do not read the crystal ball, but I think that this child is no ordinary baby, no ordinary princess. My people are good at hiding, good at lying, good at what it takes to survive the treachery of others. Not that some royal people are not also good at those things, but not you, Bronwyn. You, who were the greatest liar in all Argonia, are too honest for the people who would harm your child. Let us help you, eh?"

Bronwyn bristled, her back braced. Rupert continued to stroke her hand. Suddenly she turned and burrowed into the pillow, her head bobbing up and down. Then as quickly, she turned back.

"But why can Rupert see her and I can't?"

"Because you would lead her enemies to her. Because, again, you are no longer a good liar. You see?"

Bronwyn glared at her, but nodded sharply. Xenobia left, looking troubled, and neither so pleased nor so sure of herself as she had looked when she entered the room.

They were interrupted again when the captain of the guard and the commander of the army arrived, but Bronwyn apologized curtly and told them to wait outside before returning her attention to Carole and Rupert.

"What of these enemies of ours? The priests, that skunk thing, and the Mukbar woman?" Bronwyn asked.

"We should cut off trade agreements immediately, of course," Rupert said. "Miragenia has held Frostingdung in an economic stranglehold of dependency ever since they began commerce. There may be some difficulty, but I think with the problems Mukbar, Mashkent, and Mirza will be undergoing with the loss of their chairman and the trade with Gorequartz, they'll be much more amenable to reason than before."

"The Mukbar woman is dead then?" Bronwyn asked.

Rupert shrugged. Carole said cautiously, "I can only say I never saw her come up."

"And the skunk thing?"

Carole shook her head.

"We'll have them searched for then. And any remaining priests. If it isn't safe for my daughter for me to find her, I'll find her enemies and deal with them instead. I'm sorry I can't thank you properly for your trouble right now, Rupert, Carole. I know you did a great deal and . . . well, but I have to *do* something now, you see, before I go mad. Ask Captain Ironbow and General Gristlebone to come in as you leave, will you?"

Grippeldice waited for them in the courtyard. Her scales gleamed with an artfully limited range of color both Rupert and Carole found restful.

Rupert was more than glad to have the interview over, its outcome more successful than he had anticipated. The sunshine warmed him to his very bones. "Would you tell my dragon she is looking more beautiful than ever?" he asked.

Carole did so, and gladly, adding her own greetings to Grippeldice to his. "It is so nice to talk with you when I can see you again."

"No thanks to you," the dragon said. "You almost turned me into one of those hidebehind things with your blasted pill. I had to fly all the way back to Wizard Raspberry's castle in Argonia to get the damned thing removed. That's what took me so long. I figured when my Prince wanted to take up with that skunk creature that my being invisible must be leaving him cold. Once the spell was off, I ran into those flying refugees from a dyepot. The had no quarrel with dragons, so they agreed to be on the lookout for you. I had no idea the sight of my sweet Prince's face would inflame them with rage that way. I circled the city several times, but I wasn't even warm. Just couldn't find you, since I couldn't see you anywhere. Those things broke into houses saying they were looking, too, but they had fish of their own to fry, I can see now. I had to stop to feed yesterday, and so I found a cozy place in the woods to nap, but when I heard my Prince speaking in that big, booming voice, I fairly smoked out of there. So how about it? Ask him if he'll come up to my cave sometime."

She set them down in the courtyard of Queenston Castle, where they barely drew a glance. Queenston was long since used to the dragons.

Rupert bowed low to Grippeldice when her question was relayed to him. "Tell her I'll be delighted to do so when duty permits. Right now, I'm on my way to the Royal Archives to see Sir Cyril. There's a little matter of a Rowan's reputation that needs to be rectified."

"I have something to add that may interest you," Carole said, and told him of her dream conversation with Rowan the Recreant.

Rupert stood scratching his head for a moment, his frown uncannily like that of his much-enlarged ancestor. "Oddly enough, I seem to have known that already. Carole, I think I shall forego making myself another rowan shield after all. If I had worn it when poor old Rowan the Recreant wanted to speak through me, I doubt he could have. I *knew* what he had to say, you see. That's why I feel that the crystal was a gift. And I seem to know a great many other things about people now— about Timoteo, and Bronwyn, and Xenobia, for instance. Do you understand what I mean? When you were back there in Gorequartz about to be sacrificed, gagged so you couldn't speak, I felt as if I were you, that I could have spoken almost in your voice and told what you were going through, because I knew. You're a witch, a priestess. Now you tell me. Is that magic?"

She considered for a moment and nodded. "The bit with Rowan the Recreant certainly was. The other could be, I think."

"Then that settles it. We Rowans have never been known as particularly magical fellows, but I can't help wondering if it's not because we're always shielded against it. I think I shall be the first to do without and perhaps I may find others who would not ordinarily be able to speak who can do so through me."

Carole squeezed his arm and said, "Come along then, and tell Sir Cyril the Recreant's side of things. I'll join you. I have a christening to record."

Grippeldice blew a warm little gust of steam. Rupert turned back to scratch her between the eyes. As he did, he felt a warm rush of affection and admiration for himself wash through him. He stared at Grippeldice for a moment and grinned, then hugged her scaley neck. Perhaps it would not be necessary to learn Pan-Elvin after all.

ABOUT THE AUTHOR

ELIZABETH SCARBOROUGH was born in Kansas City, KS. She served as a nurse in the U.S. Army for five years, including a year in Viet Nam. Her interests include weaving and spinning, and playing the guitar and dulcimer. She has previously published light verse as well as four other Bantam novels, *Song of Sorcery*, *Bronwyn's Bane*, *The Unicorn Creed*, and *The Harem of Aman Akbar*. She makes her home in Fairbanks, Alaska.